THE PHANTOM DETECTIVE

February 1933 Issue

(Volume 1, Number 1)

THE PHANTOM DETECTIVE
(February 1933)

Pulp Classics #7
Series editor: John Gregory Betancourt

New elements copyright © 2005 by Wildside Press.

Published by:

Wildside Press, LLC
www.wildsidepress.com

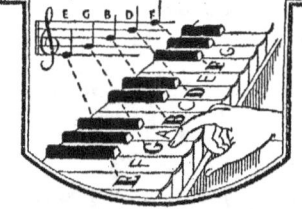

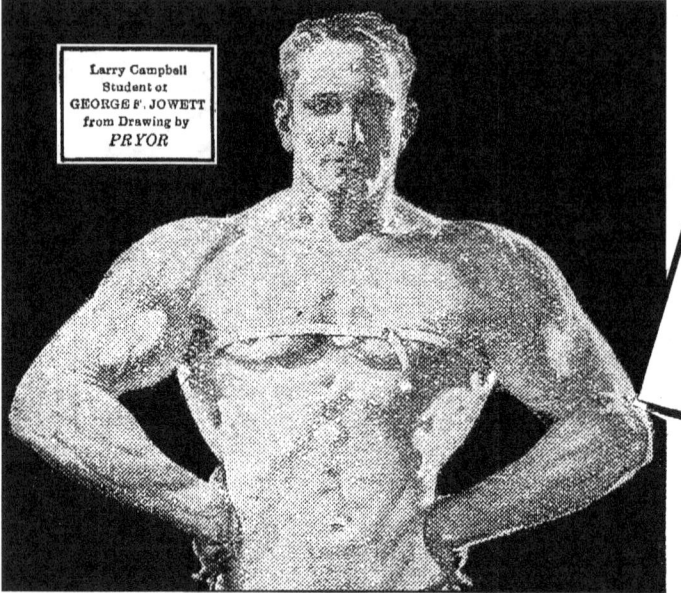

Larry Campbell
Student of
GEORGE F. JOWETT
from Drawing by
PRYOR

"I have added 7 inches to my chest 4 inches to my biceps 5 inches to my neck . . . by using the Jowett System of Physical Training"

Larry Campbell

Larry Campbell came to George Jowett for help when he was 20 years old and weighed only 110 pounds—a weak, underdeveloped stripling. TODAY he is a perfect physical specimen—a strong man who has won many strength competitions.

» I Guarantee To Add At Least...

3 INCHES TO YOUR CHEST 2 INCHES TO YOUR BICEPS

...or it won't cost you one cent! Signed: GEORGE F. JOWETT

WHAT I did for Larry Campbell—I am sure I can do for you! I wish you could see Larry in action today—a perfect example of my weight resistance method—the only method that gives the true weight lifting muscles. I've seen Larry lift more than 225 pounds overhead with one hand—and Larry is only one of hundreds of my pupils who have excelled as strength athletes.

I want to tell you fellows—there's something about this "strong man's business" that gets you—*thrills* you! You'll get a great kick out of it—you'll fairly see your muscles grow—and in no time at all, you too will be doing the one-arm-press with a 150 pound weight!

All I want is a chance to prove to you that I can add 3 inches to YOUR chest and 2 inches to each of YOUR biceps. Those skinny fellows that are discouraged are the men I want to work with. I'll build a strong man's body for them and do it quickly. And I don't mean cream-puff muscles either—you will get real, genuine, invincible muscles that will make your men friends respect you and women admire you!

Test my full course, if it does not do all I say—and I will let *you* be the judge—then it won't cost you one penny, even the postage you have spent will be refunded to you.

I want you to send for one of my test courses NOW!

"Moulding a Mighty Chest" A Complete Course for only 25c

It will be a revelation to you. You can't make a mistake. The guaranty of the strongest man in the world stands behind this course. I give all the secrets of strength illustrated and explained as you like them. In 30 days you can get a mighty back and a Herculean chest. Mail your order now while you can still get this course at my introductory price of only 25c.

I will not limit you to the chest. I can develop any part or all of your body. Try any one of my test courses listed in the coupon at 25c. Or, try all six of them for only $1.00.

Rush the Coupon Today

Mail your order now and I will include a FREE COPY of "NERVES OF STEEL, MUSCLES LIKE IRON" It is a priceless book to the strength fan and muscle builder. Full of pictures of marvelous bodied men who tell you decisively how you can build symmetry and strength the equal of theirs. Reach out—Grasp This Special Offer.

LET THE MAN with the STRONGEST ARMS IN THE WORLD SHOW YOU THE WAY!

His free book is included with your order. It describes his rise from a puny boy to one of the world's strongest athletes with a chest measure of 49 inches and an 18 inch bicep! His book explains why he is called "Champion of Champions"—and there is a "thrill" in every page!

Drawing of
GEORGE F. JOWETT
by PRYOR

FREE BOOK WITH PHOTOS OF FAMOUS STRONG MEN

"Nerves of Steel, Muscles like Iron" SENT FREE!

JOWETT INSTITUTE of PHYSICAL CULTURE
Dept. 110ND, 422 Poplar St., Scranton, Pa.

George F. Jowett: Your proposition looks good to me. Send, by return mail, prepaid, the courses checked below for which I am enclosing_____

☐ Moulding a Mighty Arm, 25c
☐ Moulding a Mighty Back, 25c
☐ Moulding a Mighty Grip, 25c
☐ Moulding a Mighty Chest, 25c
☐ Moulding Mighty Legs, 25c
☐ Strong Man Stunt Made Easy, 25c
☐ All 6 Books for $1.00.

Include FREE Book "Nerves of Steel, Muscles Like Iron"

Name_____ Age_____

Address_____

Vol. I, No. 1   February, 1933   Price 10c

—A Full Book-Length Novel—

THE EMPEROR OF DEATH

By G. WAYMAN JONES

From the Case-Book of Richard Curtis Van Loan

(Profusely Illustrated)

GRIPPING SHORT STORIES

PHANTOM FEATURES

Published monthly by PHANTOM DETECTIVE, INC., 570 Seventh Avenue, New York, N. Y. Entire contents copyright 1932 by PHANTOM DETECTIVE, INC. Subscription yearly $1.20, single copies $ .10, foreign and Canadian
postage extra. Application for entry as second-class matter pending.
Manuscripts must be accompanied by self-addressed, stamped envelopes, and are submitted at the author's risk.

Introducing

Richard Curtis Van Loan—The Phantom Detective.

The greatest sleuth of all time! A worthy successor to Auguste Dupin, Sherlock Holmes, Arsene Lupin and Philo Vance.

With this issue we open his case-book to you.

You will read the exciting, sensational story of his single-handed war against rampant banditry in America.

His courageous "Lone Wolf" campaign to rid the nation of organized crime and big time racketeers.

His identity known to only one person—this masked enemy of crime is a product of the cataclysmic World War.

Born to the purple, wealthy beyond all avarice, the war made him realize the futility of his pampered life. Daily face to face with death on the flaming Eastern Front, peace-time activities seemed too tame for him after his career as a "war bird" was over.

Others, seeking readjustment vainly, took

the PHANTOM

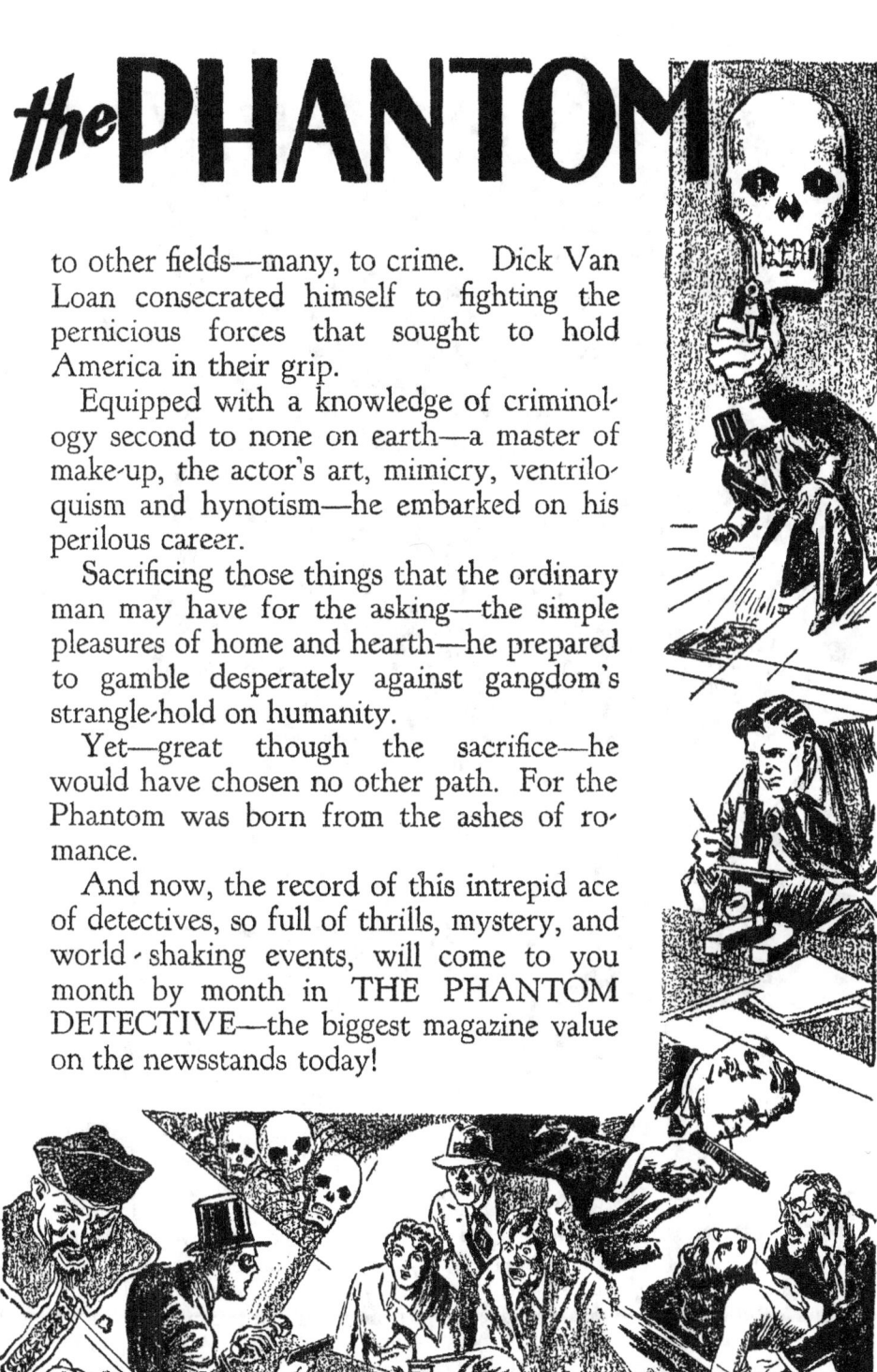

to other fields—many, to crime. Dick Van Loan consecrated himself to fighting the pernicious forces that sought to hold America in their grip.

Equipped with a knowledge of criminology second to none on earth—a master of make-up, the actor's art, mimicry, ventriloquism and hynotism—he embarked on his perilous career.

Sacrificing those things that the ordinary man may have for the asking—the simple pleasures of home and hearth—he prepared to gamble desperately against gangdom's strangle-hold on humanity.

Yet—great though the sacrifice—he would have chosen no other path. For the Phantom was born from the ashes of romance.

And now, the record of this intrepid ace of detectives, so full of thrills, mystery, and world-shaking events, will come to you month by month in THE PHANTOM DETECTIVE—the biggest magazine value on the newsstands today!

The Emperor

By
G. WAYMAN JONES

Taken from the case-book of Richard Curtis Van Loan

CHAPTER I

TREASON!

RICHARD CURTIS VAN LOAN stood in the friendly darkness of a tenement doorway, his face buried in the ample collar of his overcoat. From time to time, his alert eyes swept the dimly lit street as if in impatient search of something.

A big black town car slowly wended its way through the traffic toward him. Van Loan sighed with the air of a man who has relieved his fears, and stepped out on the edge of the curb. His slouch hat was pulled down over his eyes, his chin still buried in his coat. The driver of the car could not have recognized him even if he had turned his well-trained head, which he didn't.

Van Loan entered the car without raising his head. He picked up the speaking tube and said:

# of Death

*Swiftly Van sprang
through the window and
held the room at bay with
his automatic.*

The Phantom Detective Plays a Lone Hand Against a Mad
Genius Plotting Wholesale Death and Destruction

"I think you know where."

The chauffeur nodded, and the purring car started forward silently through the streets of Baltimore.

As they passed through the town, Van Loan thrust his hand in his coat pocket, and, pushing back his head, hastily adjusted a black silk mask across his eyes. Now satisfied that he was beyond recognition, he no longer sank his firm, square chin in his collar.

He leaned back in the seat and lit a cigarette, secure in the knowledge that he had not been observed, quite confident that this esoteric mission of his was not known to his enemies. He smoked placidly, utterly unaware that peril, in the form of a black Lincoln sedan, followed close behind him.

They were but twenty miles out of Washington when the Lincoln swept in to the attack. A motor pounded somewhere behind them. A horn blared raucously. A blackness, darker than the darkness of the night, swept along the road, swerved inward forcing Van Loan's car to the dangerous soft shoulders of the Number One Highway.

Brakes locked, screamed, and threw an acrid stench into the air. A man's voice shouted. Both cars stopped dead, the hood of Van Loan's car touching the Lincoln's mudguard.

Cursing the false sense of security which had paralyzed his normal alertness, Van Loan sprang to the door of the car, a snub-nosed automatic in his hand. His mouth was set in a grim white line as he stepped out onto the running board to challenge his enemies of the night.

BUT those enemies, apparently, were more than willing to meet him. Three black shapes whirled through the darkness. Van Loan's gun spat twice. Red streaked black. He heard a cry of pain. Then the trio of flying shapes completed their journey. They landed upon him, knocking the breath from his body, seizing the wrist that held the weapon. A fist sank deep in the pit of his stomach. He went down as if an avalanche had struck him.

Yet he retained his consciousness. He heard a harsh voice cry: "Get the cars out on the road. Hurry. There's little time to waste."

Van Loan lay on the ground held there by one man now. The others had gone in answer to the orders of the harsh voice. In Van Loan's consciousness there remained a single salient thought, a command which every living nerve in his body knew that it must obey.

He must not let them take his mask from his face!

Already his captor was bending over him, an evil grin on his face, his hand outstretched. He assumed evidently, that his victim was already knocked out. His fingers touched the edge of the black silk mask, for the retention of which Dick Van Loan had already resolved to give his life.

He summoned up every ounce of his energy, every tithe of his strength. His clenched fist came up from the ground. His knuckles crashed into flesh. The other man yelled, and fell backward. Van Loan sprang to his feet fighting for the wind that had been knocked from his body a moment before. He heard an alarmed voice from the car say: "What the hell—?"

Then he waited no longer. He ran from the road—ran as if all the hounds of hell were at his heels, and disappeared into the friendly foliage whose concealing qualities were enhanced by the heavy blanket of the night.

Their voices followed him, though their feet could not. A string of oaths ripped through the night. "You fools. He's gone. We've lost him. Get that car out. Tie up that chauffeur. There's one thing we can do before he gets to Washington. Hurry!"

Van Loan ran on. He turned, essaying to keep a course parallel to the road. A root suddenly snaked across his instep. He fought desperately to keep his balance. Then he fell. His head struck something hard and metallic. Blackness which put the night to shame flooded his brain. He lay there quietly, silent as the woods which surrounded him.

A HALF an hour ticked past. Thirty minutes of time of which Dick Van Loan would never be conscious. Then he stirred, groaned. His eyes opened. For a moment he lay perfectly still, orienting himself, collecting his faculties. Then his hand shot to his face.

His mask was still there!

But the momentary exultation that followed the realization of that fact was short-lived. In a single mental picture he abruptly recalled the events of the evening. He sprang to his feet, disregarding the dull twinging pain in his head. Then he plunged through the underbrush toward the road again.

His automatic had been lost in the brawl of half an hour ago. But nestling comfortably in his snug shoulder holster was another. He reached for it as the white line in the center of the highway became visible through the trees.

Half a dozen big cars whizzed by him. Then he saw the Ford. It was a dilapidated affair, though capable of forty miles an hour. As it came nearer, he stepped into the center of the road and waved his hands, taking care that the headlights should play upon his weapon.

The Ford stopped and an alarmed black face thrust its head from the open window.

"Listen, mister, I ain't got nothin'. It ain't no use holding me up."

Van Loan took no notice of his words. Instead, he climbed into the car beside the negro. He brandished his gun menacingly.

"I'm not holding you up," he said. "I want you to drive me to Washington as fast as you can. Do it and you'll make twenty dollars. Stall and you'll get into trouble."

The negro became affable. "Twenty bucks? Shre, boss. I'll take you to Florida for that. What part of Washington does you want to go to?"

VAN LOAN'S eyes twinkled behind the mask. In a low tone he whispered the address of his destination.

The negro's eyes popped, and the fear that had been upon him now evolved to amazement—and a tremendous respect. The car rattled on toward the capital.

The black limousine that Van Loan had left Baltimore in rolled silently down Pennsylvania Avenue. It slithered to a stop. A man of Van Loan's height and build got out. On his face was a black silk mask. He and the limousine moved in opposite directions.

The masked man walked along beside a grilled fence until he came to a sentry in a marine's uniform. The man approached the gate that the sailor guarded. A rifle barred his way.

THE masked man met the sentry's inquiring gaze.

"Andrew Jackson," he said quietly.

The rifle was replaced on the marine's shoulder.

"Pass," he said.

The masked man walked through the gate along a gravel path that apparently led to the rear of a large house. He climbed four steps to a small porch at the back of the house. A burly man in evening clothes put a hand on his wrist.

"Who are you?" he demanded.

The masked man's lips smiled ever so faintly.

"Andrew Jackson," he said again.

The burly man's hand left his wrist and respectfully touched his forehead. "Go ahead," he said. "He's waiting."

The masked man entered the house. It was a large house with mazes of stairways and doors. Yet the nocturnal visitor did not falter. He walked with the air of a man who knew every vagary of the mansion's architecture.

On the third floor, he left the stairs and walked down a long corridor. Before a closed door stood a hard-faced man wearing a derby. The masked man approached him.

"Andrew Jackson," he said confidently.

The man in the derby nodded, then tapped deferentially upon the door. A tired voice said: "Come in."

The masked man disappeared and the door closed behind him.

He stood just inside the doorway. It was a large well-lighted room with drawn curtains. In the far corner was an enormous desk, behind which sat a kindly-faced elderly gentleman, with weary, very tired eyes. The man in the mask bowed, walked across the room and took the proffered hand of the other.

"It is an honor to meet such a courageous gentleman as the Phantom," said the man behind the desk. "I am glad you have come."

The masked man bowed again. "If you think I can serve my country, I am only too glad to put myself at your service."

The other nodded, then lapsed into a thoughtful silence. Then he cleared his throat and spoke.

"You have been called in," he said, "at the suggestion of Elmer Havens, who is the only man in the world knowing your true identity. I know your reputation, and it is my belief that you are the one man who can aid us in our fight."

The masked man said simply, "I shall do my best."

THE other nodded approvingly. He continued: "Two things beset our country today. One is the world-wide financial depression, the other, the dominance of the criminal and gangster. The power of the underworld must be broken. Recently, a man has risen to combine all the nefarious forces of crime. Thus far the one point in the favor of the law has been the jealousy, the lack of organization of the criminal. But now this man—this genius, has come to rally all the armies of crime to his banner.

"I called him genius. He is. I have here the reports from our agents. I can give you no further information than these reports. I cannot help you officially. I place my trust in you. I place the trust of the country in you. You must do your best with little information against terrific odds. Here are the papers. Are there any questions?"

THE masked man took the leather despatch case which the elderly gentleman with the very tired eyes handed to him.

"No questions," he said. "However I pledge you all my resources. My life, if need be."

The elderly gentleman rose and extended his hand. The masked man accepted it. For a moment they stood there gazing into each other's eyes.

"Well, good luck, Mr. Phantom," said the man behind the desk. "May God be with you. Good-by."

The masked man bowed. "Goodby," he said. He half turned toward the door, then suddenly catching himself, he faced his host once more and backed slowly from the room, opening the door behind his own back.

It was not an empty gesture, rather an adherence to ordinary etiquette. For no citizen may turn his back on the President of the United States!

The gentleman with the weary eyes watched the door close, then with a sigh turned back to the affairs of state.

The man in the mask retraced his steps through the White House, down the gravel path, until at last he came into the street again from the gate at which the marine kept his untiring vigil.

He walked slowly down Pennsylvania Avenue which was now deserted. The only sign of life he saw was the burly figure of a traffic cop some two blocks away.

He started suddenly as he saw a movement behind one of the stretching trees that lined the avenue. His hand fell to his hip pocket. But too late. A figure took shape in the gloom. Sprang. Something black and heavy hurtled through the air and came down on the masked man's head. A hand snatched the leather dispatch case from under his arm. Two blocks away, the policeman's whistle blew.

And Dick Van Loan, regretting that he did not have time to search the man further, took a hasty glance at the policeman who raced toward him, then started off almost twice as fast in the opposite direction. As he went he thanked his lucky stars that he had been in time; and also that the reputation of the President of the United States was not one of loquaciousness.

CHAPTER II

THE EYE OF DEATH

VAN LOAN ceased his contemplation of the locuments on his desk and lighted an Egyptian cigarette. A frown wrinkled his brow, and for a moment he stared blankly into space. He was frankly worried. Apparently there was more in this affair than he had thought at first.

When Havens first suggested he take this job, he had done it in the spirit of a lark, the same spirit that had prompted him to handle other cases which had made his name a byword among decent people and a Nemesis to the underworld.

It was Havens, the publisher of a dozen newspapers, who had suggested that he become the Phantom and attempt to solve certain cases for the papers that the police had failed upon; and it was Havens who had suggested this latest undertaking.

Yet Van Loan was positive that only three living men had known of his appointment with the President—the latter, Havens and himself. Yet he had been waylaid by someone who seemed to know as much of his plans as he did himself.

IF this super-intelligence, regarding whom the meager documents on his desk concerned themselves, had so easily discovered what he had regarded as a secret impossible of transpiration, the task he had so lightly assumed would probably prove to be the most dangerous adventure in his checkered, perilous career.

However, if he was worried he was most certainly not afraid. Richard Curtis Van Loan had stood shoulder to shoulder with the reaper too often to fear anything living— or for that matter, dead.

Born to society and wealth, the War had taught him the utter futility of the pampered life he had lead in his youth. On the flaming Eastern front he had learned to grapple with death daily. Further, he had learned to like it.

Peace-time adjustment was hard— impossible. That was the reason he had so eagerly jumped at his best friend's suggestion to combat crime in the rôle of the Phantom. And as the underworld would attest vehemently, he had been thoroughly successful.

To alleviate the boredom that attacked him he had thoroughly studied and no less thoroughly mastered the various arts which would render his war on crime more effective. His knowledge of criminology was perhaps equaled by only one man—the incomparable Lombroso.

His histrionic ability, and his talent for make-up were not surpassed by any actor that ever trod the boards. He had cultivated a gift of mimicry and ventriloquism which had stood him in good stead on more than one occasion. He had but to hear a voice once, in order to be able to imitate it perfectly.

Thus it was that the Phantom had been signally successful when lesser sleuths had failed. Van Loan had perfected his chosen art to such a point that beside him the average professional detective was a lumbering tyro.

Yet, despite the fact that he had risen to the top of his chosen profession, he was not altogether happy. In order to pursue the hazardous career of the Phantom, which he created, he was compelled to forego the things which any normal man may have for the asking. Love, romance, children, a home—these things were not for Richard Van Loan. These tranquil joys were not for a man who faced death daily, who gambled his life with criminals every moment. No, all life is a compromise and the compromises which he had been compelled to make in order to create the Phantom were no small things.

YET, he would rather have it this way. Though at times when he thought of Muriel, his heart lay heavy within him. Muriel was Frank Havens' daughter, and under other circumstances, Van often thought of her as his bride. She possessed all the charms and virtues that he would have asked in his wife. But he realized he could never realize that dream. For the Phantom had been born from the ashes of romance.

He sighed and glanced impatiently at the clock. Havens should be here by now, and he was eager to report the events of the night before to his friend, the only man who knew the true identity of him who the world called the Phantom.

He lit his third cigarette from the butt of its predecessor, when the phone jangled impatiently and the operator announced:

"Mr. Havens is calling Mr. Smith."

"Havens? Good. Send him in."

He hung up and a few minutes later the door opened to admit a tall gray-haired man of about forty-two. Van sprang to his feet and greeted his visitor cordially, with an extended hand. Rather, to his surprise, Havens made no move to take it. Instead the publisher sat down on the couch, and said in a low, hoarse, tone:

"What's the time?"

Van glanced at his watch.

"Ten to twelve," he said casually. But his eyes studied the other's face with concern. Havens did not look like his usual self. His normally keen eyes were dull and glazed. His voice, usually alive and animated, was sodden, expressionless. Further, he who had yesterday been so excited about the Phantom's latest adventure seemed to have little concern with it today.

Van puffed at his cigarette slowly. "Feeling a bit under the weather?" he asked.

Havens raised his eyes and stared at the speaker. As Van met his gaze he felt a little chill run down his spine. For if ever hate and murder were written in a human face they were indelibly stamped on the features of Havens at that moment.

VAN LOAN was puzzled and his worry increased.

"Well," he said with a nonchalance he did not feel, "I had something of an adventure last night."

"Yes," said Havens in a horrible monotone. "What time is it?"

That made the second time he had asked that question in five minutes. Van decided to humor him until he found out what the trouble was.

"Five to twelve," he said quietly. Then he crossed the room and dropped a fraternal hand on the publisher's shoulder.

"Listen, Frank," he said. "We've been pals a long time. Now tell me what's the matter with you? You look all in."

AGAIN that chill ran down his spine as Havens looked up at him. A cruel smile distorted the publisher's lips. He rose slowly to his feet. His hands trembled. He seemed in the grip of some terrible emotion.

"It's nearly twelve o'clock," he said thickly.

For the third time Van glanced at his watch. Then there came to his ears the slow tolling of the sonorous bell in the Metropolitan Tower.

Havens stood stock still listening. For twelve long seconds he did not move, save for the slight tremble in his hands. Then, at last, as the final note reverberated and died away, he uttered a shrill cry. His hand flashed to his pocket in a lightning-like gesture. It came into view again holding a slim pearl-handled revolver.

He whipped it up and, aiming point blank at his best friend, he pulled the trigger.

"There," he cried, in a mad frenzy, "you die at noon. Master, I have obeyed."

But Van Loan was not taken unawares. He had been expecting something to happen, and the fact that he did not know what it would be did not render him any the less ready for it.

He leaped aside with the speed and grace of a panther. The steel slug from Havens' revolver whizzed over his head and buried itself in the wall. Then, in a flying tackle, Van crashed against the other's knees and brought him to the floor.

And in that second, in that instant when his life had hung in the balance, he knew the answer. In a single swift illuminating flash, his brain saw the only possible explanation.

Havens lay on the floor with Van's strong arms still about his thighs. The revolver had slithered underneath the couch. Havens stared blankly up at the ceiling. Then suddenly Van released him. He bent over the publisher, staring steadily into his eyes.

"Listen, Frank," he said. "Listen to me. It's Van. Van. Do you understand?"

He bent closer and struck Havens twice on the cheek with the flat of his hand. Then he snapped his fingers in front of the other's eyes. During this peculiar process, he kept up a steady stream of words.

"Frank! It's Van! Van! Come out of it. Out of it."

HE accompanied the last word with another stinging blow on the cheek. Then he breathed easier as he saw the dull glaze suddenly leave the other's eyes. Life seemed to return to his dead irises. His face lost cruel relentlessness. Van helped him up and sat him in a chair.

Normal once more, Havens stared at his friend in a bewildered manner.

"Van," he said in a questioning, puzzled voice, "where did you come from?" He looked around the room, recognized it, and went on: "How did I get here. What—"

"Take it easy," said Van gravely.

"I'll explain everything to you. You see that?"

He pointed to the revolver on the floor. Havens' eyes followed his hand. The publisher nodded.

"Well," said Van, "you just tried to kill me with that."

Horror shone in Havens' face. "What?"

Van nodded. "It wasn't your fault, though. You were hypnotized."

"My God," said Havens, now thoroughly comprehending. "Go on, man. Tell me what happened."

Briefly Van told him of his own deeds since he had arrived in the apartment. When he finished, Havens stared at him aghast.

"But, good heavens," he exclaimed. "Why? Why should anyone hypnotize me? Why should anyone want to make me kill you?"

"Because," said Van gravely, "you are the only living person who knows the identity of the Phantom. They can't kill the Phantom, because they don't know who he is. But they could hypnotize you and while under the influence tell you to kill the Phantom, because you knew what they did not. *You knew that I am the Phantom!*"

HAVENS nodded slowly as the reason of Van's explanation came to him.

"But who?" he said. "I appreciate the fact that you've made enemies among crooks. But who is so diabolically clever to be able to conceive and carry out a scheme of this sort?"

"The same person that waylaid me last night."

"But I sent my car for you? Didn't it get there? If not, where's the car? Where's the chauffeur?"

"The car picked me up in Baltimore as per schedule," said Van, "before we got waylaid. Your chauffeur is probably a corpse somewhere in Maryland. God knows where the car is."

Havens nearly bounced out of his chair.

"What? You mean you never saw—"

"No. I never saw him."

"But I received a confidential message from Washington late last night saying that you had been there."

"Not me," said Van grimly. "That was the enemy impersonating me."

"But who? Who is this enemy?"

"That," said Van very gravely, "is what we must find out if we care at all about living."

There was a short grim silence in the room.

"Now," said Van, "you're beginning to realize what I came to realize last night. We're dealing with a great man. A man capable of giving genius to crime. A man capable of welding the whole underworld together in a war on society. I have some papers here which give me certain information. Not a great deal, but at least something to work on."

He broke off for a moment, then told Havens the whole story of his adventures of the night before.

"Now," he went on, "if we can find out who it was that hypnotized you, we have a real first-class clue. Think, now! Did you come in contact with any suspicious characters this morning. Anyone at all, who you think might have hypnotized you?"

HAVENS wrinkled his brows and thought profoundly for a minute or two. Then he shook his head.

"No-o," he said slowly. "I can't say that I did. I—I've got it. The cripple!"

Van leaned forward in his chair. His eyes shone eagerly.

"Go on," he said excitedly. "What cripple?"

"Well," said Havens, "of course, I've no evidence to go on. But his eyes. I'll never forget his eyes. I grew dizzy looking at him."

"Go on," said Van. "Give me all the details you can think of. Where did you meet him?"

"I ran into him as I was leaving the Pneumatic Rubber Company's director's meeting. I left with Bursage—you know Bursage. He's head of the board. Well, we were going out of the building together when this cripple beggar came up to us whining something about a nickel for a cup of coffee."

Van nodded and scrawled something on a desk pad. Havens continued: "I reached in my pocket for some silver before I really saw him. Then when I looked at him, I noticed his eyes. He was dirty and unshaven, yet those eyes stared out of his head like glittering diamonds in a setting of mud. I never saw anything like it. They were filled with hatred—hatred and dominance."

"Dominance is hardly a quality you'd expect to find in the eyes of a bum," observed Van.

"True. I thought of that. As I handed him a quarter, his hand touched mine, and our gazes met. As he looked at me I got a trifle dizzy. My head buzzed. It was all over in a minute and I paid no attention to it. But I distinctly remember that I was frightfully dizzy at the time."

VAN nodded. "Did Bursage notice anything?" he asked.

"No. I mentioned the cripple to him as we walked away. He dismissed my ideas. Said the man was just an ordinary tramp. He saw nothing out of the ordinary about him."

"Did you notice anything out of the ordinary about him, except for his eyes?"

"No. But, God, Van, those eyes were enough. I tell you, I've never seen anything that had such a weird effect on me. It was awful."

"Awful enough," said Van grimly. "They were the eyes of death. The eyes that we must find if ever we are to break the power of the man who plans to devastate society."

CHAPTER III

THE PHANTOM MEETS THE FOE

HAVENS sat silent for a moment, as his mind absorbed the dire situation that they faced. When he spoke his voice trembled slightly, for Havens was a man of imagination.

"Does anyone know you're here, Van?"

"Not a soul. I checked in early this morning, under the alias of Smith. You're the only living soul who knows it."

Havens nodded, satisfied. Then he asked with a clouded brow:

"But what are we fighting, Van? Who is it? What is his aim? Have you no information?"

Van jerked his thumb in the direction of the papers that scattered the escritoire.

"Only what's there. His name's Hesterberg. From those Department of Justice reports, he's mad, and he's a Red. They've got a good line on him up till three years ago. Then it becomes mostly guess work. Anyway, he's got a good head on him. But it seems he's hipped on Communism. He's drawn pay from Russia for years. And since he quit the university, where he was Professor of Economics, he's devoted himself to breaking down all American ideals.

"He's plotting a tremendous world

wide revolution. As I understand it, his aim is to get all the civilized nations at each other's throats through his machinations; to tear down governments and law by his alliance with the underworld, and then, when we're weak and impotent, to crush us all with the mighty Red armies."

Havens reached for a cigarette. "A nice customer," he said. "God, Van, if he can force his will on people as easily as he did on me, we're done for."

A vague fear was reflected in the publisher's eyes as he spoke. Van Loan crossed the room and slapped him confidentially on the shoulder.

"Don't let it get you, old man," he said. "You're naturally upset after what you went through this morning. Hesterberg hasn't won yet. He—"

His words trailed off into nothingness as there came a sharp staccato rap at the door. Havens' eyes stared into the detective's.

"Who's that" he asked in a low tense voice.

VAN LOAN stood perfectly still for a moment, yet the complete immobility of his body indicated that his mind was functioning smoothly, rapidly.

"You've been followed," he said in a low voice. "Some one's followed you to see if you really killed the Phantom. Open the door. I'll stand back here. Pretend you're upset. Act as if you'd really killed me, until I think of some way to turn this break to our advantage."

Havens rose and walked toward the door, while Van carefully flattened himself up against the heavy drapes near the window. Havens opened the door, and did his best to look like a man who has just slain his best friend. His hands trembled as he held the door ajar.

His head was hung on his chest, and his voice broke as he asked:

"What is it?"

A burly man pushed past him, and glanced around the apartment.

Havens clutched at him.

"What is it? What do you want?" he demanded in a shrill voice.

THE other pushed him aside brutally. "I'm looking for a corpse," he said callously. "Did you do your little job?"

Havens uttered an exclamation of fear and shrank up against the wall. The visitor laughed harshly.

"Where's the body?" he said.

Havens caught Van's eye. With the air of a man who has been cornered he nodded his head toward the bathroom. The stranger took a step in that direction.

Van Loan made a swift movement with each hand. His right whipped an automatic from his shoulder holster, while the left slipped a black silk mask over his head. Unconcerned, the intruder walked toward the bathroom and looked in. Then he turned savagely to Havens.

"You rat! Don't lie to me. Where's the body? Where's the Phantom?"

"The Phantom's here. Both his body and his soul. Put up your hands!"

Havens laughed grimly. Their visitor turned an astonished face to the masked man who held the gun aimed directly at his heart. For a moment, Hesterberg's henchman was too utterly amazed to move. Then an exclamation fell from his lips.

"God!" he said. "God!"

"So you're rather surprised that I'm alive?"

"It's never failed before," said the man speaking more to himself than the others.

"But it's failed now," said Van. "But there'll be another killing here that won't fail unless you give me some information. Now talk."

By now the stranger had taken a grip on himself.

"Talk?" he repeated. "About what?"

"Just talk," said Van softly, but his eyes were hard. "About anything. But particularly about a Mad Red called Hesterberg, or about a cripple with remarkable eyes that impels men to go gunning for their friends. Best of all, tell me where I can meet these charming gentlemen."

The stranger frowned, opened his mouth, then closed it again. He stared steadily at the gun.

"I'm not talking," he said laconically.

"Yes, you are," contradicted Van. "You're talking or you're dying. I don't bluff. I mean it."

THE other gazed at him steadily. Whatever his faults may have been, cowardice was not among them.

"I die anyway," he said simply. "If I do talk, I'll get worse from someone else than you can ever give me."

"I'll count three," said Van, and his voice was jagged ice. "Then you get it."

He began to count in a slow deliberate voice, and for the second time that day, death was in the room.

But the henchman of Hesterberg was not of the breed that waits for the reaper supinely. With a sudden swift motion he ducked his head. At the same moment his hand flashed to his hip. Something black and ominous appeared in his hand. Two staccato reports ripped through the room. One steel slug tore angrily through the plaster of the wall. The other crashed into human

The Phantom bent swiftly over the corpse and ran facile fingers through the gangster's pockets.

flesh, ripped a heart to shreds and wrenched a life from a body.

Van stood over the crimson torso of his fallen foe. He spoke rapidly to Havens.

"Get out," he said. "I can handle this better alone. I'll communicate with you through our usual channels."

FOR a moment Havens thought of protesting, but he had learned that when the Phantom issued orders it was expedient to obey. Silently he let himself out the door.

Van Loan bent swiftly over the corpse and ran facile fingers through the other's pockets. He piled up on the table the articles he took from the dead man, then regarded them with no little wonder.

First, there was a red band, about six inches wide, with the Number 8 painted on it in white. Its use he could only conjecture. But he was quite familiar with the second object, though it was difficult to understand what a man was doing with it in the heart of New York at high noon.

It was a small rubberized silk gas mask of the type which covers the nose, leaving the mouth free. Van stared at these for some time. Then he began to go through the sheaf of papers that he had taken from the man's inside pocket in the hope of finding some clue that would put him directly on the trail of the Mad Red.

Luck was with him. His pulses pounded with excitement as he stared at the yellow slip of paper in his hand. Typed neatly upon it was the message that would, God willing, give him the first personal contact with the man who had twice tried to slay the Phantom.

It read:

INSTRUCTIONS FOR NUMBER 8

You will appear at midnight at the Morton Bank. You will wear your identification band. You will bring your gas mask. I shall lead the horde in person. You shall wait for me and remain by my side while the work is done.   O.

Van Loan sat down. He lit a cigarette and for a long time remained lost in thought. He was impervious to the bloody figure upon the floor. Impervious to everything save the fact that at midnight he was prepared to risk his life in order to come close to the man that he had vowed to track down.

The message was by no means clear to him. Then, too, there was always the alternative of calling in the police. Undoubtedly, the bluecoats, massed in sufficient numbers, could frustrate whatever plan Hesterberg had made. Yet that course

would get the Phantom no closer to the Red madman.

No, to be successful, he, the Phantom, must play it alone. Number 8 had probably been sent to see that Havens carried out the instructions of the crippled hypnotist. Or, if not, he had come on his own to see the Phantom's finish. In any event, it was a break Van could not afford to pass up.

HERE at last was the chance to meet Hesterberg, to find out the man's plans, and then to foil him. Once again, the Phantom would play a lone hand, spurning the aid of the police of the city, spurning all aid save that which his keen alert brain and his steady, courageous heart and hand could give him.

He glanced at his watch. It was almost five o'clock. That gave him over seven hours until his rendezvous. Until then he would rest, he decided. He might need that rest later. He glanced down at the body on the floor, and shrugged his shoulders. He had no time to bother with that.

He would check out and leave it there. After all, who could connect the entirely mythical Mr. Smith who had registered that morning with the Phantom?

He threw away his cigarette, removed his coat and lay down upon the bed. It was characteristic of him that neither the hazard that lay seven hours before him, nor the ugly shattered thing that lay on the floor, prevented him from falling into peaceful, untroubled slumber.

He awoke shortly before eleven o'clock. Rested and fresh, he sprang from the bed. After attending to his ablutions, he sat down before a mirror, and opened a black make-up box on the dressing table. Deftly his fingers drew the sticks of grease paint across his face.

His complexion slowly changed color; his features gradually became those of another man. And when at last he had finished, he stared into the mirror carefully scrutinizing his disguise. And the face that stared so grimly back at him was the face of Number 8 of Hesterberg's henchmen, whose corpse lay stiff and stark in the other room.

As he rose from his seat his eyes fell on the photograph of Muriel Havens on the table. Her limpid eyes stared at him from the brown paper. For a moment, he stood stock still. A sigh escaped from his lips. His heart was heavy. Then with the air of a man resolved to return to duty, no matter where his heart lay, he turned abruptly away, and, going into the other room, occupied himself with the gruesome task of divesting the dead man of his clothing.

At exactly three minutes before midnight the Phantom shot a quick glance out of the window of his cab at the illuminated dial of the clock that decorated the marble façade of the Morton National Bank Building. He was two short block from his destination; two short blocks from his mysterious rendezvous with Hesterberg, the Mad Red.

HIS lips curled in a thin, ironical smile. So be it! At last he was to come to grips with the fatal personality that hung like an oppressive pall over the money marts of the world.

The ornate pile of the bank loomed up a block away. The Phantom rapped smartly on the glass partition that separated him from the driver with hard knuckles. His cab wheeled into the curb and pulled up short with a harsh grinding of brakes.

One eye on the hands of the clock that slowly jerked over to three minutes of the hour, Van flung a bill at the cabbie, heard him shift into gear and wheel away. He paused a moment, irresolute, at the curb. The minute hand of the clock moved over another notch. Two minutes to go till the fatal hour struck.

He experienced a sharp tightening of the nerves along his spine as he traversed the last block on foot. He was aware of a strange eerie tenseness in the air; the atmosphere was super-charged with an uncanny chill of portentous doom.

SUDDENLY there was a black hole in the night where the brilliantly illumined dial of the clock had been but a moment before. The abrupt failure of that symbol of financial integrity that had shone down on Wall Street for the past sixty years, came as a ominous signal—a potential warning.

But of what?

The Phantom paused in his strides for a moment. And it was then that he realized for the first time that not only the lights of the clock had failed but all other lights along the canyoned thoroughfare as well. The knowledge came to him as a distinct shock. For a panicky second he stumbled forward in an abysmal tunnel of stygian gloom. What a moment before had been a mazda spangled street of granite was now empty of all light.

Empty of all light, yes; but not of life.

The nerves of the Phantom snapped out of their momentary lapse. He was distinctly aware of a horde of strangely masked figures rushing by him with purposeful haste. They seemed to materialize out of the very gloom of the street, that a moment before had been empty of all save himself.

They brushed by him, grotesque,

goggle-eyed, long-nosed gargoyles in the heavy pall of darkness. The Phantom sensed without seeing that they were all converging on the massive doors of the bank building.

He measured stride with the surging throng about him, vainly trying to estimate their numbers. Then, a moment later a sound—a strange and sibilant sound—a sinister sound, pierced through the mental arithmetic of his brain. His finely arched nostrils quivered; his throat was suddenly parched with an acid streak of fire!

Gas! He understood it all then—those hideous masks for faces. Hesterberg was martialing his forces to the attack under a barrage of gas. The noxious poison flicked at the lining of his lungs. With a practice and skill perfected in the Argonne he laced his own gas mask over his head and charged up the granite steps of the bank on the double quick.

A sharp pencil of light from a pocket flash played over the fantastic group of six around the bank's door. The Phantom's heart kicked out a steady hundred and thirty as it finally came to rest on him, picking out the bold letter eight on the sleeve of his coat.

A sharp cultured voice drilled into the Phantom's consciousness — a voice he was never to forget.

GOOD! Number 8! What word have you received?"

Some instinct, some cunning premonition told the Phantom that he was being addressed by the Mad Red himself. Twin pulses beat at his throat; the knotted veins of his gnarled hands stood out like whipcords. Fo a moment he was assailed with a swirl of mad chaotic emotions. Why not whip the automatic from his shoulder holster and

empty its load of lethal death into the madman's heart?

Then with Hesterberg's sharp reiterated phrase came sanity. Van had no desire to commit suicide just then.

"Well, Number 8—what word— what word?"

The Phantom knew now that the inquiry concerned his own demise.

"Dead!" he answered in a clear monotone.

A sharp breath whistled through Hesterberg's nostrils.

"Magnificent, Number 8. Stand by my right. Details 1 and 4 are in the bank by now. 5 and 2 have the building surrounded and are holding the street." A sharp grating as of steel on steel came from behind the massive doors of the bank, to be greeted by another sharp exhalation from Hesterberg's nostrils. "So—the door opens to us—like all other doors in the world shall open at my command."

The six-inch portals swung slowly inward. Hard at Hesterberg's right with the detail of men close behind them, the Phantom moved swiftly across the threshold of the bank.

CHAPTER IV

PAPERS OF DEATH

HIS keen analytical brain was working at high speed. It was quite obvious from the few words that had passed between him and the Mad Red that the Number 8 he was impersonating was of some importance in the Hesterberg councils.

A lieutenant, an adjustant of crime! So much the better! If he had been ordered to stand hard by the Master's right, he would stand there—with his index finger coiled around the trigger of his gun.

But all such thoughts were momentarily wiped from his mind. Hesterberg's pocket torch was darting like a hungry tongue of flame around the vaulted quadrangle of the bank. In weird, lurid flashes it depicted scenes of fantastic unreality.

Off to the right, behind a steel shield, three men worked with torches and explosives on the combination of a safe. Behind the grilled windows squads of men systematically rifled cash boxes. At every point of vantage, at every window and door stood a gas-masked giant with a gaping mouthed submachine-gun crooked in ready hands.

Through the murky haze of the cloud of gas the scene was bizarre. At Van's feet a blue uniformed watchman writhed in agony as the poison gas settled in a ball of fire in his chest. The Phantom's first impulse was abruptly checked by the cursing snarl of Hesterberg as the latter stumbled over the prone body.

"Fool of a Bourgeois!" spat out Hesterberg. "Slave for a pittance to guard the treasures of your betrayers. You have suffered blindly long enough. Suffer now for a cause. The glorious Red cause of Alexis Hesterberg."

BEFORE the Phantom was aware of what was happening the Mad Red whipped out a heavy German Luger and, aiming it point blank at the convulsed chest of the watchman, fired twice in quick succession.

Two jets of smoke coughed from the nozzle of the gun; but there was no explosion. The gun was silenced. The Phantom's eyes were twin gimlets of steel behind his protecting gas mask but his voice was calm, impersonal when he spoke.

"A good end for the old fool. But it was gold that killed him—not steel!"

"Red gold!" chortled Hesterberg.

"Come, Number 8, we have work to do."

Not quite knowing what his cue might be, the Phantom strictly obeyed his first order and kept close to the side of the Mad Red. With rapid strides they traversed the broad marble floor of the bank.

The Phantom's keen eyes took in the scene of frenzied activity about him; corrected his first impression and realized that though the masked figures were working at top speed there was an assurance about their movements that could only come from organization, precision and a technique dominated by a supermaster mind.

HE was only permitted a few brief glimpses of the systematic looting of the bank. Hesterberg with a show of arrogant contempt at such a mad scramble for the evil yellow metal—led the way down the broad flight of steps at the rear of the building.

He never hesitated once; and the Phantom, living up to his grim appellation, followed close on his heels. With unerring stride, as if he were a daily familiar of the bank, Hesterberg led the way to the vault that sheltered the safety deposit boxes of the bank's depositors.

Two of the Russian's henchmen stood before the ravaged door, their work completed. The ponderous steel portal hung awry from one hinge, neatly and expertly blown from its moorings. With an avid eye on the dim-lit interior beyond, Hesterberg dismissed his two henchmen with a grunt and with two long eager strides swept into the interior of the stronghold.

For a second time that night the Phantom was tormented with the mad desire to call for an immediate showdown; to reveal himself to the Mad Red, not as Number 8, but as the Phantom himself. The momentary advantage was his. They were alone together, those two, deep in the subterranean vault. To him would be the vantage of a surprise attack. All he would have to do would be to draw his automatic.

But then sanity again asserted itself. To kill Hesterberg was one thing; to get out of the bank was another. And anyway, Mad Red or no, he couldn't shoot the Russian down in cold blood. Time for gun play later, he decided. First he had to discover what mad enterprise brought Hesterberg to that particular vault of the bank.

He was not left long in doubt as the pencil of light from the pocket torch in the other's hands came to rest on a brass plate above a huge strong box which bore the following legend:

IMPERIAL JAPANESE EMBASSY

FOR the first time the Phantom was given some inkling of the magnitude of the plunder. Let his henchmen loot the money coffers! He, Hesterberg, was interested in far more important things. State documents, State papers, secret files! Who could tell but that the balance of world power lay concealed behind that enigmatic locked door?

The looting of a bank was one thing, but the disrupting of international relations was another and far more important one. What was behind that locked door guarded by the seal of the Japanese Embassy? What contents lay within that little, two by two cubby-hole, that Hesterberg should have planned so minutely, risking so much to discover?

Hesterberg, too, was impatient with curiosity. With a hand that trembled slightly and an eye that gleamed fanatically even through the vizor of his gas mask, he fitted a slender, tapering key into the lock of the box and turned it. The door swung open at his touch.

All thought of the automatic clutched in his right hand forgotten; all thought of an immediate showdown swept from his mind, the Phantom leaned eagerly over the Mad Red's shoulder and peered eagerly into the dim recess of the stronghold.

Neat bundles of heavily sealed, official documents met his eye. Hesterberg plunged two rapacious hands into them; pulled them out to the probing light of his torch.

The first he discarded with a grunt of disdain. The Phantom noted that it was a list of the secret operatives of Moravia. The second and third packets Hesterberg swept from him with ill-concealed rage. They fell unnoted at his feet.

So intent was he on the remaining packets that he failed to note that his good right hand —Number 8—had stooped to retrieve the fallen documents. While Hesterberg was avidly scanning the remaining papers, the Phantom managed to scribble a few words on the face of one of the packets and stuffed it into his inside pocket.

AN ironic smile played on his lips for a moment. For the first time since assuming the role of Hesterberg's henchman he felt sure of himself. He was playing his old game again; using his old style, his old technique.

His mental gloatings were cut short abruptly by a throaty chuckle of satisfaction from Hesterberg.

Hesterberg thumped the top packet in his hand with an enthusiastic fist and permitted the remaining ones to trickle through his fingers to the floor.

"Capital! Excellent! Tremendous!" he exalted. "This night's work will carry us well along the road to success, Number 8!"

In vain the Phantom essayed to read the inscription on the topmost sheet of the papers clutched in Hesterberg's hand. Before he could decipher the minute script the Russian thrust the documents in his pocket with one hand and pounded the Phantom affectionately on the shoulder with the other. He hooked his arm under Number 8's and led the way out of the vault.

"Our work is done here, Number 8," he enthused. "Come, comrade, you are strangely silent tonight. Give me the details of the climax of that little scene I so subtly arranged for our friend the Phantom."

WITH Hesterberg's words came a new worry for the Phantom. He had no qualms concerning his disguise. He was a past master in the art of makeup. And into the bargain his face was effectively concealed by the gas mask. Unfortunately, however, his acquaintance with the legitimate Number 8 had been of too short duration, had terminated so swiftly and tragically, that he wasn't quite familiar with the other's voice.

Though the mask that fitted snugly over his head would muffle his words, he realized the necessity of caution.

He tried to dismiss the affair with a shrug and a word.

"Havens was an excellent shot. Through the heart."

Hesterberg grunted his satisfaction and with his arm still crooked under the Phantom's led the way up the stairs to the main floor of the bank.

Though Van was guarding every word, his keen, analytical brain was functioning smoothly. He realized that if the Mad Red couldn't recognize him through his disguise, by the same token the features of the Russian were concealed from him. His voice he would always remember; it was imprinted indelibly on his memory.

However, he determined before the night's adventure was over to secure at least one glimpse of Hesterberg's face. That he would find it interesting, he was sure. But before that, he had work to do; delicate work. He still had in the breast pocket of his coat the packet of documents he had retrieved from the floor.

A suspicion of a smile flitted across his thin lips as he recalled the hasty words he had scrawled on the topmost sheet.

They were on the main floor of the bank now. The Russian's henchmen had completed their systematic looting of the bank's treasure room.

The Phantom's arm was still crooked under Hesterberg's. He led the latter to a marble-topped table to the left.

"Why not leave a little memento for the directors of the bank?" he suggested.

Hesterberg got the idea at once. He chuckled sardonically to himself, stepped to the counter and picked up a pen.

AN excellent idea, Number 8," he began. Then paused as he concentrated on the message he was to leave. The Phantom leaned familiarly over his shoulder and watched the pen as it scrawled in a fine hand:

"Morton: You are the king of finance, but you lose to the Emperor of Death."

But the Phantom was not interested

in any message that Hesterberg was to leave behind him. While the Russian chuckled over his wit, the Phantom's hand with the finesse and lightning speed of a magician, eased the packet of documents from Hesterberg's pocket and substituted in their place the one he, himself, had filched.

The operation was executed in the twinkling of an eye before Hesterberg had dotted the final i of his message.

Then a swift change came over Hesterberg. His old aggressive manner asserted itself and he issued a series of crisp orders to his men. Like a well-drilled army corps they martialed themselves at their leader's words and beat a hurried retreat from the bank.

Outside, the darkness still hung over the street like a black mantle. The cloud of gas laid down at the first attack was slowly rising. From a short distance away came the confused murmur of many voices and the heavy tramp of hurrying feet.

Suddenly the stillness of the night was shattered by the shrill blast of a police whistle directly ahead. It was repeated, first from the right and then from the left.

Hesterberg paused a moment on the topmost step of the bank and surveyed the scene and his men. He issued his final order, sharply, explicitly.

"The police are amassing at last," he said lightly. "But as usual, they are too late. The gas barrage won't have lifted for another minute."

HE turned to Number 8 at his side. "The Council of Five will repair with me to headquarters at once. Pass along the word."

The Phantom turned to the man next to him and repeated the order. Hesterberg was addressing his men.

"The police will charge in ex-actly forty seconds. I am leaving the scene of action now. Cover our retreat. Meet the police in massed formation. Depend on your sub-machine-guns. Hold them for at least two minutes, then disband to your stations. Await there for further orders through the regular channels."

THE Phantom gambled on giving his identity away, but boldly assumed that he was one of the Council's Five. He stuck close to Hesterberg's right, his gun hand hovering in the region of his automatic.

A moment later his assumption proved correct as he was wedged into the rear of an ebony limousine between Hesterberg and another helmeted figure with the numeral 12 emblazoned on his sleeve band. A man was at the wheel with another beside him. With a roaring exhaust the car pulled away from the curb and careened down the deserted canyon of Wall Street.

As they sped from the scene of the looting of the bank, a staccato rumble of gunfire told the Phantom that the police had charged.

Massed around the steps of the Morton Bank two score grisly, gas-masked men, awaited the charge of the police. The heavy odor of gas had cleared away now, and the rumble of speeding automobiles came to their ears distinctly. That meant reserves.

They waited tense, expectantly, fingers wrapped around the trigger guards of their sub-machine-guns. No man stirred; no man grumbled. Though they well knew that their position was precarious in the extreme; though they well knew that they would be outnumbered by ten to one, they held their ground. Hesterberg had given them orders and they obeyed them.

Suddenly, swiftly the attack began! Under a covering barrage of flying steel the minions of the law charged on the run. Fifty yards down the street a street-lamp, spluttered, then flashed on. Then another and another in quick succession.

Hesterberg's men held their fire. The police were charging madly now, guns spewing flame, concentrating on the bank. The masked men crouching at the steps of the marble edifice massed closer together. Lead whined and screamed shrilly over their heads; razor-like slivers of marble, chipped from the face of the bank, exploded in their eyes.

And then the first burning lead took effect. With an inarticulate scream a masked figure in the front ranks of the besieged men threw up his hands and plunged to the pavement.

That death cry was the signal for a counter-attack!

A score of fingers constricted on as many triggers. A withering barrage of lead carried sudden death into the ranks of the police. The surging line of the blue coats faltered, stopped, crumpled.

The charge of the police was stopped. Hesterberg's men continued their barrage and before their withering fire the police broke ranks and sought what shelter they could find in the bullet-riddled street.

FROM behind refuse cans, fire plugs—they blazed away at the huddled mass of helmeted men on the steps of the bank. From the protection of doorways they hastily reloaded their guns only to empty them again in venomous bursts of lead.

Outnumbered as they were, Hesterberg's men put up a valiant defense. But slowly their forces were decimated. They had held their position for more than the two minutes ordered by the Russian. The order for the retreat was given.

Forming their lines again they amassed their machine-guns before them and began their death march to the rear. Their Thompsons held off the police; prevented the blue coats from closing in and surrounding them. But one by one the machine gunners were killed off. The retreat became a rout, the rout annihilation.

Of the two score men left behind him, only a handful escaped to report back to their respective stations. But in the Russian's colossal scheme what mattered the sacrifice of a few dozen men?

CHAPTER V

THE MEETING

THE moment the Phantom had been waiting for since twelve o'clock came at last. Secure in the private sanctum of Hesterberg, with the door locked and guarded behind them, came the order to unmask. With a heart that was even and firm and a hand that was never more steady, Van unstrapped the buckles of his mask and flung the contraption onto a near-by table. So intent was he on the face of the Russian that was about to be revealed that he never gave a moment's thought to the dire peril he would be in himself if his disguise broke down. Fortunately the room was dimly lit. The Phantom sensed more than saw the luxuriousness of his surroundings. And Hesterberg—Hesterberg was so elated with his accomplishments of the night that he became expansive, bombastic, off guard. The Phantom grinned to himself derisively as he anticipated the shock the Russian would receive in a few short minutes.

Hesterberg took his place at the

head of a long mahogany table. By simple elimination the Phantom realized that his place was at the Master's right. Insolently he kicked out his chair, felt in the pocket of the coat he had taken from the dead Number 8, found a packet of expensive cigarettes and lit up. His iron nerves were on edge, not from fear but from anticipatory excitement.

Through a hazy pall of blue smoke he scrutinized the sharp features of Hesterberg. A huge domed head, he saw, dominated by a pair of large, luminous eyes. The nose was high beaked and finely chiseled; the lips, thin, red and cruel. A handsome face in an arrogant, dominant way; a handsome face ruined by mad, fanatical eyes.

THE Mad Red reached a long, claw-like hand inside his coat. The Phantom's nerves tauted. The blow-up was to come sooner than he had expected. The hand came to light a moment later clutching the substituted packet.

Hesterberg laid the document on the table before him and pounded them with an enthusiastic fist. He spoke and the crisis was delayed for a moment.

"Gentlemen," he began in a ringing voice, "let me congratulate you. The work we have accomplished tonight is tremendous. These documents here"—and again he pounded the official documents before him— the official papers before him— "these documents here mean more to us than gold. They mean power!"

The vaulted room echoed somberly to the word. The mad light in Hesterberg's eyes flared up more brightly. And it was then that the Phantom realized that the Russian's strength lay in that word "power." His strength and his weakness.

With an eloquent arm Hesterberg swept his Council of Five with an inclusive gesture.

"Gentlemen, with these papers here we have the world at Japan's throat. They have merely been waiting for an excuse. And tomorrow I see Kemmel, the Andorra Ambassador." He paused dramatically. "He either does as I order him to do—or dies. Yes, dies by his own hand. Phagh! This childish international tradition of honor plays right into our hands. It relieves us of the detail of executing these greedy pigs when they are discovered in their treachery."

Though caution dictated that he keep his mouth shut, the Phantom could not resist the temptation to bring the little comedy he had precipitated to a climax. Flicking the ash nonchalantly from his cigarette, he inquired casually:

"Excellent, but just what are these papers?"

Hesterberg swept them up in greedy fingers.

"These papers mean more to us than the downfall of Japan. With them in our possession we have the torch to set the world on fire. These papers are the secret—" He glanced at the packet in his hand and his voice broke off abruptly. A tense, ominous stillness vibrated in the room for a moment.

WATCHING Hesterberg keenly through a cloud of smoke, the Phantom saw a score of frustrated passions race across the Russian's face. He, the Phantom, was enjoying the situation immensely. He set himself for a jeering bellow of rage from the Mad Red. But the vocal storm was never delivered.

Instead, when Hesterberg spoke some few panicky seconds later, his voice was a dead calm monotone; a voice far more deadly and sinister than any bellow could have been.

Through the distinct, unemotional enunciation of each syllable the words dripped with a deadly venom. A venom, as Van sensed, that made itself felt with terrible effect on the other four members of the Council of Five.

They were four simple words. Appallingly simple. But death was the answer to the question they propounded.

"Who is the traitor?"

Silence ensued; a foreboding silence that clutched at even the Phantom's throat.

Hesterberg, in the same dead monotone, repeated his question. But the question now had become a flaming accusation.

"Who is the traitor?"

Then abruptly his nerveless calm was shattered. He exploded in a torrent of inflammatory denunciation. Shaking two claw-like fists in the air the packet of documents in his hand thudded to the glass top of the mahogany. Five heads bent over as one to read the laconic message penciled on the topmost sheet. The taunting words stared up at them:

Your second failure at the hands of—the Phantom!

A NERVOUS voice from one of the Council of Five broke in on the Russian's ravings. "The signature of the Phantom, but—but—"

"But there are no buts!" stormed Hesterberg. "These are not the papers I took from the strong box of the Japanese Embassy. These are some insignificant statistics on tariff duties. Phah! There has been a substitution, a trick!" His voice rose high on a storm of passion. "Fools! Madmen! Idiots! So there is one among you who would match his wits against Hesterberg. You are babes, children. Without me you are lost. Empires topple and crash at my machinations!"

"Mad, completely mad," commented the Phantom to himself, as he lit a fresh cigarette. With cool eyes he surveyed the strained faces around the table. Though the others, too, might have had a suspicion of the Russian's dementia, they feared him none the less. They looked questioningly, uncertainly, at one another.

THEN as suddenly as the torrent had come, it abated. Hesterberg led off on another tack. His voice became wheedling, his words dripped honey—but the flame in his eyes never died. He essayed a laugh and the sound grated in the stillness of the room like the shattering of glass.

"Of course," he began, spreading his hands depreciatingly, "if this little farce is someone's idea of humor, I have a few tricks of my own I can play. Perhaps you have witnessed some of them, my friends?"

In the grim silence that followed the Phantom felt the shudder that raced around the council board. Despite his iron nerves and steady self-control, he was visited with a vague, momentary doubt as to the wisdom of the course he had pursued.

Then came the anxious voice of Number 4. "But what if it was the Phantom?"

"This farce has gone far enough," grated Hesterberg. "There is treachery here. That packet of documents was purloined from me. And I suspect that one of the five here—" He broke off abruptly. His voice was jagged ice when he continued again. "Gentlemen, I am sorry to report that one of us here is a traitor to the cause. Those papers must be found. Now. We will have to search, gentlemen. We will have a very thorough search—and it will begin with me."

He turned to the Phantom on his

right and with a steady hand Van extinguished his cigarette in a hammered bronze tray.

"We will stand in a circle," continued Hesterberg. "To show that there is no prejudice, you, Number 8, will begin the search by going over me."

VAN nodded his understanding and the council around the table arose as one man. They formed a tight circle. The Phantom was about to go through his role when suddenly the Mad Red wheeled on him. A strange glint was in his narrowed eyes.

"But it was you, Number 8, who reported to me that the Phantom was dead!" he grated.

The long deferred climax was at hand.

"Then I lied," snapped Number 8. "The Phantom lives. I am the Phantom!"

The savage nozzle of his automatic was grinding at Hesterberg's groins. In the sudden silence that descended on the room at his declaration, he heard the breath whistle sharply through Hesterberg's nostrils.

The two men confronted each other, the demoniacal fury in Hesterberg's eyes challenging the mocking glint in the Phantom's.

"I am sorry to break up your little meeting this way," continued the Phantom. "But it was unavoidable. My gun is an inch deep in Hesterberg's flesh. One overt act from any of you, and I squeeze the trigger."

His simple statement was met by silence from the Council of Five. With a supreme effort Hesterberg regained control of himself. His smile was an unpleasant thing to behold.

"So I meet the Phantom at last?"

"In person."

"So?" continued Hesterberg. "What do you expect to achieve by these melodramatics?"

"I have achieved much already," replied the Phantom blandly.

Hesterberg's lips curled with scorn.

"Fool! Riddle me this: How are you going to get out of this building alive? Though your automatic is pointing at me, it is you who are in the trap—not I."

"I have been in traps before."

"But never in any of mine," replied Hesterberg triumphantly. "I have just pressed a button at the foot of my desk. By now every door, window and exit is guarded. My men have orders that no one is to enter or leave this building until further orders from me."

"Fine," replied the Phantom. "I see you have a Callophone there. What is to prevent you from countermanding your order? Nothing! If you refuse—"

He emphasized the implied meaning in his unfinished words by ramming the nozzle of his gun another half inch into the Russian's stomach.

"You are right, Hesterberg," he continued. "I have been in traps before. But I have gotten out of them—with lead." The bland note abruptly left his voice. It became hard, bitter, dominating. "You will pick up that Callophone and order your men to—"

FOR a brief second a flash of cunning glinted in Hesterberg's eye. He shrugged his shoulders in a gesture of defeat.

"The trick is yours," he said simply.

The Phantom's lips curled in scorn.

"I am no fool, Hesterberg. Your scheme is to rescind the order, permit me to leave the room—and then countermand it again. No—no, my dear colleague. Nothing quite so simple." His voice spat out in staccato orders. "Hesterberg, I will give you five seconds to pick up that Callophone and tell your men that both *you* and I—that both you and Number 8 are going to leave the room.

"You understand? My gun will be grinding at your ribs. Like the perfect host you are, you are going to escort me personally to the door."

A mask of livid hate descended on the Russian's face. His eyes challenged the Phantom's, but all he read in the other's—was death.

The calm voice of the Phantom burst like a bomb in the tense silence of the room.

"One!"

Hesterberg did not move, but a thin yellowish froth collected on his twitching lips.

"Two!"

Silence in the room save the whistling breath escaping from the Russian's distended nostrils.

"Three!" There was death in every syllable. The Phantom's finger tightened on the trigger. Hesterberg read the signs aright. With a convulsive movement, like an automaton on strings, he jerked over to the Callophone.

"Hesterberg speaking," he croaked into the transmitter. "Number 8 and myself are going to leave the council room. The preceding order is rescinded."

THOUGH the Phantom's lips curled at the words, his finger never relaxed on the trigger of his gun.

"You are a wise man, Hesterberg," he said. "We will leave at once. I don't need to remind your men that if anything should interrupt our progress, you will be the first to go."

He half bowed ironically to the Russian, prodded him with the gun and indicated the door.

Their progress across the room was a death march. The Phantom had to risk turning his back to the remaining members of the Council of Five. An icy chill raced down his spine in anticipation of a barrage of lead from the rear. But of one thing he was determined; if he took the long journey that night, he would not go alone. Hesterberg would be there to keep him company in hell.

THE door opened before their advance. Out of the council room, they traversed a long, broad hall. Eyes alert, nerves on edge, the Phantom was surprised and slightly worried at seeing absolutely no one along the way. Some psychic instinct warned him that Hesterberg hadn't yet played his last trump. Things were progressing too smoothly. The door to the street beyond was a short ten feet ahead, flanked on either side by narrow stained glass windows.

Then—like the stroke of doom—appalling darkness!

The broad hall was thrown into stygian gloom. The Phantom was momentarily thrown off guard and Hesterberg was quick to take advantage of that second. He dropped to the floor, avoiding the slug of lead that tore from the Phantom's automatic.

Something smote Van on the back of the head. He staggered; struggled with a lean hand that clutched at the papers in his pocket. He felt them wrench and tear; felt the packet part, half remaining in his possession and half in the hands of the Russian.

Then the engulfing blackness was shattered by flashes of scarlet flame. The Russian's men were going into action at last. The Phantom had to get out to the street beyond. The door was one way but a barrage of avid lead blocked that means of exit.

So much the better. The Phantom smiled to himself bitterly and held his fire. He side-stepped quickly to the left, judged the distance to a nicety, took two long strides, then leaped.

He caught the stained glass window that flanked the door on the left in dead center with his shoulder. Midst a flying shower of splittering glass he hurtled through the air, landed like a panther on the street beyond and for once in his checkered career took to his heels.

CHAPTER VI

ENTER THE DOPE

THE night clerk looked up angrily, annoyed that a potential guest should presume to disturb his slumber at this ungodly hour. Even a cheap hotel on West Twenty-third Street should merit some sort of respectable treatment, and this overalled young man facing him seemed anything but respectable.

"What do you want?" he grunted.

The stranger, apparently a worker from the docks, smiled pleasantly.

"A room," he said.

"Dollar, two dollars, three dollars. Which do you want?" asked the clerk—anticipating the answer, he reached for the dollar room key.

Dick Van Loan took it from him, paid the dollar in advance and climbed the three rickety flights of stairs. The room was small and dingy. As a residence it was rather abject, but as a place for complete privacy, which the Phantom desired very much at that moment, it was a first-rate bargain for a dollar.

He lit a cigarette and threw himself upon the mattress which smelt of insecticide. He stretched luxuriously. He was tired. Since evading the henchmen of Hesterberg, he

had traveled quite a distance. He had also stopped off at Grand Central Station to retrieve a suitcase that he kept checked there against emergencies, changed his clothes in the lavatory, and came to this obscure hostelry to rest and to think.

Suddenly he sat up and withdrew from his pocket a handful of papers. They were torn almost in half. He bent forward and carefully studied the documents in his hand. Most of the inscriptions thereon he could not decipher. They were written in Japanese. Then down at the bottom typed in French, were the words:

Then, it is agreed between the Imperial Japanese Empire and the—

At this point the paper was ripped off jaggedly. Van lit another cigarette and pondered for a moment. Obviously, these documents, whatever they were, were calculated to cause an international upheaval in his mad plan to conquer the world.

And undoubtedly this was just the beginning. Hesterberg and his mighty criminal army could loot the banks of the world, could pillage the treasuries to pay their way while Hesterberg himself gave State secrets to those who would blow weaker nations to pieces.

HIS arch plot was transparent to Van now. God only knew what other papers he had in his possession. Van remembered his remark his threat about the minister from Andorra. If Hesterberg had access to every hiding place in the world, he could blackmail and bribe his way to power.

Van sighed and gave himself over to another angle of the affair. This time, in his first meeting with the Mad Red, he had at least given him a temporary setback. The half of the Japanese documents that were in his possession probably nullified the other half that Hesterberg had snatched from him.

True, the Phantom had again escaped from the relentless clutches of his maniac, but in so doing he had lost the trail. Hesterberg and all his army now knew that the Phantom still lived. The whole underworld would be suspicious, wary.

Even if Van attempted to enter the world of crime disguised, in an endeavor to pick up the Mad Red's trail, he would not be readily accepted if no member of standing in crookdom would vouch for him.

No. If he were to get in touch with Hesterberg again, if he were to learn beforehand the plans of his foe, if he were to frustrate them, then he must be introduced into the underworld with as much endorsement as any debutante crashing the portals of Park Avenue.

But where was he to get this endorsement? Who would take an unknown into their confidence? And if he should make his true identity known, if he should inform the underworld, that he, the Phantom, desired safe conduct into their midst—?

HE smiled grimly as he thought of the answer. He carefully stowed the papers in his pocket again, and lay down full length on the bed. For a long time he thought, thought thoroughly, and in great detail. But there seemed no way to pick up the trail of the Mad Red again, unless chance should come to his aid.

Then, when it seemed that his mind had for the first time in his life failed him, he was struck with an idea. An idea so paradoxical, so obvious, that he burst into hearty laughter as he saw the beautiful simplicity of it all.

Next to its own members, there was one group of people that had easy access to the underworld. And those people were the police!

The police always had their stool pigeons. The stools might, undoubtedly did, hold out information. But still they had the entrée. On that entrée their jobs—and lives depended. If the Phantom could prevail upon the police to send him to their stools as another stool, his purpose had been accomplished.

SUPERFICIALLY there was always the danger that another stool pigeon might betray Van. But that peril was not as great as it seemed. Stools are loyal to each other. They have to be. It is an immutable law of self-preservation. They may double-cross the crook, they may double-cross the police, but they never double-cross one of their own kind. Death would be too sure, too swift.

Van grinned and yawned.

Thus it was that while the slimy army, the murderous horde of Alexis Hesterberg combed the city to deliver a message of death to the Phantom an overalled dock worker slept soundly on a dirty bed in the West Twenties; slept deeply, renewing physical and mental tissues for his next encounter with the Mad Red.

The following day the Phantom rose early and took the subway downtown. In a dilapidated rooming house on the East Side, he saw a dirty sign in a dirtier window which proclaimed that here there were rooms for rent.

He nodded his head. But instead of entering the house he went to a telephone booth on the corner and called Police Headquarters.

"Hello," he said suavely. "Give me the commissioner."

"Yeah?" said a gruff ironic voice at the other end of the wire. "And who the hell are you?"

"This is the Phantom, Mr. Commissioner. I'm giving you a tip that would be wise to act upon."

"This," said Van curtly, "is the Phantom."

There was a startled silence at the other end of the phone, a click as connection was made.

Van heard a distant voice say in awed tones:

"It's the Phantom, Chief;" and a second later the crisp incisive voice of the commissioner himself trickled over the wire into Van's ears.

"Hello!"

"This is the Phantom, Mr. Commissioner," said Van. "I'm giving you a tip that would be wise to act upon. At Number 8765 East Third Street there lives a dip known as the Dope. He's a snow addict and will do anything to get the stuff. He has connections and will make an excellent tool. If you handle him properly, he'll be able to get you some remarkable information."

"But, what—? Who—?"

Van Loan had already hung up.

Detective Sergeant O'Neal was used to strange assignments. His principal duty was to keep the many stool pigeons that the department used in line. He knew many strange and unsavory characters, and of all the officers in New York, O'Neal was closer to the nether world of crime than any other.

It was almost sunset on that day when his chief called him into the private office, handed him a cigar, and said:

"O'Neal, we've got a new stool pigeon for you. One that promises to let us in on a lot of things that we should know."

O'Neal, phlegmatic and unmoved, raised cynical eyebrows. "They're always touted," he said. "But few of them deliver."

The chief smiled.

"This one ought to deliver," he said. "He was recommended by a co-worker of ours—a co-worker by the way, that we've never met."

O'Neal's eyebrows raised again, this time inquiringly.

"Yeah," continued the chief. "The Phantom."

Even the stolid O'Neal was startled out of his customary stolidity. Every member of the police department had heard of, and respected the Phantom. True, none of them knew his identity, none of them had ever seen him. Nevertheless, they were grateful to him for more than one piece of work which had solved what to them had seemed utterly unsolvable.

"The Phantom?" he said. "What's his game?"

THE chief shrugged. "I don't know. But a tip from him's good enough for me. This guy's a cokey and a dip. Get to him right away. Line him up. Tell him who to report to. Get to it at once."

O'Neal puffed at his cigar, waved the chief a farewell and disappeared through the door, a puzzled frown playing over his brow.

The frown was not engendered by any apprehension of the result of his mission. It was simply that for the Phantom to work like this with

the department was most unorthodox. It had never been done before. Little enough they knew of the elusive detective who masked his identity so well, but included in that little was the fact that he was a lone wolf. That never before had he asked the aid of the police, never before had he even given them a tip.

O'Neal threw the cigar away, and walked slowly uptown.

He stopped before a dirty brick tenement house. Before he entered his eyes carefully scrutinized the building—its adits and exits. Then, after completing an act born of lifelong habit, he entered.

A frowzy landlady showed him the door that led to the Dope's room. O'Neal stood on the threshold and knocked imperiously. A moment later the door was slowly opened.

DESPITE his callousness, despite his phlegm, O'Neal recoiled as his eyes gazed at the horrible emaciated figure that opened the door. The Dope's face was a yellow distorted thing. His hands were bony claws, and his arm from wrist to shoulder, was perforated with a hundred little punctures.

He shrank back as he stared at the bulky figure of the policeman. O'Neal, overcoming his natural revulsion, strode into the room. The Dope's abject eyes followed him in fearful apprehension.

"So," said O'Neal, with heavy affability. "So you're the Dope?"

The man addressed twisted his fingers nervously. He swallowed twice, but said nothing.

O'Neal pulled back the lapel of his coat. In the dim light of the room, his police shield gleamed there.

"I'm O'Neal of Headquarters," he said. "I want to talk to you."

The vague fear in the Dope's eyes crystallized. His pupils dilated. His jaw dropped. When he spoke his voice was an abject whine.

"I ain't done nothing, Sergeant. Honest to God, I ain't done nothing."

"No," said O'Neal with irony. "They never have. But don't get panicky. This is just a social visit. I'm just here to look around."

He walked slowly about the room, his roving eyes covering every inch of the bare chamber. At last his eyes fell on a hypodermic syringe, lying on the table. He smiled mirthlessly. The Dope, following his gaze, gasped.

Their eyes met.

"So," said O'Neal. "So that's it."

Utter panic shone in the Dope's glazed eyes.

"No, no," he screamed. "That ain't mine. I'm no junkie. A pal left it here. It ain't mine, I tell you."

"No," said O'Neal very slowly, very deliberately.

He reached into his pocket and withdrew a small bottle filled with white crystals. He held it out toward the Dope.

The sight of the bottle sent the Dope mad. He charged across the room, a horrible inarticulate cry emanating from his loose lips. His fingers clutched convulsively for the bottle which O'Neal held tantalizingly out of reach.

"For God's sake," he whined. "Give me a shot. Just one shot."

O'Neal laughed mockingly.

"Yeah?" he said. "And I suppose that needle there still belongs to a pal, eh. A pal who left it here. In that case what does a decent, clean-living citizen like you want with this nasty stuff?"

HE replaced the bottle in his pocket and made as if to leave the room. But the Dope, shrieking and drolling, threw himself upon the plainclothes man.

"No, no," he cried. "It's my needle. I lied to you. But for God's sake give me a shot. Just one shot."

O'Neal sent him sprawling on the floor as he pushed the revolting figure from him.

"Lay off me," he growled. "And listen. I'll give you a shot. I'll give you all the shots you ever need, if you do what I tell you."

The Dope stared at him painfully.

"I've heard," continued the policeman, "that you know a lot of things that the police would be interested in knowing. I've heard that you can bring us some valuable information. I've heard that you're a first-class stool pigeon."

THE Dope's eyes reflected furtive terror. He crouched against the wall.

"No, no," he whimpered. "Not that. Don't ask me to do that. I can't. I won't. They'd kill me."

O'Neal laughed unpleasantly.

"You're in a tougher spot if you turn it down," he said. "The man who recommended you for this job doesn't take refusals."

The Dope raised his eyebrows inquiringly.

"Who—" he began.

"The Phantom!" said O'Neal.

The fear in the Dope's eyes crystallized into an appalling terror. His hand trembled and his mouth opened. But the dryness of his throat absorbed the words before they were spoken.

"You see," went on O'Neal, "you are in a spot. A sweet spot. So if you want your snow, if you want to keep clear of the Phantom, you'd better come through."

"All right," said the Dope abjectly. "But, now, for God's sake, give me a shot."

"Okay."

O'Neal handed him the crystal filled bottle.

"I'll expect to hear from you," he said. "Give your reports to 'Cokey' Day who runs the joint on Hester Street. Send me something within a week or else—"

He glared at the miserable figure of the Dope threateningly, then with a free stride left the room. The door closed behind him.

For a long moment the Dope did not move. With avid eyes he took the hypodermic in his trembling hands; then watched it as it slowly trickled through his palsied fingers to the table.

A shudder wracked his emaciated frame; a hand that was suddenly steady made a swift pass across the Dope's face. He jerked erect; miraculously inches were added to his stature. The loose lips ceased their trembling and the strong line of an iron jaw stood out boldly in the vague light of the room.

Eyes that a moment before had been bleary and wild, cleared up, brightened. From them shone the clear, cold light of a man with one set purpose; a man driven forward to his goal by an indomitable will.

The transformation was complete. In the place of the drug-ridden Dope, stood the grim, determined figure of—the Phantom!

CHAPTER VII

THE CRIPPLE

HE lost little time. O'Neal, the hard-boiled policeman, had given him the information he wanted. Cokey Day was the man who could steer him back to the lost trail of Hesterberg. Now that he could go to Cokey as a fellow stool, the owner of the joint would vouch for him to the underworld.

Swiftly he ripped open a shabby suitcase. From its interior he took an automatic and tucked it away in the holster under his shoulder.

Then he sat down and smoked a cigarette meditatively, the one moment of relaxation that he allowed himself before resuming the rôle of the Dope, and venturing forth in search of the Mad Red.

HE threw the butt on the floor, stepped on it, then sat down before the mirror. Once more he adjusted the little pieces of wax on his face. Yellow grease paint streaked his face, giving it that dead doped look. He scraped the floor with his nails until they were black. In the mirror the features of Richard Van Loan evolved slowly and completely to those of the Dope.

Then he went out into the street.

Cokey Day's joint was, as a matter of cold hard fact, the meeting place for the dregs of humanity. If you waited in Cokey's barroom long enough your eye would fall on almost every criminal in the world. It was their sanctuary.

In its grim walls many a deed of violence had been plotted or discussed. Accustomed as its habitues were to seeing peculiar people without asking questions, or even glancing askance, the Dope made his entrance unnoticed.

He weaved his way through the dotted tables toward the bar. Then, leaning confidentially over the mahogany, he asked the bartender for Cokey Day.

A fat finger indicated a door at the rear. The Dope shuffled toward it slowly. He knocked softly and a gruff voice said:

"Come in."

The Dope entered to see an evil-faced, hard-eyed individual seated behind a battered desk.

"Is this Mr. Day?" asked the Dope, wheedling respect in his tone.

Day nodded. "What the hell do you want?" he said. "Who are you?"

"They call me the Dope."

"So what?"

The Dope lowered his voice and spoke confidentially.

"O'Neal sent me."

Those three words seemed to have a thunderbolt effect upon Cokey Day. He half rose to his feet, fear and wrath flaming in his little eyes. Then he sat down again and beckoned his visitor closer.

"Shut up, you fool! Do you want the whole world to hear you? Now, what do you want?"

The Dope shrugged. "Nothing," he said. "I just dropped in to get acquainted. O'Neal said I would report through you."

DAY swore a mighty oath, and raised his hands appealingly to heaven.

"My God," he said. "Is O'Neal crazy? Sending a dope like you. Does he want to queer the racket? A mug like you'll talk for the first shot anyone offers you."

The Dope smiled craftily. "I thought maybe you'd want to keep me supplied," he said with a leer.

Day glared at him savagely. "All right," he said. "I'll look after you. But for God's sake keep your mouth shut. If you don't, you'll die. And," he added ruefully, "so shall I."

The Dope nodded and turned toward the door. "Mind if I hang around a while?"

Day shook his head. "No. But don't talk, that's all."

The Dope nodded. His hand reached out for the door knob. But he never completed the gesture.

The door suddenly swung open so violently that it almost knocked him over. Something silken and white and fragrant swept past him. He turned his head to see a girl, slim and blonde, bend over Cokey Day's desk. Her pupils were dilated. Her hands trembled and there was agony, supplication in her voice as she addressed the dive keeper.

"Cokey, for God's sake give it to me. He's cut off every supply. Not a dealer in town's got the guts to let me have any. Cokey, for God's sake. Just an ounce. Just an ounce, Cokey."

THERE was something terrible in the spectacle of this beautiful girl, humbling herself to a beast like Day. Yet it was evident that as long as her tearing nerves cried for the drug that would bring them surcease, there were no lengths to which she would not go. She looked appealingly in Cokey's eyes.

"No," said Cokey laconically, with an air of irretrievable finality.

With trembling fingers the girl fumbled in her bag. Something green and yellow fell on the desk.

"That's all I got," she said. "There's enough dough there to buy ten pounds of it. And all I want's one ounce. One little ounce, Cokey."

Cokey Day eyed the money greedily. Avidity and fear of reprisal shone in his eyes. The fear won. He shook his head.

"No," he said. "Now, get out."

The girl turned a beaten, suffering face away from the desk. The Dope still stood at the door. As she passed the girl turned to him, desperately, as if she knew there were no hope, but any chance was better than none at all.

"Sell me some snow," she said. Then as she really saw him for the first time, her hope grew. For in the Dope's face she recognized the ravages of cocaine. "Don't tell me you don't take it. Give me a shot; I'm dying. Give me a shot."

The Dope's brain moved swiftly. He was eager to understand this little drama. Why it was that a girl with money could not buy dope. Who it was that had forbidden the dealers of the underworld to sell it to her? Who had enough power to frighten Cokey Day away from money?

"Well, yes," he said slowly. "I guess I can spare you one shot."

"O-oh!" The girl fell upon him gratefully. Her arms went around his neck. Tears streamed down her cheeks, and her trembling fingers stretched out for the soothing powder which would miraculously silence the shrieking of her nerves.

The Dope reached into his vest pocket and withdrew the bottle which O'Neal had given him. He held it out to the girl. She snatched it, and fumbled in her bag. She produced a hypodermic needle.

"Lay off, you fool!"

Cokey Day rose from his desk and threw himself across the room. The girl, seeing him coming, uttered a shrill cry and fled, still holding the bottle and the needle in her hands. The Dope slammed the door hurriedly, thus effectively checking Cokey Day's pursuit.

"You fool. You fool!"

Cokey was beside himself with rage. The Dope turned an ingenuous face toward him.

"Why? The kid was dying for a shot. I'll give anyone a shot. I know what it is to go without it."

"You'll never give her another shot if the boss finds out about it. You idiot!"

"What boss? Why?"

DAY seized him by the arm, wrenching it brutally.

"Listen, mug. How the hell O'Neal picked out such a fool as you I don't know. But if you care for your worthless life, mind your own business in here. You'll be lucky if the boss doesn't find out where Ruby got that stuff."

He opened the door and pushed the Dope through it roughly. Once outside in the large room, the disheveled figure of the dope fiend shuffled over toward a table and sat down. He lit a cigarette and alertly watched the people around him.

HE started as a hand tugged at his threadbare sleeve, then looked up into the eyes of the girl called Ruby. Her whole demeanor had changed now. Her eyes were bright and sparkling. Her hands were steady. Her voice was husky, but firm. Cocaine, that insidious robber of the mind and body, had enhanced her youthful beauty.

"Thanks," she smiled at him. "Thanks a lot. You've done me a favor, and I'll never forget it."

The Dope was about to ask her to sit down. He wanted to see if he could extract any information from her. Perhaps Day's mention of the boss who had cut off her dope supply was knowledge he could use in his own grim game.

"Won't you sit—" he began. But suddenly the invitation froze on his lips.

He inhaled deeply, and his heart picked up a beat as the picture of a familiar face filtered through his retina. In answer to a friend's hail, Ruby walked away.

The Dope made no move to stop her. He sat immobile and tense at his table watching a figure walk across the floor. The man walked slowly, heavily, as if in a daze—like a drunk or a person under the influence of some soporific drug.

And deep inside the Dope's brain something clicked, something whispered: "Danger!" For the man who shuffled so lethargically across the floor was Frank Havens!

Van Loan fought down his impulse to stand up, to call out to his friend. Something sinister was about to happen. Death skulked unseen as Havens shuffled aimlessly and dully across the room.

Then Van was aware that another person had entered the room and was following Havens, some few feet behind. Swiftly he glanced at the second man, and then, in a flash he understood. For the second visitor to Cokey Day's was a cripple— a little unshaven cripple with eyes like diamonds in a setting of mud.

Havens had again been hypnotized by the little man with the eyes of death. For what motive, what purpose, Van did not 'know. But both his heart and mind told him that jeopardy was imminent.

Havens and the cripple disappeared around a white pillar at the far end of the room. It was then that Van arose. It cost him something to maintain the slow, dragging walk of the Dope at that moment when every nerve in his body was counseling him to run. But he did not increase his pace one iota.

ARRIVING around the pillar, he was just in time to see the cripple slowly stumping up a rickety flight in the rear. Havens was already out of sight. Van cast a hasty glance about him. No one was in sight.

It was then that he cut and ran. He came breathless but silent to the foot of the steps. With a cat-like tread he slowly made his way up the creaking, rickety stairs. At the third landing he stopped. He heard a door open. He heard a babel of voices—and in that babel one voice stood out saliently. It said:

"So you have him? Good. Now we can strengthen the one weak link in our chain."

The door slammed again, but not before Van had recognized the voice of Alexis Hesterberg!

For a moment he hesitated. Should he leave Havens there and go for help? That way was too big a gamble. What would happen to Havens in the meantime? Further, there was an excellent chance that Hesterberg would be warned in time, so perfect was his sky system.

No, Van put his loyalty to his friend first. He, the Phantom, would see this through alone.

CAUTIOUSLY he mounted the remainder of the stairs. By dint of applying his ear to each of the three doors on the landing, he ascertained by the low rumble of voices from within which room Havens was in.

He hesitated no longer now. Swiftly he mounted the iron ladder that led to the roof. Once there, luck came to his aid. At the side of the building was another ladder of iron which led to a fire escape landing below at the very window of the room where Havens was held prisoner.

Like a feline he descended, wrapped his arms tightly around the iron half-way down, and hung like a monkey where he could observe whatever went on, hear whatever was said.

His mouth became a grim, thin line as he took in the scene below him.

Havens sat still as death in an arm-chair in the middle of the room. Behind him stood Hesterberg. In the foreground, his glittering snake-like eyes never leaving the publisher's countenance, was the cripple. Two other men stood near Hesterberg. The Mad Red spoke.

"Then, this," he said "is the end of the international angle. Once I procure the torn half of those papers from the Phantom I am ready to plunge Europe and America into war. Then, I shall embark on the financial angle. Then, I shall force the bankers to send gold to Russia. Then, THE DAY!"

Van Loan nodded grimly. So, it seemed, Hesterberg was as eager to see him again as Van had been to see Hesterberg. The Mad Red wanted those papers, and he could not get them without getting the Phantom first.

"Yes," said Hesterberg inside the room. "This is the end. Now we have in our power the one man in the world who knows the true identity of the Phantom. He shall tell us who he is. Then we shall get the papers and the Phantom shall get—death!"

He paused a moment. Van strained his eyes so that he could see the dramatic tableau more clearly. Hesterberg's guttural voice continued:

"So, Sligo, keep your wicked eyes on him and ask him who and where the Phantom is?"

The iron rung of the fire escape cut deeply into Van's arm. Now he understood. Hesterberg had sent his hypnotic cripple to bring Havens here. Now, while he was under the cripple's influence they were asking him who the Phantom was. That should, as Hesterberg had said, be the end. But Van reflected grimly that the Phantom was by no means through yet.

Sligo, the cripple, with the eye of death, took a step toward the helpless Havens. His gleaming agate gaze bored into those of the newspaper man. Hesterberg moved forward impatiently.

"All right," he said testily. "Ask him, Sligo."

Sligo nodded. Never taking his eyes from Havens' face, he spoke. "Listen to me," he said.

HAVENS answered in a dull lifeless monotone.
"Yes, Master."
Van's blood boiled, to think that

Havens should address this rat of the underworld as "Master." Still he bided his time.

"Tell me," went on the cripple. "Tell me, who is the Phantom?"

"The Phantom?" Havens repeated the name hesitatingly as his subconscious fought against his revealing the secret. Van could see the beads of sweat on Sligo's brow as he used every ounce of his will to wring an answer from Havens' lips.

"Yes," he said, "the Phantom. Who is the Phantom? What is his name?"

"Ah, yes, the Phantom," said Havens in that inanimate tone. "The Phantom, Master is R—"

THAT was enough for Van. He dropped down upon the iron rung. He leaned through the window with his gun in his hand. The automatic spoke once. Sligo, the cripple, uttered a sharp cry of pain and fell to the floor, the blood that ran from his temple crimsoning the rug.

Swiftly Van sprang through the open window and held the room at bay with his automatic.

At the moment that Sligo had lost consciousness and fallen to the floor, Havens had started up in his chair. Now, no longer under the baleful influence of the cripple, he blinked his eyes bewilderingly and stared blankly through the room.

One of Hesterberg's men shouted:
"The Phantom! It must be the Phantom!"

"Shut up," said Hesterberg. "That little coke fiend is not the Phantom. "Now"—addressing himself to Van—"what does this mean? How dare you intrude here?"

Van knew that there would be little chance of winning a battle here with Hesterberg. He had too many allies in the building for that. If the crazy Red had not recognized him so much the better.

Cokey would know him only as a stool of O'Neal's. If he could get out of this room with Havens before the alarm was given, they could chance a run for it.

Still keeping everyone in the room within range of his automatic, Van backed slowly toward the door. Havens was staring at each person in the room blankly and in turn. Van smiled faintly as his best friend ran his eyes over the face of the Dope without recognizing him.

"What's this mean?" said Havens suddenly. "Who are you, men? Where am I?"

Thus far Van had not spoken a word. Now he answered the other's question.

"You're in a den of cutthroats," he said quietly. "So am I. Let's try to get out."

Hesterberg laughed unpleasantly. "Listen," he said. "No stranger can get out of here without trouble. Now, what the hell do you want?"

The Dope grinned, and for a moment an intelligence that was alien to a snow addict gleamed in his eyes.

"I want to get out principally," he said. "And I'm taking him with me."

He indicated Havens, who still sat with a blank expression on his face, not quite oriented to his environment yet.

"Put that gun away," said Hesterberg," or you'll never get out of here alive."

HE walked slowly toward Van, holding him with his eyes. Slowly his hand crept toward his hip pocket.

"Don't do it," said Van. "Stand back. All of you stand away from that door."

His voice rang with purposeful command. They obeyed. Van jerked his head toward Havens.

"Come on, you. Stand up. Get over by the door. When I tell you, open that door and run like hell."

Havens did as he was told. Though he by no means understood how he had come here, who these people were, he realized that he could not go far wrong with a man who wanted to get him out of this room which seemed to hold him captive. He stood with his back to the door, his hand on the knob.

"Now," said Van coldly, "we're leaving. I'd advise you not to follow too quickly, or else I shoot from the stairway on the way down. Give us a full minute. It'll be much safer for you if you do."

HE turned to the still slightly bewildered Havens.

"All right," he shouted. "Now!"

The door swung open. Two flying figures raced through it. It slammed behind them. As they gained the stair head, Van heard Hesterberg's voice roar through the panel of the door.

"Go on, you fools! After them, quick!"

Apparently the Mad Red had little compunction about risking the lives of his men. He had no intention of giving the Dope the full minute that he had demanded to make his getaway. And so great was Hesterberg's power, so great was their fear of their master, that his henchmen did not hesitate to choose between his wrath and possible death outside that door.

For a second time the portal swung open. Two more figures raced through it.

As they turned the landing at the top of the second flight two staccato reverberations boomed above them. Steel ate into the crumbling plaster of the walls. Van pushed Havens ahead of him down the stairs and, taking hasty aim, pressed the trigger of his automatic.

One of the men staggered, but recovered and came on. Now there was an enraged shout from the top floor, and Hesterberg joined the chase in person.

FOUR revolvers roared. Three from the pursuers and a single automatic took up the defense. The hallway echoed grim crashes, and the air was acrid with the stench of powder.

Van and Havens leaped like cats down the last flight, with such speed that they gained the ground floor some thirty feet ahead of their pursuers. Once there, Havens ran toward the front door of the dive. But Van's hand caught his flying coat-tails and pulled him back. He had a better plan than that.

To run through the room, to enter the street was to court disaster. Gripping the publisher's wrist, Van rushed along the wall toward Cokey Day's office.

He dragged the breathless Havens through the door, slammed and locked it. Then, even before he turned around he heard a vaguely familiar voice say:

"Oh, Cokey, I've wanted—"

What she wanted he never knew. Ruby stood at Cokey's desk slowly turning her head. Then surprise showed in her brilliant eyes.

"Oh, it's you. I thought it was Cokey. What—"

"Listen," said Van swiftly. "Get us out of here. Hesterberg's behind us. He'll kill us if he finds us. There must be an exit from this office. Cokey's not the kind to let himself get trapped in an office like this. Get us out."

Already the patter of running feet could be heard without. Hesterberg's voice demanding informa-tion as to where the quarry had fled boomed through the panel.

"Hesterberg—" Ruby repeated the name and her voice was pregnant with hatred and loathing. "Quick! Here!"

She turned, walked to the south wall. Her slim hand lifted a litho-graph from its place. Her finger touch a small button imbedded in the wall. Slowly a huge bookcase moved outward. Then with a jerk it stopped, revealing an aperture some five feet square in the center of the wall behind it.

Van shoved Havens into the black opening. Then he stopped a second and took the girl's hand in his.

"Thanks," he said. "I'll repay you for this some day."

Her shapely lips were distorted by an evil smile.

"If I've crossed Hesterberg." she said bitterly, "that's payment enough."

Van squeezed her hand quickly, and a moment later joined Havens in the pitch black of the secret exit. The bookcase swung into place be-hind, just as Hesterberg's imperious knock crashed against the locked door.

CHAPTER VIII

THE MAD RED STRIKES

VAN LOAN'S flashlight picked out a yellow path through the labyrinth of underground pas-sages beneath Cokey Day's dive. Of course, Van realized that if Hester-berg knew of this exit, he would post his men at all its adits, and the pair of them were no better off than they had been in that top-floor room.

Yet, he reasoned, it was unlikely that Cokey Day had told anyone of the passage. In fact, he was a little surprised that Ruby knew of it. In Cokey's precarious position—that of playing fast and loose with both the underworld and the police—he had to be prepared for any emergency.

The flashlight revealed six wooden steps leading to a trap-door. Van preceded Havens up the stairs and cautiously pushed the trap open. A gust of clean night air swept into his face. His eyes strained into the street beyond. They saw nothing.

"Come on," he said to Havens.

The publisher followed him into the dingy deserted street of tenements. The trap-door slammed shut behind them. They walked in silence down the street. A vagrant taxi passed, and Havens hailed it. He gave the driver an address, then turned to his savior.

"I'm still by no means sure what happened to me tonight," he said, "but I *do* know that I've you to thank for getting me out of it. You must come home with me and tell me who you are. Perhaps I can do something for you."

Van laughed, then for the first time that evening spoke in his natural voice.

"You can give me a drink and a bath, Frank," he said with a smile. "I can't think of anything else I want just now."

Havens gasped. His jaw fell, his eyes gleaming mirrors of utter amazement.

"Van!" he exclaimed. "You! But how? What—?"

"I'll tell you all about it over the drink," said Van, grinning at his friend's stupefaction. "I can talk better with this wax out of my handsome features."

VAN peered carefully through the rear window of the cab to make sure that they were not being followed, then gave the driver the address of the secret apartment which he and Havens kept for just such exigent occasions as these.

In fact, even now, they had the cab stop a block or so away. In their position they could afford to take no chances. Once inside the apartment, Van removed his disguise, bathed and donned one of the suits that was always waiting there for the day when their owner, pursued by danger, should need them.

AS he dressed, Havens related as much as he knew of the circumstances which had brought him to the dive of Cokey Day as he remembered. Then with the story almost finished, he broke off and exclaimed excitedly:

"Oh, Van, I forgot to tell you. I haven't seen you for a few days. Isaac Block's been killed."

Van's fingers stopped in the adjustment of his collar pin and turned his head ever so slightly.

"Block?" he said. "Killed? Why?"

"As a warning. He was found shot in his library yesterday. The news was suppressed because of the panic his death would cause in the Street. But it'll break in the papers tomorrow. Probably the bulldog editions have it now."

"But why? Why was he killed?"

Havens shrugged, and his voice was bitter.

"No reason. Simply as a warning."

"A warning? From whom?"

But Van knew the answer to that even before the publisher had said that one word which the Phantom had learned to know meant death.

"Hesterberg."

Van's own eyes stared at him grimly from the mirror as he brushed his hair. His mouth was set and hard. He turned to Havens.

"So," he said. "He's killing merely to terrorize the community now. He must feel damned sure of himself."

The two men looked at each other, worry and apprehension in their gaze; each thoroughly conscious that the thought in his own head was also in the others. Thus far, despite all their efforts, Hesterberg had covered his trail. More than that, his hand had stretched forth from his inaccessible concealment to strike down his enemies.

"Let's go up to your place," said Van. "I need that drink more than ever now."

Silently Havens rose and the pair of them cautiously made their way to the street. Though now, as they hailed a passing cab, no habitue of Cokey Day's would ever have recognized the well-dressed young clubman who climbed into the taxi, as the abject dope fiend who had fled the East Side dive a scant hour before.

Despite the lateness of the hour, Muriel Havens was still up when they arrived at the publisher's home. She greeted her father affectionately, then turned to Van.

"Hello, stranger. I haven't seen you for a long time, and now you come visiting at this late hour. Well, I'll forgive you. Sit down and talk to me while Daddy mixes one of those cocktails for which he's more famous than for his newspapers."

Havens smiled, and entered the butler's pantry to mix the drinks, while Van sat down and gave his undivided attention to the girl opposite. Animatedly she indulged in small talk, while he silently feasted his eyes upon her.

HE was aware of a vague regret as he sat there—a regret that he had sacrificed his right to make love to this bright young creature that sat before him.

Little did she realize as she sat there in the security of her own home talking to the most eligible bachelor in the city, that only a short while ago, he had been engaged in fighting for his life in a section of the city that she could not have known existed.

Then suddenly he heard her mention two words which abruptly took his attention from her beauty and riveted it to her phrases.

"Yes," she said, "of course, the Phantom's a hero and all that, but I certainly wouldn't want my husband rushing around fighting those crooks. It's romantic and all that, but I think I'd prefer security."

VAN LOAN smiled a smile that did not come from his heart. He felt dull and heavy within. Yet when he spoke his voice was as bantering as her own.

"A husband as good as they say the Phantom is," he said with a laugh, "would have no trouble sneaking the house at night when you were waiting for him with a rolling pin."

She joined his laugh.

Havens entered with a tray of cocktails. Muriel drained her glass and waved her hand to Van.

"Well," she said, "if you insist upon calling at this hour, you won't see very much of me. I must get along to bed."

She kissed her father, and ran lightly up the stairs. Van shook his head and sighed.

Havens nodded proudly, then suddenly realized that they had things to talk about.

"How do you figure tonight's episode?" he asked anxiously.

"Well," said Van, "your part of it is easy to explain. Hesterberg evidently needs those papers I have. He needs them badly. Having no idea where to get hold of me, or even who I am, he sent his cripple out again to hypnotize you, to bring you to him. They were just asking you to reveal my identity to them when I shot. The moment the cripple became unconscious, of course, you come out of the trance."

Havens nodded slowly. "God!" he said. "It was a close squeeze, Van. If you hadn't been there in time, I would have told him. That would have been the end of us."

VAN nodded. "It surely would," he said. "He'd have sent us to the same place that he sent Block."

In the next room the phone jangled harshly. Havens excused himself and went to answer it. Van remained seated in silence, two images struggling for dominance in his brain. First, the figure of the swarthy Russian, and, second, the seductive picture of a charming young girl to whom he could never declare himself.

A moment later Havens burst excitedly in upon his reverie.

"That was Bursage," he said breathlessly. "He's just received a death threat from Hesterberg."

Van glanced at him keenly. "What sort of a death threat?"

"He got a phone message tonight. He was told at once to float a Russian loan to the extent of ten billion dollars. He was ordered to have arranged the credits by midnight tomorrow. If he failed he was to be killed at exactly midnight."

"Well," said Van, "I expected something like this. Only tonight, I overheard Hesterberg say that as far as his international machinations were concerned he was ready, save for the piece of paper that I possess. He's now after money and products. He's going after the bankers now. He must have money and supplies if his schemes are to work. That accounts for Bursage. He's an international banker. Hesterberg's selected him as the second victim. This time he means business. Block was killed simply as a manifestation of power."

"Well," said Havens, "what do we do? Bursage wants me to talk to you. Frankly, he's pretty panicky. What shall we do?"

"First," said Van, "we'll sleep. Then you can tell Bursage to forget about the loan. Tell him to remain at his bank—The Second National— after hours tomorrow. Tell him to remain there until I arrive. You meet me there, too. I've got a scheme to stop Hesterberg at this particular game—and if he beats me here, the man's a genius."

And Van slept well that night. First, he knew that Hesterberg would seek him out as long as he held his torn half of the Japanese papers. And second, his keen brain had already evolved a plan to frustrate any attempt on Bursage's life —a plan so sound, so fool-proof, that even the Mad Red with all his distorted genius could never carry out the threat he had made.

The next morning, the papers screamed forth the news of the elusive maniac who had slain Isaac Block two days before. In the news columns, the rewrite men ran riot describing a murder, which they had not witnessed, in minute and conflicting detail.

EDITORIALS demanded that the police apprehend the murderer, who apparently was attempting to terrorize the entire metropolis. Leaders condemned the officers of the law as grafters and cowards, even hinting that the whole department was in the pay of the madman who struck at the foundations of the government.

In short, the papers ably assisted Hesterberg to do exactly what he was essaying to do. If it was his intention to strike fear into the hearts of the residents, the newspapers with their lurid stories helped matters considerably.

The murder of Block was on every tongue, and somewhere in the dark recesses of the underworld, the perpetrator of the deed skulked, awaiting the night when he would go forth to strike again.

It was four o'clock in the afternoon of a gray autumn day. The metropolis lay listless and dull under a leaden sky. The very weather seemed to cast a vague undefined shadow of apprehension on the city.

In an office on the second floor of a building which towered haughtily into the sky, sat a man whose mood reflected the atmospherical condition without. He sat leaning over an expensive shining desk. His brow was marred by a worried frown. His hands moved nervously, aimlessly, and in his eyes was the look of a man who awaits a visit from death.

For the first time in his successful career, Silas Bursage felt that he was incapable of dealing with a problem. All the things that he had learned to hold sacred, inviolate were about to fail him. The police, the sacred rights of an American citizen—it seemed these things could avail him nothing now that he had been singled out by the Mad Red to do a deed which would be impossible to do with honor.

OF course, it was possible for Bursage to yield to Hesterberg's demand. It was possible for him to float the loan which was demanded. Furthermore, it was possible for him to do it in such a manner that few people would know that he was actually betraying his country, compromising his own honor.

Bursage was not a man lacking courage. Cowardice had not enabled him to reach the pinnacle that he occupied today. No, that was

not it. But, he reflected bitterly, it was hard. He had made his fortune by obeying the rules that society laid down. Now it was about to be taken from him by a man that flouted those rules.

YET though he toyed with the idea for a while, he already knew deep down in his heart that he would die if need be, before he would accede to the demands that Hesterberg had put upon him. But, suppose he died? What then?

He was not the only banker in America capable of performing the task demanded of him. There were others. And would they all stand as firmly for the right as Bursage was prepared to do?

He raised his eyebrows and shrugged his shoulders. After all, that was not for him to answer. He could go no further than his own specific case.

The jangle of the telephone brought him out of his moody reverie. Havens' welcome voice came over the wire. Bursage eagerly greeted him.

"Hello, Frank. Have you found the Phantom?"

Havens' answer lifted the banker's spirits considerably.

"Good," he said. "What does he advise?"

"Stay in the bank," Havens advised him. "Remain there after hours. Have your watchmen doubled. Both the Phantom and myself will be there before midnight. If anything breaks in the meantime, the Phantom will get in touch with you himself."

"Good!"

They bade each other good-by and hung up the receivers. Bursage leaned back in his padded swivel chair and lighted a cigar. As he exhaled the expensive smoke, he smiled faintly, and realized that now the

Phantom was in the struggle as his ally, he felt reassured. He opened a drawer of his desk and, taking a revolver therefrom, slipped it into his pocket.

If Bursage, the banker, had to die, he would go out fighting. He smoked the cigar down to its last inch and was just reaching a stage of complete relief when the phone rang for the second time. A metallic voice said:

"Bursage?"

"Yes."

"This is Hesterberg. Have you decided to accede to my demand or have you decided to die?"

Despite the relief Bursage had left at the news of the Phantom's aid, the steely tones of the Mad Red on the other end of the wire sent a little chill running down his spine. He forced the quaver out of his throat as he replied:

"I have decided," he said evenly, "to do neither, Hesterberg. I most certainly shall not float the loan, and at the present moment I have no intention of dying."

A SHORT, sharp laugh trickled over the wire.

"No," said Hesterberg. "Few people have. Is your answer final?"

"It is."

"Very well. You shall die at midnight. No matter where you are; no matter who guards you, you shall die precisely at midnight tonight. No one can stay the hand of Hesterberg."

The click of the receiver was the exclamation point of the sentence. Bursage wiped the perspiration from his forehead and sat back once again in his chair. Now he was frankly afraid. There was something in his enemy's voice, something cold and hard and inhuman that had sent an icy chill into his heart.

Despite the fact that with the proper precautions it would be impossible for any foe to come close enough to kill him, Bursage was afraid, and in his mind's eye he already saw the gaunt finger of the Grim Reaper approaching.

CHAPTER IX

HESTERBERG'S WORD

OUTSIDE the skies were slowly evolving from gray to ebony as the early night fell like a silent blanket over the city. Lights twinkled from a thousand buildings, and to Bursage, it seemed that they were winking obscenely at him, challenging him to gaze upon them for the last time. Bursage shuddered.

The door opened and his secretary entered. He laid an envelope on the desk.

"A messenger just left this for you personally. And when you have time, there's an invalid outside in a wheel-chair to see about the Drake account. Mr. Wheeler suggested you see him personally."

Bursage nodded and dismissed him. His fingers trembled slightly as he ripped open the envelope to find a single sheet of paper and another sealed envelope with a black serried border. He read the message and smiled.

Bursage:

Don't worry. I can take care of tonight's affair. Put the enclosed envelope in your pocket. Give it to me when I ask for it tonight.

THE PHANTOM.

Bursage rose from his desk. He thrust the envelope in his pocket as per the Phantom's written instructions. What the mysterious detective's plans were, he had no idea, but he had implicit faith in him. After all, what could possibly happen to him? Here in his own bank, under the protection of the keenest detective that had ever lived.

He was almost restored to normal as he strode from the room to interview the man about the Drake account.

The night had come. She had cast her concealing cloak about the city, the cloak which is kind to lovers and law breakers. The infinity of the sky was broken by no star's gleam. The gray clouds which had obscured the sun all day, now destroyed the radiant beauty of the night. It was an evil night. A night redolent of psychic wickedness.

PRACTICAL and prosaic as Dick Van Loan was, he was aware of the peculiar atmosphere. He strode briskly through the lighted streets toward the bank where Bursage and Havens waited for him. His route was neither the shortest nor the most direct. He walked east, west, north, south; then, certain that he was not being followed, he doubled back on his trail and entering a cigar store made his way to the rear and closeted himself in a telephone booth.

Following the instuctions on the outside of the phone book, he said to the operator:

"I want an ambulance. At once. The Second National Bank. Hurry."

He hung up before anyone could ask embarrassing questions and continued his walk toward the bank. Within a block of it he slowed down and did not increase his pace again until he heard the legato jangle of the ambulance's bell. He smiled as he thought of the interne's discomfiture when he realized the false alarm. But it was the most expedient method he could think for getting the Phantom into the bank, unobserved.

The shiny black car pulled up before the bank. The interne joined by the policeman on the beat who loitered near-by walked up the granite steps and tugged the night bell.

After a short pause the door was opened cautiously. Already the curious crowd that always flocks about such scenes had begun to gather. Van joined on the bank steps.

Evidently satisfied that this was an honest error and not a trap, Bursage and Havens came to the door and chatted for a moment with the interne. By now the crowd had grown to large proportions. They overflowed the sidewalk and streamed up the steps of the bank. The more curious peered inside.

Van found himself so close to Havens that he could have reached out and touched him. But the publisher, in earnest conversation with the interne, paid him scant attention.

Cautiously Van thrust his hand in his pocket and withdrew his mask. He turned his back on the crowd so that only Havens and the policeman could see his face. Then he boldly crossed the threshold.

"Hey, you," said the policeman.

Van turned. Havens saw him. Van made a swift motion of his hands which meant nothing to anyone save the publisher. It was a secret signal they evolved which was used when he wanted to make his identity known to Havens.

"It's all right," said the publisher. He put his mouth close to the policeman's ear. "It's the Phantom."

THE policeman touched his hat respectfully, and a moment later, the heavy door closed shutting Havens, Bursage, the Phantom and six watchmen in the bank.

"Well, gentlemen," said Van easily. "Sorry to have caused all this commotion but in case the building was being watched, I preferred not to be seen entering."

Bursage came forward and wrung his hand.

"Thank God, you're here," he said, husky relief in his voice. "I was afraid—"

His voice trailed off. He did not say what he was afraid of. But the look in his eyes made that fact clear enough.

DON'T be afraid of anything," said the Phantom. "Now, if you'll take us somewhere where we can talk privately, I'll tell you my plan."

Bursage led them to his own office. He took a box of cigars and a bottle of cognac from a cabinet and offered them. Over the fragrance of both, Van explained the cast iron scheme he had evolved.

"Of course," he said. "It seems impossible for Hesterberg to gain entrance to this bank. However, the man's got a mind which might be able to overcome any obstacle. But I've got a real problem for him. At precisely ten minutes to twelve, you're going into the biggest vault you've got, Bursage. We'll lock you in for twenty minutes."

"You mean—" began Bursage eagerly, but Van interrupted him.

"I mean that if Hesterberg or any scheme he can evolve can break into this bank through the doors through the watchmen, through Havens and myself, and then crack into a three-foot thick doored vault without keys or combination, he's more than a genius, he's a miracle worker."

Bursage sat back, a smile of relief wreathing his features. After all, his faith in the Phantom was being exonerated. No one that ever lived could pass through all the obstacles that Van had mentioned. No one could break into that new steel burglar-proof vault. First, its stone walls were over a yard thick, as was the steel door. It was locked by twelve locks, each of which had a different combination. He was safe! Hesterberg was foiled.

Havens sat forward in his chair.

"But," he objected. "Suppose the entire threat is a trap? Suppose Hesterberg has no intention of fulfilling his threat at midnight. Suppose he has merely mentioned the time to throw us off the trail, to leave Bursage unprotected at the hour when he really plans the killing?"

Van considered this for a moment, then shook his head.

"No," he said decisively. "That's not like Hesterberg. I know him pretty well. He's crazy and an egomaniac. If he said midnight, it's a matter of pride with him to make it midnight. There's no doubt about that. It isn't so much the murder he's interested in. It's the show of power. He wants to make us fear him, to show us that nothing is impossible to him. That's why he warned us he would strike at midnight. Then he can show us, that despite that warning, despite all our precautions, he can accomplish his purpose."

"But," said Bursage, his face pale. "Can he?"

Van laughed. "I doubt it," he said. "I can't explain how he'll ever get into that vault. Can you?"

And when the banker was compelled to admit that he could not, he felt reassured.

FOR some time they sat there, drinking and smoking congenially, not at all like three men who were awaiting a visit from the bony reaper who had been sent to them by the distorted mind of the Mad Red.

Out in the night somewhere, a clock tolled eight chimes. Havens consulted his watch.

"Eleven-thirty," he said. "Shall we start?"

Van nodded, and the trio of them rose. Bursage hastily scribbled something on a piece of paper.

"The combination," he said. "You'll need it to get me out."

VAN nodded and thrust the paper in his upper vest pocket. In the silence they walked through the gaunt marble and steel corridors of the bank. Finally, Bursage stopped before a tremendous impregnable portal of steel.

"This is it," he said.

He bent down and proceeded to twist the first series of dials. So difficult was the door to open, that it took him all of fifteen minutes to accomplish his task.

At last he reached out for the handle and gave the door a tremendous tug. Slowly it swung open, revealing a dark, cadaverous interior. Van entered first with a flashlight. The yellow beam of the torch carefully scrutinized every square inch of the huge safe. There was no sign of anything untoward there.

"All right," he said to Bursage. "Get in. Don't be afraid. You'll be out in twenty minutes or less. Good luck."

Bursage took his hand, then after gripping the hand of Havens for a moment, he entered the safe.

"Are you armed?" asked Van.

Bursage nodded. His face was drawn and pale. His eyes glittered nervously. But he kept a grip on himself. He essayed a short forced laugh.

"Sure," he said. "I'm armed. That ought to clinch it. Shouldn't it?"

Van agreed that it should, then slowly they swung the enormous door closed behind him. With unhurried fingers, the pair of them shot the heavy bolts into their sockets. Then Van gave a quick twist to the dozen dials which effectively locked the metal portal. He glanced at the piece of paper in his hand, and his retentive mind immediately memorized the score of numbers written upon it.

Then he tore the paper into a hundred pieces, crumpled it into a tight ball and thrust it into his pocket. He turned to Havens.

"See that the watchmen are at their places," he said. "Then come back here."

Havens walked briskly across the high ceilinged vault room, and Van, a thin smile of triumph flickering over his face, took up his position with his back to the steel prison which held the president of the Second National Bank within its invulnerable walls.

The Phantom's hand was in his coat pocket, resting on the butt of a .38. For the first time since he had come to grips with Hesterberg, he felt thoroughly confident of the result. Think as he would, he could find no flaw in his protection of Bursage.

IT was humanly impossible to gain access to that vault. It was difficult enough to enter the bank building itself. The watchmen had had their orders. But to pass the .38 in his pocket, then to pass that yard of steel which shut Bursage off from the rest of the world was utterly, absolutely, and apodictically impossible.

Havens returned.

"Everything okay," he reported. "I guess this is one time we've beaten Hesterberg. It was a swell idea."

Van nodded. High up on the wall a clock relentlessly ticked off the minutes. From without, midnight struck, and the chimes reverberated through the night over the city.

Instinctively, Van's hand tightened on the butt of the weapon in his pocket. He felt his heart pick up a beat as the moment when Hesterberg had threatened to kill, arrived. His keen eyes swept the vault room. A shadow passed the door.

He started into complete alertness, then relaxed again, as he realized it was only one of the watchmen making his rounds. Havens stood at his side. His hand was also in his coat pocket and for a similar reason.

Both of them stared at the clock. The minute hand moved slowly, almost imperceptibly. Five minutes past twelve. Havens glanced inquiringly at Van.

"Shall we open up?"

Van shook his head. From the holes in his silk mask his eyes gleamed triumphantly.

"We'll make sure of it," he said. "We'll give him five more minutes."

Those five minutes took five hours to tick their way into the chasm of time which houses the past. Then when the minute hand stood directly over the numeral 2, Van turned to Havens and nodded.

"Now," he said. "Come on."

HE twisted the dials rapidly, and as soon as the combination was released, the publisher tugged back the heavy handles which drew the bolts. It took ten minutes more to accomplish their task of releasing Bursage.

Van pulled the heavy portal open slowly. A smile was on his lips. He was human enough to take a keen personal relish in outwitting the man who had escaped him so often. The door swung open all the way. Van said:

"Okay, Bursage. You're safe. It's twenty minutes past twelve. Come on out."

There was no answer!

Van Loan felt an icy hand clutch out from nowhere and touch his heart. For a moment he stood transfixed on the threshold of the vault. Had, then, all his elaborate precautions failed? Had Hesterberg achieved the utterly impossible? He heard Havens' ejaculation of anxiety at his side.

"God, is he all right?"

VAN whipped his flashlight from his pocket, and pressed the button. Then he fell back a step. Horror and amazement dilated his eyes. Havens swore a mighty oath. Van's nails bit into the palms of his hands and he was aware of an eerie sensation of the supernatural as his gaze followed the yellow beam of the flashlight.

For there, revealed blatantly in the yellow halo of light, lay Bursage. Blood gushed from a hole in his chest, and the glittering jeweled hilt of a dagger protruded from the crimson flow. His was a crumpled, bloody body that needed no closer scrutiny to make sure that he was dead.

The Mad Red had kept his word. He had struck as he had promised!

Van thrust the flashlight into Havens' trembling hand. He stepped forward into the vault and bent over the body. Bursage's coat lay open, and peeping from the inside pocket was the edge of an envelope, with a black serried border.

Without quite knowing why, the Phantom bent down and extracted the envelope from the dead man's pocket. It bore no inscription. Hastily he ripped it open, and holding it so that the beams of the flash played upon it, he read the scrawled message on the dirty paper within.

He died at midnight!
        Hesterberg.

Slowly Van backed out of the
vault. His eyes flashed with baffled
rage, and a tremendous desire for
vengeance upon the murderer who
had once again outwitted him. Havens clutched his arm with a shaking
hand.

"What happened? Is he dead?
How? How could anyone get in
there?"

"He's dead," said Van grimly.
"Hesterberg kept his word. How, I
don't know. But, by God, I'll find
out if it's the last thing I ever do
in this world. I swear it, so help me
God."

He raised his right hand and his
eyes to Heaven as he swore an oath
by the God he believed in, that he
would eventually bring the Mad Red
to justice.

Havens bent over and read the
message Van still held in his hand.

"He died at midnight," he said
aloud.

Van turned to him. "Aye, he did,"
he said. "He died at midnight, and
so, I swear shall Hesterberg. By
everything sacred I swear. Hesterberg shall die at midnight and by
my hand."

Then with his eyes burning terrible holes through his mask, he
turned and walked from the room.
Havens followed him, trembling with
the air of a man who had just met
death face to face—as indeed he
had.

CHAPTER X

HEARING BUT NOT SEEING

THOUGH a pale dawn had
streaked the East before
Van Loan had found a
troubled slumber the night before,
he awoke promptly at ten. He was

*Blood gushed from a hole in his chest,
and the glittering jeweled hilt of a
dagger protruded.*

immediately assailed by the events of the night before and the tragic end of Bursage. He was oppressed by a sense of failure. A man's life had been entrusted into his hands and he had failed—miserably.

He picked up the few clues to the baffling mystery where he had left off a few short hours before. One question confronted him; one question to which he could arrive at no satisfactory answer.

L OCKED in a vault alone—how was Bursage murdered?

He could find no answer. At last he dressed and went out to telephone Havens. He dialed a number and a moment later the familiar voice of Havens trickled into his ear.

At the first words of his friend, his physical and mental lassitude swept from him. He kicked his feet out of bed and sat bolt upright, gripping the telephone with tense fingers.

"What," he barked into the transmitter.

Havens' voice came to him again; calmer this time, more distinct.

"Hesterberg has sent his second warning. Clairborne, this time!"

"When did Clairborne get it?" snapped Van. "Give me the details."

"Ten minutes ago. I'm just through talking to him on the phone. He's heard of Bursage's death, and he's terribly upset. Wants to know what's he to do."

"What did you tell him?"

"Nothing, yet."

"What was the message?"

"No ultimatum; no demands. Simply that at twelve midnight, Clairborne would be killed. Good God, Van, this—this is terrible. We've got to do something; got to do something at once!"

The tone of the voice told Van that Havens was a very frantic man. And with good cause, too. With each suc-ceeding event, he, Van Loan, was realizing the terrific power he was pitted against. A power that could pronounce sentence on a man and then execute it within sealed, bank vaults.

He whipped his brain into feverish activity.

"What are we to do?" came Havens' voice again, strained and halting.

A half-formed plan began to mature in Van Loan's brain.

"Get in touch with Clairborne at once. Tell him to go to his Club tonight. The Union. Have a party of friends there. Have him get in touch with the Commissioner and have him throw a cordon of police around the building. I'll be there. Tell Clairborne that. I'll be there—and I won't fail!"

"You're coming as—?"

"No—I'll be there, but you won't know me. I'll be there as the Phantom!"

Van heard Havens' short gasp over the wire, but before waiting for more questions, he snapped his last order.

"Get in touch with Clairborne at once. And tell him if he wants to live he must be at the Union."

A CAB crawled slowly down Fifth Avenue toward the Union Club. Leaning against the cushions in the rear, with a forgotten cigarette between his fingers, Van pondered this second warning of Hesterberg.

That he should threaten Clairborne, he could understand. But to threaten him without making some demand was altogether unintelligible. It seemed incredible that Hesterberg was killing again, merely for a show. Hesterberg's insanity didn't run to murder for murder's sake. No; there was something more behind it than that. Find the motive behind that second warning and he would have the key to its frustration.

But the motive was as elusive as Hesterberg himself.

His taxi pulled up to the canopied entrance to the Union Club. Richard Van Loan assumed his most debonair, nonchalant air and strolled into the luxurious smoking room of the establishment. He waved a cheery greeting to a few fellow members; sank into a deep leather-cushioned chair by an open window and rang for a drink.

Sipping the high-ball, he studied the interior of the room. He found himself scrutinizing the pictures as if he half expected to see the fanatical eyes of Hesterberg stare out at him from the portrait of old Peter Schyville, the founder of the club. He caught himself searching the oak panels of the room for some indication of a secret door.

Van swore softly to himself and downed the rest of his drink. He was acting ridiculous—like a cub detective on his first case.

But what *was* the answer to Hesterberg's threat of death?

THE perplexed state of his mind made him restless. He rose from his chair only to sink into another on the opposite side of the room. It evolved down to this. Hesterberg wasn't one to threaten idly. At twelve o'clock precisely, an attempt would be made on Clairborne's life. And unless he outwitted the Russian, the attempt would succeed. It was a grim responsibility to carry around for twelve hours, especially since he had no plan of attack or defense.

If Clairborne came to the club—and he would—the attempt on his life must of necessity take place there. How—or through what devious cunning, Van did not know. Of

only one thing he was certain. He, too, must be there prepared for any emergency.

The Phantom, too, must keep that rendezvous at twelve.

VAN ordered another drink. For the next hour he kept the steward busy. Then with the fifth drink came the glimmering of an idea. He heaved a grateful sigh of relief, puffed out a blue cloud of smoke with vast contentment.

A moment later he repaired to the restaurant on the second floor and with the lightest of hearts, ordered himself a substantial lunch. He dwaddled through the meal; topped it off with an excellent bottle of wine.

One o'clock found him in a drug store at Sixth Avenue and 42nd Street. After making several purchases, he returned again to the Union, but this time he avoided, with extreme caution, the main entrance to the club. Instead, he made his way to the rear of the building and with the greatest circumspection slipped quietly and unobtrusively into the trade entrance.

He spent an interesting half hour examining the labyrinth of narrow hallways and back stairs that made a catacomb of the cellars of the Union Club. He found, that if need be, he had fourteen different ways of reaching the main floor of the club. What was more, he discovered a small locker for cleaning supplies that gave directly on to the lobby of the club, beneath the broad stairs leading to the second floor.

It was small, musty, smelling of damp rags and soap suds. But it would have to do. Van closed the door behind him, locked it and dropped the key in his pocket. Stuffing the crack beneath the door with old rags, he snapped on a fly-specked light bulb, settled himself as comfortably as possible on a soap box, drew out a deck of cards from his pocket and began a game of solitaire.

Van had a ten hour vigil before him, but with the philosophy of a stoic, he waited for developments.

He slept through the major part of the afternoon and the early hours of the evening. At seven he awoke, stretched his weary limbs and risked three swift inhales on a cigarette.

The increasing hub-bub of noise outside the door of his self-imposed prison, told him that the night's activities at the club were beginning. Around eight, on hearing the voices of Havens and Clairborne, as they entered the Union, he was tempted to come out of his place of concealment. But only for a moment. He realized that the strength of his plan lay in absolute concealment until the time for action had arrived.

The first step of his plan had been fulfilled. He had brought Clairborne to the club; to strike, Hesterberg had to reach him there. And he, the Phantom, was laying in wait to see that the Russian was foiled.

Footsteps drifted by his door. Snatches of conversation, broken and disrupted came to his straining ears. But slowly, piece by piece, he pierced together the information that Clairborne had taken his advice and had called in the police.

The Union Club was surrounded by a cordon of stalwart bluecoats. The minions of the law were stationed at every point of vantage outside the building. And in personal charge of the police contingent was Inspector Demaree.

THE Phantom didn't have much faith in the strong arm of the law, but when it came to a massing of numerical strength and a pitched battle, they had their advantage.

Nine o'clock came; ten. By the sounds of revelry that floated down to the locker, from the dining room, Van surmised that Clairborne was throwing a party as a gesture of disdain at Hesterberg's threat.

The party was almost too gay; he realized that there was a note of hysteria in it.

For a moment all thought of Clairborne and his party was wiped from his mind. Footsteps approached his hiding place, stopped. He heard voices; one voice first and recognized it as Havens'. He pressed his ear against the door and listened.

"You are prepared for any emergency, Inspector?"

"Any, sir. But just what do you expect to happen here tonight?"

The Phantom didn't hear Havens' reply that followed immediately. His every nerve was consumed with liquid fire; his lean muscles knotted to whip-cords. It was not the question Inspector Demaree had propounded that had wrought this sudden change in him. No. It was the voice that had asked the question.

The Phantom had heard it before. He would never forget it. Its accent was impressed indelibly on his mind.

IT was the voice — of Hesterberg! Hesterberg—Detective Inspector Demaree! No! The thing was impossible—mad!

The men moved on, their voices faded. The Phantom heaved a long sigh and relaxed. He realized then that it was time to come out of his place of concealment. He had to take a look at this Inspector Demaree. But he feared the worst.

Awaiting his opportunity he slipped from the locker room a moment later, slithered like a shadow behind the shelter of a marble colonnade. A swift survey of the scene told him that the club was in the hands of the Russian.

THE Phantom shrank back against the marble column as Havens and another man marched out of the smoking room. They headed his way, deep in conversation. Half-way across the lobby, the man at Havens' side, stopped and rapped out a terse order to a man at the door.

That voice again! The voice of Hesterberg; the voice of Detective Inspector Demaree. The Phantom didn't get the key to the puzzle immediately. It came to him a few seconds later as Havens and the Inspector stopped a few feet away from him. He now managed to secure a good look at the face of the man at his friend's side.

There was no denying those eyes. There was no mistaking that high-domed head and arrogant lips. The Phantom was staring at Hesterberg —Hesterberg, the mad Russian.

Then in a flash of inspiration he comprehended the stupendous cleverness of Hesterberg. Van had to admit the genius of his foe. The Russian had staked all on a colossal bluff. He himself had impersonated Demaree; they were his men in blue, planted around the building, not the police.

And quick on this realization came a second. There was a traitor close to Havens or Clairborne. Someone who had—

But time to analyze that situation later. The Phantom realized that he had to completely change his plans. And then came the bitter truth that he had no last ace up his hand to trump this last move of the Russian.

He stood frozen to his place of concealment behind the colonnade. His mind worked at top speed. With Hesterberg in person on the job;

with his minions surrounding the building in the guise of the police, he was at a terrific advantage.

Unquestionably, in the role of the Police Inspector, Hesterberg had given the order that no one was to leave or enter the building; undoubtedly he censored all incoming and outgoing calls.

It was so simple, so perfect it would have been ridiculous if so much wasn't at stake. The Russian had the entire building and all its occupants at his mercy. All he had to do was to wait till the fatal hour of his message and then carry out the execution. But that brought the Phantom back to one of his earliest questions. Just what was behind this particular move of the Mad Red?

He wasn't to know until an hour later.

It was eleven o'clock.

TEN minutes later a tall, cadaverous man in the uniform of a steward entered the dining room on the second floor of the Union Club, bearing a tray and a bottle of whisky. He was lost, unnoted in the bevy of hurrying waiters. He served drinks casually to half a dozen beckoning fingers, but slowly he worked his way to Havens' chair.

He bent over to fill the newspaper man's glass. And in the babel of voices around the groaning board the words he whispered in Havens' ear was unnoticed.

"Van. Make no sign. Locker room—lobby—beneath stairs. At once."

Havens' momentary confusion was covered by a peel of laughter that rang out in appreciation of some witty story just told by Clairborne. The cadaverous steward passed on to the next reveler, and by the time he had reached the end of the table his bottle was empty.

Loading his tray with empty glasses, he made a slow, leisurely exit from the room.

FIVE minutes later Van was offering Havens a drink from a gold inlaid pocket flask.

"Here—take a swallow of this," he urged. "You'll need it."

Havens raised the flask to his lips and took a long pull. Excitement gleamed in his eye. From Van's manner and the method he had taken to communicate with him he was morally certain that something exceptional had developed.

"Well?" he demanded eagerly. "What is it? What have you discovered?"

"Plenty," replied Van grimly. "How's your nerve?"

The publisher essayed a confident laugh that didn't quite come off.

"With another swallow from your flask I think I can rise to the emergency. What is it?"

"Good," answered Van. "Prepare yourself for a shock." He paused dramatically for a moment and then gave it to his friend straight from the shoulder. "Your pal, Inspector Demaree — is Hesterberg himself!"

Havens recoiled at the information and before he had a chance to recover, Van delivered his second thunderbolt.

"And what is more," he continued bitterly, "the hordes of policemen around the building are all fakes, also. They're the Russian's men. He's pulled a master stroke."

"Then there's no way we can save Clairborne?"

"Yes—there is. A plan just as daring as Hesterberg's. You have to carry it out."

Havens' lips clamped together and his shoulders straightened.

"Right. I'm ready."

Van slapped him on the back affectionately. "Of course. I knew you would be."

"What do I do?"

"Sorry, old man," replied Van. "You got to play this blind. You've got to trust me."

"Implicitly. What do I do?"

"Something very simple. At a quarter to twelve, on some pretext or other, get Hesterberg or Demaree, as you will, away from the mob in the dining room. Corner him down here in the lobby. Hold him there till I offer you a tray with a bottle and two glasses.

"I will pour two drinks from the bottle. Down yours at a gulp. Hesterberg will follow suit."

For a moment Havens was tempted to ask questions. He restrained the impulse.

"That is all?"

"That is all."

Their hands came together in a firm clasp. No further words were said between them. The bargain was sealed. Each man knew that their fate to say nothing of the stupendous ramifications of Hesterberg's plans— lay in a mutually implicit faith in each other and chance.

But no matter which way the breaks went, Death was holding the trump Ace.

THE party in the dining room on the second floor was continuing with ever wilder abandon. At eleven-forty, Havens pushed back his chair and strode over to where Inspector Demaree was seated at the opposite side of the board.

He nodded to him significantly and indicated the door. Demaree followed him out of the room. Havens held his peace till he had reached the lobby below. He glanced at his watch.

"It's eleven forty-two, Inspector," he began. "The Russian was to strike at twelve. You are sure your plans are all completed?"

Demaree smiled ironically. "Quite sure. Don't worry, Mr. Havens. Events are going to develop exactly as I have mapped out."

"I feel a great deal of responsibility in this matter—"

DEMAREE again assured him that he was master of the situation. "I have every detail taken care of; my men are at every point of vantage around the house. No one can get in or out without orders from me. Hesterberg will have to do business through me."

Listening to the diabolical words of the Russian, Havens could not help but admire his colossal nerve. A vague feeling of doubt swept over him. Would the Phantom, after all, be able to outwit this master criminal, with the cards all against him.

Failure tonight—when, if Clairborne was murdered, Hesterberg would have a terrific psychological advantage in his campaign!

It was just then that a tall, cadaverous steward passed across the far end of the lobby, headed for the stairs.

"Steward," called out Havens.

The man turned, crossed over to the group of two. He held a tray in his hands on which was a bottle and two glasses.

Havens licked his lips and with an apologetic cough turned to the police officer. "You know, Inspector," he said wryly, "I'm just a trifle nervous. A good drink of this will be a help, eh?"

The Inspector laughed confidently, while the steward poured two drinks, but his eyes never left the bottle. He watched Havens closely as he lifted a glass from the tray, before taking his own; he waited for a brief moment while Havens downed his drink at a gulp, before tossing off his own shot of Scotch.

The steward offered to fill the glasses again, but Havens waved him aside. He was playing his part up to the hilt. Hooking his arm under the Inspector's, he led the way again to the dining room.

CHAPTER XI

A BARGAIN FOR LIFE

WITH the first stroke of twelve, an expectant hush fell over the revelers in the dining room of the Union. All eyes were on Clairborne where he sat at the head of the table. The knuckles of his hand stood out in white relief as he gripped the stem of his wine glass and looked defiantly around the table.

The second stroke of the clock, and the hush in the room became deeper, more strained.

Havens' heart was pounding furiously in his breast. He felt helpless, weak, impotent. Van! Where was Van?

With ominous fatality the succeeding strokes of the clock filled the room with dread. Everyone there expected something to happen. Their eyes were riveted on the face of the marked man, with fascination.

And on the final stroke of twelve, something did happen. But not to Clairborne.

Detective Inspector Demaree kicked back his chair. Twin automatics were in his hands as he confronted the table. Gone was his mask of easy affability. In its place the cruel features of Hesterberg dominated the table.

"Gentlemen," he began in a mocking voice. "Let me introduce myself. *I* am Hesterberg!"

His startling declaration was received in appalling silence.

The sudden revelation of Demaree's real identity; the knowledge that all those in the club were trapped and at the mercy of the Mad Red, froze the hearts of those present. Only Havens had a faint glimmer of hope—a faint glimmer that was fastly fading.

THE wine glass snapped in Clairborne's fingers; his eyes gazed with fascinated horror at the twin automatics in Hesterberg's hands. His lips worked convulsively but no words came.

The Russian did the talking for him.

"Let us be calm, gentlemen," he went on with mocking contempt. "And as for you, Clairborne, your hour has not yet struck. But there is an 'if.' A big 'if' for all of you."

"Speak! What—for God's sake, what," panted Clairborne hoarsely.

Hesterberg swept the men around the table with eyes of fire.

"This little gathering which I have so adroitly arranged for tonight, was not to murder you, Clairborne. That was only bait. I have come here for the Phantom!"

An audible gasp rose from a score of lips at his words.

"Yes—the Phantom," continued Hesterberg in a metallic voice. "I know that one of the men here in the Union Club is the Phantom. I knew if I threatened to kill Clairborne at midnight, the Phantom would be at hand to protect him. Unfortunately for you. I don't know which one. But I *do* know the Phantom is here, and he dies tonight and by my hand!"

Silence; silence, broken only by the sound of heavy breathing.

"I have no wish to commit wholesale murder. I have a proposition to make. Let the Phantom declare himself and the rest go free. Let the Phantom hold his peace—" his fingers tightened on the trigger of the gun in his hand—"let the Phantom hold his peace and all of you here die.

"That is the only way I can make sure. The Phantom must die!"

Hesterberg's proposition was received in dumb silence by his listeners. Mutely, wonderingly, pleading, they stared at one another. No one spoke.

"Come, come!" snapped the Russian. "I warn you gentlemen, that unless the Phantom discloses himself immediately, I will begin with the man on my left and blow his brains out."

The gun came up menacingly—stopped, wavered for a fraction of a second.

The door had opened, closed. A masked figure stood on the threshold and despite the gun in Hesterberg's hand, dominated the scene.

No one there in the room, least of all the Russian, needed an introduction.

"Lo! The Phantom discloses himself!" rapped out the masked figure. "But not at your command, Hesterberg. At his own bidding."

THE flames of triumph lit up the smouldering eyes of the Russian, but before he could give vocal expression to his victory, the Phantom was speaking again.

"Wipe the arrogant smile off your lips, madman. Two guns in your hands and you are utterly helpless, powerless. You are blowing no one's brains out tonight, unless your own. In fact, you can't lift the automatics in your hands an inch further."

As if drawn by a magnet, all eyes in the room riveted themselves on Hesterberg. And the Phantom's words proved true. Even as they watched, in speechless bewilderment, a filmy haze clouded the fire in the Russian's eyes, he swayed slightly, tried with a supreme effort to raise the guns, only to see them slip from his nerveless fingers.

A SECOND later Hesterberg collapsed in a limp heap on the floor.

The downfall of the Russian threw the room into a ferment of excitement, but the next moment, the Phantom's voice restored order again.

"We are not out of the woods yet, gentlemen. This is just the first step. We have Hesterberg momentarily in our power. But how are we to get him out of here to the police? How are we to get out of here ourselves? His men have the place surrounded. All exits are guarded by his men."

This statement of the facts of the case threw the gathering into another alarmed silence.

"We will charge out," declared Clairborne.

The Phantom held up his hand. "In a physical encounter with Hesterberg's men we would be wiped out. No. Let me think. There must be some other way."

For two full minutes the Phantom wrestled with the problem of escaping from the club with Hesterberg. There was only one possibility, a slim chance fraught with danger. Under no circumstance dared he remove the silken mask from his face. Therein lay the rub. But he had to risk it.

It was no time now for hesitation. He jumped into action, strode over to the fallen body of the Russian and began to disrobe.

"I'll impersonate the Russian. Follow me out. Let me give the orders."

"But your mask," protested Havens.

"It is dark outside. I will try to conceal it. It is our only chance.

The change of clothes and shoes was effected in a minute. With the hat of Inspector Demaree pulled low down over his face, partially concealing the mask that hid his features, the Phantom turned to the group of hesitant men that surrounded him.

"Wait here. Say nothing," he ordered.

Swiftly he stepped to the door and flung it open. He blew sharply on the little whistle he had taken from Hesterberg. The knot of men gathered around the doors looked up at him.

Masking his voice, the Phantom spoke.

"Send the squad on duty inside the club up here," he called down imperiously.

Six men detached themselves from the group around the door, one remaining behind on guard. They pounded hurriedly up the broad steps, barged into the dining room.

THE Phantom met them at the door with leveled automatic. The men looked at him with puzzled frowns. Hesterberg in a mask? Then slowly it dawned on them. They were not looking at their chief; they were gazing into the eyes of the Phantom. Something had happened to Hesterberg.

The Phantom never gave them a chance to get over their surprise.

"One word from you and it will be your last," he ordered. "Now march!" Prodding the last man with his gun, the Phantom forced the prisoners across the dining room to a small serving pantry. He forced them into the small cubby hole, closed and locked the door behind them, snapping the key off in the lock.

Then he turned back to Havens, Clairborne and the rest. He indicated the body of Hesterberg at his feet.

"We have to get Hesterberg out with us. We have to get him to the police." He knelt down and felt the Russian's pulse. "Pick him up, some of you. Throw his coat back over his face. Then form a tight circle about him, and follow me."

Like a funeral cortege carrying the dead, the procession was formed and with the Phantom in the lead, they left the dining room.

Their progress was uninterrupted all the way down the broad stairway, till they reached the hall below. Here the one man who had remained on guard came up on the run. The Phantom knew that the moment for the big test was fast approaching. It was ten feet away; five.

Assuming an attitude of profound meditation, he bowed his head as if he were concentrating deeply, placed his left hand up to his eyes. By this simply expedient he hoped to cover the silken mask that still concealed his features.

The guard pulled up shortly.

"What's wrong? Chief? Where're the men? What's the idea of changing the plans?"

STILL assuming deep abstraction, the Phantom kept his left hand to his head and waved his right one irritably.

"I've made a mistake," he mumbled. "Send the men back to their stations. Permit these gentlemen to go unmolested. Pass along the word."

It was a magnificent bluff, but would it work.

The Phantom felt rather than saw the suspicion that sprang to the man's face. He waited tense

for a moment, prepared for instant action.

"There's something screwy here," snarled the lieutenant. "That ring! Hesterberg never wore a ring. You're not—"

HE never finished the sentence. With a warning bellow to his men, he sprang to the limp figure carried by Havens and the others, and threw back the coat that concealed the features of Hesterberg.

The Phantom knew that he had made one slip and he cursed himself bitterly. In changing clothes with Hesterberg, he had neglected to take off the Masonic ring on his finger. And that small detail overlooked, had again thrown him and the men he was pledged to protect into the power of the enemy.

But he was not the one to accept defeat without a struggle. Quick as Hesterberg's lieutenant had been, he had acted more quickly. Even as the coat fell from the Russian's features, the Phantom jammed the nozzle of his automatic against Hesterberg's skull.

The wolves closed in from the street, guns drawn. The Phantom's finger tightened on the trigger of his automatic.

"Call off your dogs," he ordered, "or Hesterberg is the first to go."

No further need for the vain attempt to hide his mask, the Phantom confronted the Russian's lieutenant. Their eyes clashed audibly.

"Back," ordered the lieutenant to his men. "But keep your guns ready for action."

"An interesting situation, but I think I hold high cards," purred the Phantom.

"Like hell you do. Not with fifty men surrounding you."

"My gun is against Hesterberg's head. It would give me great pleasure to shoot."

"Shoot—and not a man of you gets out of here alive."

"Exactly. I shoot Hesterberg—you shoot me and my friends. One overt act from you, and I dispatch Hesterberg to hell. It's a stalemate. I shall keep my guns against Hesterberg's skull until we are safely on the outside. Then—"

"To hell you say," swore the gangster. "I'm no fool. It's no difference to us whether you kill Hesterberg here or in the police station. If you kill him on the outside, we've gained nothing. If you force my hand and kill Hesterberg here — you and your friends get wiped out. That evens the score."

THE Phantom realized that they had reached an impasse.

"What is it you want?" he demanded.

"Hesterberg—and you."

"On what terms?"

"The only terms. If you don't agree you're all wiped out. You —Hesterberg—and all this crowd."

The Phantom was in the most difficult situation of his career. Gladly would he have laid down his life if in doing so he could have wiped out the menace of the Mad Red. But to lay down the life of his friends, the men he had sworn to protect—that was something else again. No matter what else happened; no matter what happened to him, they must escape.

"I agree," he said at last. "I will agree to turn over myself and Hesterberg to you—on one condition."

"And that is?"

"These men here go free. I was the only man Hesterberg wanted tonight. Is it a bargain?"

"Agreed," replied the lieutenant grimly. "You stay with Hesterberg. The others can go."

Havens started to protest but the Phantom cut him short with a word.

Though on the surface his bargain appeared to turn him completely over, into the power of Hesterberg, he still had a last trick to play. He had to get Havens, Clairborne and the rest free before the lieutenant discovered it. He turned to the gangster:

"I am ready. I shall leave with you and Hesterberg. But to insure that there be no treachery, my gun stays at Hesterberg's head. If you betray our bargain, I shoot. If anyone attempts to lift my mask, I shoot. This problem shall be resolved between myself and Hesterberg when he comes to."

This was an angle to the matter that the lieutenant had not foreseen. He had to save Hesterberg's life at any cost; failing this, their entire plot crumbled. He realized bitterly that the Phantom had not gained his reputation for naught.

As long as he held the gun to Hesterberg's head, even though he was a prisoner, the Phantom was master of the situation. But just how long could one man hold a gun to another man's head, surrounded by a score of hungry wolves? Yes —the Phantom was asking himself that self-same question!

CHAPTER XII

THE VIGIL

IT WAS a grim, bizarre and altogether insane procession that marched out of the lobby of the Union Club a few minutes later. First went the mock police, the rank and file of Hesterberg's forces. Bringing up the rear, two men supported the limp body of the Russian, with the Phantom still masked, holding a gun to his head. And he, in his turn, was menaced by the gun of Hesterberg's lieutenant.

Cars were waiting at the curb; the men dispersed. A minute later the Phantom found himself in a speeding limousine, alone with Hesterberg and the lieutenant.

The car pursued a zigzag course through the city. The curtains were down and the Phantom lost all sense of direction. Once by the rhythmic flashes of blurred light, he realized that they were crossing a bridge. Which one, he knew not. Corners were turned in rapid succession; long stretches, continuous driving along straight roads were traversed.

Then at last, with a sudden jerk, the car came to a halt. The door swung open. Hesterberg was stirring, breathing heavily at the Phantom's side, whose grip on the automatic tightened as he pressed it against the Russian's head.

Hesterberg groaned, opened his eyes, winced under the drilling pressure of the automatic.

"It's a gun, Hesterberg—my gun —the Phantom's gun," grated Van.

The Russian's lieutenant went into a hurried explanation. "It was my only out, sir," he concluded. "I had to save you at all costs. "But it is just a matter of time until this fool here is unmasked."

THE Phantom commented grimly to himself that it was undoubtedly the truth, but his only chance was in continuing his bluff. Though he hadn't the vaguest idea how he was to get out of this desperate situation, he had a tremendous advantage so long as his gun was at Hesterberg's head.

He kept it there, relentlessly. The Russian before him, a man at his own side, they entered the shadowy portal of a darkened building.

The scene was set in a large room on the ground floor. As long as his trigger-finger was steady, the Phantom was in a position to make demands. He made them. A chair was placed for him—his back to the wall. Directly in front of him sat the Russian, lolling in confident ease in a large cushioned chair. Before them stood a group of six— tense, watchful, waiting—each man armed with a vicious sub-machine-gun.

The vigil began.

ONE moment off guard, one sleepy nod of the head and the Phantom knew that finis would be written to his career. At the very most, he had twenty hours in which to extricate himself from an impossible situation.

He had had little sleep the night before; he had been cramped for the greater part of the day in a stuffy locker. How long would it be before outraged nature exacted her toll; before sleep overcame his already shattered nerves?

He dared not think of it; he had to keep awake. He had to find some way out of that room, despite the six sub-machine-guns trained on him.

Hesterberg removed the plump panatella from his lips and exhaled a pungent cloud of blue smoke. He settled himself more comfortably in his chair, heaved a sigh of contentment and satisfaction.

"Comfortable, my dear Phantom?" he inquired ironically.

"Quite," purred Van.

"Excellent. I only hope that your vigil will not be too long."

"You're keeping it with me."

"But you forget that I can doze off. Sleep, my dear Phantom— sleep. A gun gets very heavy after an hour or so. Muscles creak and strain. Sleep is a sweet thing— but the sleep of Death is sweeter."

The Phantom realized that Hesterberg was baiting him. Already the gun in his hand was getting heavier. Fine beads of sweat stood out on his forehead; he clamped his teeth together until he was aware of a physical pain.

He said nothing. Hesterberg would soon tire of his little game if he did not rise to the bait. And anyway, he had to think, think! He had to concentrate on those six men before him! He had to concentrate on those four walls surrounding him!

WHERE was his escape? How was his escape.

An hour dragged by on never ending minutes and the Phantom was no nearer the solution of his problem than when he had entered the room.

The six guards opposite him were changed. Food was eaten in his presence; wine drunk. Men went to sleep in chairs, on cots before him. Snores filled the room. With every faculty at his command, the Phantom fought off the sleep that was slowly numbing his senses.

The automatic in his hand was a leaden thing of almost incredible weight. A thousand flashes of light danced before his eyes. It seemed to him that irresistible forces were slowly pulling down on the lids of his eyes.

His muscles became cramped; the twisted cords in his neck was a living torture. His whole body cried out in anguish for sleep. But there was no sleep.

With an ever increasing sense of the inevitable doom that was closing in on him, the Phantom realized that only three short hours had passed. Three hours! How many more before he nodded off and the wolves pounced in?

By the sheer power of his will he lashed his mind to renewed efforts. He went over the bare four walls for the hundredth time. He stared wide-eyed into the blazing

mazda lamp that lit up the scene. Was there no possible way he could compromise?

Hesterberg groaned, opened his eyes, and winced under the drilling pressure of the Phantom's automatic.

Another hour went by. Hesterberg awoke in his chair and continued his taunting tactics of before.

"If nothing else, my dear Phantom," he mocked, "I can assure you an untroubled slumber at the end of your vigil. The peace of the grave."

Hot words rose to the Phantom's lips; in an insane frenzy he was tempted to empty his automatic into Hesterberg's skull; tempted to still forever that taunting voice.

But with an iron will, forged in the fires of hell, he restrained the impulse. Hesterberg should die. He had sworn that. But the Mad Red's hour had not struck as yet. First he had to learn more of the Russian's plans; find out how far they had matured, whom they involved.

Let him once get the key figures in Hesterberg's colossal organization and he would not hesitate to be the one to wipe out the madman himself. He mentally lashed himself to an emotional frenzy in imagining the sadistic pleasure he was to get some day when finally he dispatched Hesterberg to hell. He reveled in the gory details of the execution he planned; he gloated over the dying anguish of Hesterberg. He—

And it was then that the Phantom called a halt. He realized that he was going a little mad, cracking under the strain. Exerting his last ounce of will power he mastered his failing brain and nerves and again concentrated on evolving some means of escape.

His fingers were numb, cold, constricted around the butt of his automatic. A terrific thirst assailed him while the beads of sweat on his forehead trickled crazily into his eyes. Hunger, thirst, sleep, slow paralysis—he had to fight them all.

Hesterberg was asleep again, his high-domed head slumped on one shoulder. In a frustrated frenzy the Phantom listened to the even breath rasp through the Russian's nostrils. And then he was suddenly calm. He had an idea!

A SLIM chance, it was true—but nevertheless, a chance. He had nothing to lose and everything to gain. For the past five hours he had been suffering the torments of hell waiting for the inevitable. Now he had a faint hope of being able to frustrate the net of doom that was slowly closing in on him.

Slowly, inch by inch, he began to put his plan into operation. Hairbreadth's width at a time he eased his body slightly forward. So slow and steady that no eye could detect the movement his right hand went out toward Hesterberg's slumped body.

It reached the Russian, crawled up the side of his coat, and with stealthy fingers probed into Hesterberg's pocket.

A WAVE of exultation swept over the Phantom. His fingers had come in contact with the cold steel of an automatic in the other's pocket. He wanted to shout; he wanted to risk all on whipping out that gun, but by some miracle of nerve he restrained the impulse.

As slowly as his hand had delved into the Russian's pocket, it was withdrawn. The Phantom knew that the six grim pair of eyes were riveted on the gun pressed against Hesterberg's skull.

They were watching his right hand, waiting—waiting until it had wavered the fraction of an inch. But his right hand did not waver and slowly, imperceptibly he removed the automatic from Hesterberg's pocket with his left.

A quick analysis of the situation told the Phantom that his only possible chance was to kill the lights. The door to freedom was on the left, equally distant from himself and the six guards. With the advantage of the surprise attack on his side he had every confidence of making it.

He had noted in the hundred times he had searched the walls of the room that a fuse box was against the far wall. This must be the focal point of his attack and there were two problems that confronted him. First, from the awkward position he was in would he be able to hit it with the automatic in his left hand? Second, did that fuse box control the light in the room?

It was utterly futile to ponder the

matter. The Phantom had to gamble and gamble then. His aching nerves reacted to the stimuli of the coming encounter; he took a deep breath; his index finger constricted slowly on the trigger of the automatic.

Four things happened simultaneously.

The Phantom shouted hoarsely. The gun in his hand exploded. The lights over head went out. And before the weird, electrical flashes from the fuse box had died away, the Phantom was streaking toward the door.

All hell broke loose in the room on a rising crescendo of noise. Hesterberg's wild bellow rang out high above the crash of the machine-guns. Chairs were overturned, tables barged into as the Russian's henchmen milled about wildly.

A savage burst from one of the machine-guns was answered by a piercing curse in Russian. Hesterberg's men were mowing down one another. Chaos; pandemonium reigned.

Hesterberg's voice shrilled out again, frantic with fear and anger.

"Hold fire, you fools! Lights! Lights!"

But when the flickering light of a match lit up the scene some ten seconds later, the Phantom was gone.

THOUGH the Phantom knew that Hesterberg and his men would have long since cleared out by the time the police arrived, he nevertheless called up Headquarters and gave them the address of his prison.

A roaring taxicab carrying him away from the scene of his late exploit, he sank back on the cushions, closed his eyes and completely relaxed for a moment. He felt strangely weak, weaker than he had ever been in his life. His muscles ached like a torment, his hands trembled, daggers of fire pierced his eyes.

There was nothing he wanted so much in the world as sleep. But bitterly he realized that there would be little sleep for him that night. Bitterly he realized that there would be little sleep for him so long as Hesterberg's mad schemes were allowed to mature.

THE dawn was still-born as his taxi, his third by this time, raced up the deserted length of Fifth Avenue. It came to a grinding halt at a block in the Fifties. Throwing a bill at the driver, Van raced up a short flight of stone steps, squashed the bell by the side of the door with an impatient thumb.

Two minutes later he was wringing the hand of Havens.

For a moment neither could speak. They merely stood there mute, dumb, staring into each other's eyes for strength.

"God, boy!" mumbled Havens at last in a broken voice. "I never— I—"

Van waved the words away with a gesture and sank wearily into a chair.

"Neither did I," he said simply. "A drink, man—I need a drink. A stiff one."

Havens busied himself with whisky and soda, Van brushed away the soda and downed the Scotch with greedy gulps.

"You look almost ten years older right now," breathed Havens in an awed voice.

"Not only ten years older, but ages older," answered Van. "I'm back to you from the dead."

"What happened?"

Van helped himself from the bottle again and in a few terse words told Havens of what he had gone through since leaving the Union Club with a gun at Hesterberg's head.

Food was brought in. Van fell to with a prodigious appetite, renewing his frazzled nerves and energy. Over his second cup of coffee and a cigarette Havens again plied him with questions.

"What has been puzzling me all along," he began, "is how you disposed of Hesterberg at the club. I know you drugged him, but how?"

Van permitted himself a smile.

"I accomplished that with your subtle aid."

"You don't mean that glass of whisky Hesterberg and I drank together?"

"Exactly."

"But then how was it that I wasn't drugged, too?"

Van lit another cigarette and smiled fondly at the publisher. "That part is very simple, old man. When you and I were having our little conference in the locker, I offered you my pocket flask. You took a long pull and along with the whisky you imbibed the antidote to the drug I put in the bottle of Scotch I offered to you and Hesterberg."

Havens looked at his friend and smiled at him wryly. "And you wouldn't tell me?"

VAN shrugged. "There was no use in putting that added strain on you. But that part is in the past, forgotten. There are other worries to confront us. Frank"—and here his voice became tense and hard—"there is a traitor close to you; someone who knows your movements and consequently mine. How did Hesterberg know so positively that I would be at the Union Club last night?"

For another hour they discussed the matter, trying to place their fin-

gers on the guilty man, but without success. For another hour they discussed Hesterberg and his diabolical plans, trying in vain to devise some master stroke to get the Russian into their power.

CHAPTER XIII

"I Can't Talk"

VAN spent the late afternoon and evening with Havens at the latter's office at the *Clarion*. He was worried, troubled. That Hesterberg was slowly maturing his plans he knew but for once he felt himself absolutely helpless to frustrate the Russian.

Though he had succeeded on occasion to turn the tables on the Mad Red, he was accomplishing nothing to put a definite end to Hesterberg's plan. Hesterberg was still at large; he still dominated his minions of the underworld. Where he would strike next, God alone knew.

At any moment Van expected to hear that another figure of international importance had received the threat of death. Until that happened he was helpless, powerless to lift a hand against Hesterberg.

He realized bitterly that that was where he was at a disadvantage. He had to sit supinely by, twaddling his thumbs until Hesterberg made the first move. He was making no moves of his own! He was the one who was on the defensive.

"Yes," agreed Havens. "But good God, man, what can you do?"

"I've got to contact the underworld. I've got to get a direct line on Hesterberg through the underworld. Can't you see it, Frank? Once I have a few strings out on the Russian, I can move myself. I will be able to act, do things, make demands."

He rose abruptly to his feet,

clenched his cigarette with determined fingers. He called for his hat.

"Where away?" said Havens.

"No place—any place. I'm on the trail of Hesterberg."

He left the publisher's office and on a hunch decided to look in on Wooley, Havens' managing editor. Some bit of crime news might have come in that would furnish him with a clue. He walked slowly through the smoke fogged city room, oblivious to the clatter of typewriters and jangling telephones about him.

He was deeply enmeshed in thoughts of Hesterberg. He was— And then a word caught his ear, snapped him out of his reverie.

"Listen, Ruby," I tell you—"

It was Wooley's voice. He was speaking to a woman by the name of Ruby. Vividly there flashed to Van's mind the wreck of a girl who had effected his escape from Cokey Day's establishment. Could it by any possible chance be the same? Could Wooley be speaking to the drug-ridden girl? Could Wooley be—

A thousand possibilities flashed through Van Loan's mind. He half concealed himself behind a filing cabinet, lit a cigarette and, cocking one ear, tried to catch the rest of Wooley's conversation.

Unfortunately he was speaking guardedly over a phone and the clatter of typewriters and the hum and throb of the presses in the basement below, drowned his voice.

HE hung up a moment later and through the cloud of smoke of his cigarette Van saw that his hand was trembling, saw that his face was pale and drawn. Wooley reached for his hat immediately, shoved back his chair and made for the elevator. Van was well to the rear of the crowded car as Wooley waited impatiently for the elevator to disgorge him on the ground floor.

Some psychic sense told Van that at last he had fallen onto a live clue. Of course, it was altogether possible he was running down a blind alley. There were hundreds of women named Ruby in the city. He hadn't the slightest thing to connect Wooley's feminine caller with the creature of the Russian.

BUT why had the newspaper man acted so strangely? Why had he trembled? And what was the message that made his face pale?

Van followed him for two short blocks, saw Wooley turn hurriedly into a small Italian restaurant. He slowed up his pace, passed the eating house once and grunted his disappointment as he saw that the interior of the restaurant was effectively curtained off.

He wondered whether it would be wise to go into the eating house and run the risk of being seen by Wooley. He decided he had to risk it. He had to know the identity of the mysterious Ruby who had called Wooley on the phone. Unquestionably the call had been put through from the restaurant.

Hesitating no longer he pushed open the door and stepped inside. While his eyes searched the tables he mumbled something to the cashier at her desk by the portal and headed for the telephone booth wall on his left. Yes, far in the rear against the wall sat Wooley. And opposite him was the girl. The girl Ruby whom he had first seen in Cokey Day's.

He made his bluff good by dropping a coin in the slot of the telephone, waited another moment and then left the eating house.

Ten minutes later he was back in Havens' office going over the personal cards of the employees of the *Clarion.*

The Phantom entered the darkened hallway of a brownstone house in the Eighties. By the flickering glow of a match he examined the names under the row of bell buttons. With a murmur of satisfaction he pressed down firmly on the one that corresponded to Wooley.

The automatic lock on the door clicked immediately in response. The Phantom pushed open the door, hurried down a long hallway and rapidly mounted the steps at the far end.

He stopped a moment before the door of Apartment 3B, adjusted with his left hand the silken mask that concealed his features, while his right went to the pocket of his coat for the reassuring feel of his automatic.

With hard knuckles he rapped smartly on the oaken panels of the door. The portal was opened to him immediately.

Wooley stood on the threshold. He took an involuntary step backward while an inarticulate cry was strangled on his lips. The Phantom stepped hurriedly across the threshold, closed and locked the door behind him.

STARK fear writhed slowly across the pale face of Wooley. He retreated drunkenly backward into his apartment as the Phantom advanced upon him. His voice trembled shrilly when he spoke.

"You're — you're the —" He couldn't find the courage to finish his words.

"Yes, Wooley, I'm the Phantom," said Van grimly.

The verification of his suspicions robbed the newspaper man of all animation. His muscles became paralyzed and he sank helplessly into a chair. His first reaction on seeing the masked figure at the door had been fear; a compelling desire to escape.

NOW even those two most driving emotions were dread. There was no fear in his voice when he spoke; no fear in his eyes as he gazed at the Phantom's as they blazed out at him from the slits of his mask. He was broken; utterly broken.

"I knew it was just a matter of time," he began in a dreary monotone.

Though all his actions wreaked with guilt, the Phantom, as yet, had nothing definite on Wooley. He had to play his cards carefully; had to get Wooley to talk.

"Why," he demanded, and his voice rasped like a file.

Wooley looked at him with dumb pleading eyes. Then a frenzied passion distorted his drawn features.

"Hesterberg—that's why!" he screamed hysterically. "Hesterberg —the Mad Red. I tell you, if you—" He broke off suddenly; his voice became dead again. "But you know, you know."

"I know that Hesterberg must die," replied the Phantom calmly.

"And I die, too," echoed Wooley.

"There is still a chance for you, Wooley."

A frantic light of hope flamed up in Wooley's eyes as he gazed at the Phantom's face. Then it died down as swiftly as it had come.

"You mean?"

"Tell me all you know of Hesterberg. I want names, place, facts. Give me what I want and the Phantom does not strike."

Wooley looked at him pleadingly with agonized eyes. Fear descended on him again, leaving him weak, convulsed, hysterical.

"But I know nothing—nothing. So help me God, I know nothing. If you don't kill me—he will. Nothing escapes him; he knows all. Now that you have discovered me I am of no further use to him. It means —death."

Despite himself, despite the fact that he knew that Wooley was a traitor to all civilization, the Phantom could not help but feel a pang of sorrow for the wreck of a man before him. But relentlessly he went back to the attack.

"You must talk," he grated.

HIS eyes were gimlets of steel behind the blackness of his mask. His words carried a compelling threat. Wooley recoiled from him, backed up to the wall.

"I—I don't dare to talk," he whispered in a cracked voice. "It means—"

"Death from me if you don't!" shot back the Phantom.

"No! No!" pleaded Wooley. "I tell you, I can't talk. I know nothing."

The Phantom's voice came in hollow tones of accusation.

"You lie, Wooley. It was you who advised Hesterberg of my trip to Washington. It was you—"

But he never finished the second charge. With a wild gesture Wooley clawed frantically at his hip. An automatic flashed in his hand. The Phantom's gun was out a second later; his finger constricted on the trigger. But only one shot reverberated hollowly in the room.

With an agonized scream Wooley had pressed the automatic to his temple and fired. The Phantom stood there, riveted to the floor and watched him with fascinated eyes. He saw the mask of fear slowly melt from Wooley's face; saw the stark mad look fade slowly from his eyes.

Wooley swayed back and forth drunkenly for a moment, then pitched forward headlong on his face.

With a weary sigh, the Phantom pocketed his automatic. Once again on the verge of gaining real information, a real clue, he had been frustrated. And though this time it was by the hand of fear snuffing out a man's life, Hesterberg was no whit less responsible for it.

The Phantom cursed himself bitterly. If he had only foreseen Wooley's only out, as he should have; if he had only been a little faster he could have saved Wooley. Again he shrugged his shoulders wearily. The dead were dead and there was no bringing them back to life again.

With a bitter sigh he realized that he still had work to do in the apartment. He set about it swiftly. There was no telling when one of the Mad Red's men would appear on the scene. Any moment now the police might come in to investigate the shot.

He risked these two possibilities, dropped to one knee beside the body and rolled it over. Stark eyes stared unseeingly at the bright light overhead. But the Phantom had stared at death face to face before unblinkingly. Swiftly he made a thorough search of Wooley's clothes. Nothing.

WITH another curse at his luck he began a thorough search of the apartment. But the Fates were fickle that night. He unearthed absolutely nothing that would give him a lead to Hesterberg. The Russian's men were too well trained to be found with incriminating evidence on them.

In two tries the Phantom had drawn blanks.

His final ace was Ruby!

He turned out the light, walked swiftly to the door of the apartment and let himself out into the narrow hallway beyond. One swift survey of the street told him that it was deserted. Whipping off his mask, he strolled casually to the nearest corner, hailed a cruising taxi and climbed aboard.

Deep lines of concentration furrowed his brow as he was carried towards his apartment. Wooley explained much; but unfortunately not enough. If only he had been able to make him talk! Bitterly the Phantom pondered the awful tragedy behind the suicide of the *Clarion's* editor. But pondering that question got him nowhere.

It was obvious now, that it had been the dead editor who had warned Hesterberg of his secret trip to Washington. At least that much of the mystery was cleared up. Little enough, but it was a beginning.

Now he had to concentrate on the girl. He had to get to Ruby—talk to her—make her talk. The girl might be able to give him the information he had failed to get from Wooley.

By the time his cab deposited him at the door of his apartment, his line of action was mapped out.

CHAPTER XIV

RUBY

A HALF hour later the Dope, with shambling gate and palsied hand, slithered into the Fourth Precinct Station House. Ignoring the profanity hurled at his head, he caught the eye of Detective O'Neal and nodded his head significantly towards the rear of the room.

O'Neal understood and with the Dope shambling after him, led the way to an empty squad room.

"Well?" demanded O'Neal. "Where the hell you been? You're a hell of a stool. I got a good idea to smack you one in the nose."

The Dope held up an emaciated arm protestingly.

"Don't hit me," he whined. "I got something good for you—honest."

"Yeah?" sneered O'Neal doubtingly. "It better be good. What is it?"

THE Dope cast a frightened glance around the room. He took a step closer to the detective and lowered his voice.

"You know that dame, Ruby— the hop-head that hangs around Day's joint?"

"Yeah——I know her. So what?"

"Pick her up?"

"What for?"

The Dope again cast a frightened glance over his shoulder as if apprehensive of the dark corners of the room. He wet his dry thin lips with the point of a red tongue.

"Listen, O'Neal, "he pleaded in a trembling voice. "I'm giving you an okay tip, see? You pick up the dame and then things will happen. Get it?"

"I'll be damned if I do," growled O'Neal. He grabbed the Dope's emaciated arm in a vice-like grip and twisted. The Dope winced with pain. "Come clean, rat, or I'll bust your arm. Spill it!"

The Dope's lips drooled with anguish as he struggled weakly against the detective's torture.

"So help me, Sarge. That's all I know. You got to pick up the dame, see? I got it from Clancy. She's hopped up to pull a job—a big job."

O'Neal released his grip on the hop-head's arm and shoved him from him. "Okay, Dope. I'm a damn fool, but I'll play your tip blind. But if you've crossed me—if you make a monkey out of me, God help you."

"I wouldn't cross you Sergeant," whinced the Dope. "Say, how about a little snow. Just one shot. I'm all a tremble for a little coke. My nerves are all shot to hell. Just one shot, Sergeant."

"Nix to you," growled O'Neal. "If this dumb tip of yours means anything, I'll see that you get your sugar. If it don't, you won't need any more sugar to back up your lies."

O'NEAL, despite his brutality, was a good man. He knew his underworld and within an hour he had located Ruby and made his pinch. True, he didn't know on what ground he was pulling her in but he felt sure that the Dope wouldn't have dared give him a bum tip.

He had just locked Ruby in a cell and was on the point of going out again to pick up the Dope when he was attracted by a commotion at the desk. He hurried up on the run, ran full tilt into a tall man with a silken mask across his eyes.

O'Neal knew without being told that he was confronting the Phantom. Furthermore he knew that the Phantom's visit to the Fourth Precinct was to do with the prisoner he had just locked up. By God, the Dope had given him a straight tip at that.

"I want to see the woman, Ruby," said the Phantom.

Hard-boiled as he was, O'Neal was somewhat awed before this almost legendary figure. By reputation the Phantom was the most hard-boiled of them all.

"I just picked her up," he said. "She isn't booked yet."

"Never mind that. I just want to speak to her. Alone."

O'Neal nodded, chewed violently on the stub of his cigar for a moment, then led the way to cell 21. He fitted a key into the lock, flung open the door. The Phantom stepped across the threshold, heard the door slam behind him.

"Holler when you want me," called the detective and stamped noisily down the corridor.

The Phantom's back was to the dark interior of the cell. He sensed more than saw or heard the living person behind him. He turned abruptly, took two swift strides across the cell and stood confronting Ruby.

Her eyes dilated with horror as she took in his grim visage covered by the mask.

"The Phantom!" she breathed in a whisper.

"Yes—the Phantom!"

"What do you want with me?"

"Plenty."

"I know nothing. I'm only an addict."

"An addict in the power of Hesterberg!" shot back the Phantom.

His accusation brought a sharp, stifled gasp from the girl.

"Then you know?"

"Some—not all. Listen, Ruby. I am here as your friend. You must believe that. Do as I say and I promise you protection. Fail me and—" He left the threat unfinished.

The girl's head came up; her eyes bored into the Phantom's.

HOW do I know you're not a phoney, a fake? How do I know you're a friend of mine. How do I know you're not one—" her voice fell to a whisper—"how do I know you're not one of Hesterberg's men? Hesterberg himself."

The Phantom took a step closer to her; lean fingers reached out and gripped her by the wrist.

"Look into my eyes," he commanded. "Are they the eyes of Hesterberg? No! For your own sake, Ruby, you've got to believe me. I am your friend. If you don't —if you fail me—so help me God, I shall forget that you are a woman!"

She shrank back from the menace

in his voice. No man had ever spoken to her before like that. She feared the man before her but greater than her fear of the Phantom was her fear of Hesterberg. In vain she tried to extricate her wrist from the steel fingers that held her. The Phantom's breath was hot on her face; his eyes dominated her.

"Speak, woman, and I give you the protection of the Phantom. Hold your tongue and all Hesterberg's power can't save you. Look at me. I am the Dope you first saw at Cokey Day's. I am the Dope who shot Sligo. I am the Dope you helped escape from the cellar that night. Remember? Ruby, you must believe me."

"I—I do believe you. But I am afraid."

"Of Hesterberg?"

"Yes. He knows all, sees all, hears all. If I talk he will—will kill me."

"But you want to talk?"

"God knows, I do. I don't dare."

The Phantom took a step closer to her again. His voice fell to a dramatic whisper. "There is Wooley," he began.

HER sharp indrawn breath and the trembling hand that gripped him by the throat told the Phantom that he had struck home.

"What—what about Wooley?" she breathed hoarsely, her voice a mixture of love, anguish and fear.

Though the Phantom had hoped to be able to keep the information from her he saw that it would be the only way to get her to talk.

"Wooley is dead," he said in a soft voice.

Ruby received the information in appalling silence.

"He killed himself an hour ago."

Then the torrent broke. An inhuman, piteous sob broke from the girl's throat, wracked her body. Hardened as he was to suffering,

torture and despair the Phantom was moved. He averted his head while the low, inarticulate animal cry of anguish continued. Then it was stilled. The Phantom felt the terrific struggle that was taking place in the girl; saw her fight for mastery over her shattered emotions.

A MASK fell over her face—a mask of hate. There were no tears, no cries. Her eyes were dry and hard—harder that the Phantom's. Her lips were firm and purposeful, matching those of the man before her. When she spoke her voice was an emotional monotone.

"I'll talk. Now that he is gone, nothing else matters. Me, Hesterberg—nothing. Only this: That Hesterberg should suffer the way I have suffered; that he should live a living death that I am now living since Carl is gone!"

Her voice and words were terrible in their consuming hate. Despite his iron nerves, the Phantom felt an icy chill course down his spine. He was suddenly aware of a mighty respect for this woman before him for he knew that Ruby was ready to lay down her life to avenge the death of Wooley.

"I tried to save him but I was too late," he said humbly.

"It was only a matter of time," answered the girl in a hollow voice. "It was inevitable. If he hadn't killed himself Hesterberg would have. First, I must tell you—Carl was no traitor; no coward. What he did, he did for me—because he loved me. He was my husband."

The Phantom nodded his head in understanding.

"Go on," he said.

"It was my fault. I was foolish, vain; wanted jewelry and clothes. Because he loved me he stole. Stole from *The Clarion*. Somehow, Hesterberg found out. That devil finds out everything!"

A sudden transformation came over her. She jumped to her feet in a frenzy, grabbed the Phantom by the lapels of his coat.

"You've got to believe me," she pleaded in a wild voice. "He stole for me. Carl was no thief!"

The Phantom nodded his head in sympathy but said nothing. The girl continued after the outburst in a dead voice.

"When we tried to pay back the money it was too late. Hesterberg had Carl in his power; threatened to expose him; put him in jail. And I was too weak, too selfish again to let him go.

"Then Hesterberg promised to release him if he did one service for him."

"That was the Washington affair!"

The girl nodded mutely.

"And then Hesterberg didn't keep his promise?"

"No; he had us deeper in his power than before. And then I—I took to drugs. It was the end!"

The Phantom bowed his head; never before had he been so moved by a confession. The girl continued:

"But you are not interested in the downfall of a foolish woman. What do you want to know? What do you want to know about Hesterberg? If I can have but one finger in his downfall, Carl will be avenged and I will die happy."

THE scene was too pregnant with tragedy for the Phantom to derive any great satisfaction from the information he was about to receive. But he had to press the issue. More was at stake than the anguish of one woman.

"First," he said tersely, "who is the traitor in Clairborne's office? Who called Hesterberg instead of the police to protect Clairborne at the Union Club?"

"The man is Mcarson—Clairborne's secretary," replied Ruby.

THE Phantom cursed himself for a fool for not having arrived at that conclusion himself. But no time now for vain regrets.

"That's the only question I have to ask now," he grated. "You speak; I want to hear everything you know."

Ruby was silent for a brief moment, collecting her thoughts. But the mask of hate never lifted from her face and her eyes were baleful pools of fire.

"First," she began, "you should know this. There is a sign—a signal that is passed between all of Hesterberg's men. It is this."

As the Phantom watched with fascinated eyes she took the ring from the small finger of her right hand and transferred it to her left.

"Whenever you see that sign you are looking at one of the Russian's creatures."

The Phantom's pulse kicked out a steady hundred and thirty. At last he was getting somewhere, learning things; concrete things.

"Fine," he exclaimed with satisfaction. "Go on."

Ruby was still marshaling her thoughts when suddenly the heavy feet of O'Neal pounded down the corridor. He stopped before the prisoner's cell, fitted a key into the lock and swung the door in.

"Sorry to break in on this conference," he said, "but there's a mouthpiece out at the desk with a writ of habeas corpus for the dame here. He demands that we produce her immediately. Order signed by Judge Pinelli."

At his words and the mention of the judge's name, the Phantom felt the girl press close to him. He was aware of the violent trembling of her body; of her panting breath as her hands went to his coat in an imploring gesture. O'Neal's message had awakened all the old fears in her.

With ill-concealed impatience the Phantom turned to the detective.

"Can't he wait five minutes?"

"Sorry," grumbled O'Neal. "But a writ's a writ. This mouthpiece is a tough guy. He'll make it rotten for me if I don't produce. Come on, Ruby—somebody's springin' you."

But despite the fact that somebody was trying to get her out of jail, Ruby had no desire to go. She clung to the Phantom.

"I'm afraid," she whispered. "Hesterberg is back of this. Follow."

THE Phantom pressed her hand reassuringly and nodded, then turned to the detective.

"Okay, O'Neal—take her. But remember, her safety is in your hands. I'll hold you responsible. Where is Judge Pinelli sitting?"

"At his home; joint up on Riverside Drive."

"Okay. Take the girl. I'll make my exit through the rear."

Richard Van Loan was standing idly at the curb hailing a cab before the Fourth Precinct Police Station, when Ruby came down the steps of the Station House escorted on each side by a burly policeman. A sharp nosed bespectacled individual, carrying a brief case, brought up the rear. Van tagged him as the lawyer who had presented the writ. As his own cab pulled up to the curb he saw from the corner of his eye that Ruby was being ushered into a high powered limousine. The car slid away from the curb immediately. Van jumped into his own taxi and slammed the door behind him.

"I'll give you twenty dollars above the clock if you don't lose that car," he snapped.

"You're on, boss," grinned the driver. "Let's go."

Despite his suspicions, the limousine ahead traveled at a normal rate of speed northward. It stopped for traffic lights, turned west on Seventy-second Street and proceeded at a leisurely rate of speed up Riverside Drive. Van's taxi had little trouble keeping its tail light in sight.

CROUCHED forward on the cushion, a cigarette between his lips, watching the car ahead, Van wondered for a moment if Ruby hadn't been wrong, her fears ungrounded. Judge Pinelli was a respected member of the bar. If her detention by the police was unlawful, he would discharge her.

And then Van understood. That was exactly it. It wasn't what would happen to Ruby before she got to Pinelli, it was what would happen to her after her dismissal.

He threw his cigarette out the window of the cab as he saw the car ahead pull to the curb before an ornate four story gray stone house.

"Here! Quick! Pull into the curb," he ordered.

His cab pulled up before the canopied entrance of a large apartment house. Van jumped out, made a great show of searching in his pocket for money while he kept his eye on the car ahead. He watched Ruby escorted out of the limousine by the two policemen; saw her, surrounded by the two officers and the lawyer, mount the steps of Judge Pinelli's home.

The Phantom was undecided for a moment as to his next course of action. As long as Ruby was guarded by the two policemen, he felt that she was reasonably safe. Still, he couldn't get out of his mind the note of fear in the girl's voice, her final word to follow. He knew enough of Hesterberg's machinations to realize that it was entirely possible that Pinelli was one of the Russian's allies.

AS he stood there hesitant on the sidewalk, a second limousine pulled up at the curb, before the judge's home. The curtains were drawn; though the streets were dry, the license plate on the rear was bespattered with mud. The Phantom had seen that trick played before.

There was something phoney about that car. Some psychic sense warned him that Ruby had been right. Strolling slowly up the sidewalk he shot a swift glance at the second car. What he saw was not reassuring. A dark, beetle-browed gangster sat hunched over the wheel, while two others sat poised and tense in the rear in attitudes of expectation.

That decided the Phantom. He crossed the street, lost himself in a dark hallway and shifted his automatic from his shoulder holster to his side coat pocket. When Ruby came out of that house he was going to escort her away—and no one else.

With his keen eyes on the doorway opposite him, he tied a silken handkerchief around his neck and adjusted it so that it could be flipped up over his face in a second.

He had just prepared himself for a long vigil when things began to happen. The door to Judge Pinelli's opened. The Phantom stiffened and his hand dropped to the pocket of his coat. But it was not Ruby who darkened the portal. The two policemen who had escorted her into the building pounded heavily down the stone steps to the sidewalk.

The Phantom hesitated. That meant that the judge had released the girl. But why hadn't she availed herself of the protection of the police and left with them? The Phantom was filled with a vague apprehension. If anything should happen to Ruby he was lost. If her suspicions were correct and the Russian was the power behind the writ, he had to go into action at once.

He crowded against the shadows of the hallway considering his next move. The two policemen had turned the corner and were by now out of sight. Then again for the second time in two minutes the Phantom stiffened while his hand dropped to his automatic.

More action on the far side of the street. The door of the limousine that had arrived a few minutes before swung open. The two occupants of the rear seat stepped out, hurriedly mounted the steps of Pinelli's house. The door was opened immediately to them and they disappeared into the dark interior.

That decided the Phantom. Something was wrong; decidedly wrong. He, too, had to get into that house.

He took the silken handkerchief from around his neck, stuffed it into his pocket and hurriedly crossed the street to the apartment house. Waiting his chance when the elevator was making a trip to the upper floors, he made a hurried exit through the trade entrance in the rear.

HE came out in a dark and shadowy courtyard, surrounded by a high board fence. Two houses away to his left was the rear of Judge Pinelli's house. The Phantom never hesitated. Adjusting the mask about his face he scaled the board fence as agilely as a cat, crossed another dark courtyard and pulled up ten seconds later before the basement of the judge's house.

CHAPTER XV

JUDGE PINELLI

IT was but the work of a minute to force a window with his pocket knife. Slowly, carefully, inch by inch, he raised the casement, straddled the sill a moment, gun in hand, then dropped softly to the room beyond.

He paused a tense moment, listening, every nerve and muscle on the alert. He was impelled forward immediately by the necessity of speed. He had to locate Ruby at once. When Hesterberg struck, he struck surely and swiftly.

He negotiated the basement rooms of the house successfully, felt his way to the flight of steps that led upward. Pushing his gun before him he mounted swiftly, came out a moment later onto a small landing on the main floor. Darkness! No lights, no sounds!

For a panic stricken moment the Phantom thought that he was too late; thought that Ruby had left the house by the front while he was effecting his unlawful entrance through the basement window. Then a harsh, grating sound set his teeth on edge. The breath whistled sharply through his nostrils and his finger constricted on the trigger of his gun.

But a moment later as his jumpy nerves settled, he smiled grimly to himself with satisfaction. He wasn't late after all. That grating sound that had made his pulses pound was the striking of a match against a wall. It had come from the floor above. Simple deduction told him that the man who had struck that match was probably on guard.

The Phantom began the ascent of the second flight of stairs. Unless he missed his guess, Ruby was in a room above him, still in conference with Pinelli and one of the men from the car. The Phantom's plan was simple in conception but not quite so simple of execution. He had to listen in on what was being said behind the locked door on the second floor.

He reached the top of the stairs, crouched low by the banister. His keen eyes were accustomed to the gloom now. He focused them down the corridor to his left. Nothing. To the right—and his teeth clamped together. He made out the scarlet tip of a glowing cigarette. Suddenly it disappeared—then after a pause became visible again.

"Pacing up and down before the door," thought the Phantom.

He counted the interval between succeeding appearances of the glowing cigarette and judged that whoever on guard was walking a post of ten paces. He himself was some fifteen paces away from the sentry when the latter's back was first turned to him.

That was all the Phantom needed to know. The red eye of the cigarette was coming toward him. He counted the paces. Seven—eight—nine—ten! And in that second that the glow of the cigarette was extinguished as the sentry turned around, the Phantom leaped.

LITHE as a tiger, swift and silent, as his name, he sped over the thick, velvet carpet on the floor. He was on his man; his gun described a swift arc through the air and descended with crushing force onto yielding flesh. Even as he smote, the Phantom's left arm went round his victim's throat in a strangle hold.

The guard slumped beneath the blow without a sound, without a protest.

"Out for a long time, fellow," whispered the Phantom as he eased his limp burden to the floor. "I'm only sorry I couldn't have given you the other end of the gun."

He wasted no further time on the guard. Straightening up, he sped swiftly back to the door from beneath which a thin blade of light cut the opaque darkness of the hallway. He pressed his ear to the jamb and listened. Voices came to him, heavy threatening masculine voices against the frightened words of Ruby.

"Now listen, baby, Carl's dead, see. He can't do nothing more for you. What we want to know is what's this gag about the pinch by O'Neal? How come?"

Ruby's voice came plaintively to the Phantom through the closed door, weak and tired from her struggle.

"I've told you, Joe, for the hundredth time, I don't know. He just picked me up and asked me a lot of damn fool questions."

"Questions about what, my dear?" came a cultured suave voice — the voice of Pinelli.

"About Carl."

"Yeah—I thought so. And you squawked."

"You lie!"

"Then what did you tell him?" pursued the judge.

HIS voice was cool, menacing— far more dangerous than the brutal accents of her other inquisitor.

"I—I told him I didn't know who killed Carl," pleaded Ruby. "Can't you believe me?" Her voice suddenly cracked and a piteous note crept into it. "Please, Joe, for God's sake, give me a shot. My nerves are all on fire. I'm all broken up. Can't you see—ah, for pity's sake Joe— give me, give me—"

Though the Phantom could not see into the room, he vividly imagined the scene that was transpiring be-

hind the door. He could see Joe tormenting the girl to a frenzy by holding a phial of dope before her; he could see the heavy form of Judge Pinelli sitting smugly back in his chair watching the woman's anguish.

"You'll get no more snow, Ruby," snarled Joe. "You're through, see. You squawked to O'Neal. Hesterberg wants you; what Hesterberg's got to say to you is plenty. And then it's the noose for you. I'm going to take you to the boss now."

THE Phantom had heard enough. His eyes were hot and dry; a hard lump was in his throat. The violent hate that consumed his heart twisted his entrails into a hard knot.

Adjusting the mask over his face with one hand, the lean fingers of the other shot out to the knob of the door. With a violent wrench and a kick of his foot he shoved the portal inward.

He stood there on the threshold, the automatic in his hand thrust forward aggressively. His sudden advent was heralded by a stifled scream from Ruby. Joe made a half movement towards his hip but pulled up short as the gun in the Phantom's hand jerked up to cover his heart. Judge Pinelli sat stupidly in his chair, eyes bulging, while the swarthy color faded slowly from his cheeks.

The Phantom looked steadily at one man, then the other.

"You're taking the lady no place," he rapped out, as he stepped into the room. "She's going out with me and if any one tries to stop her, God help him."

"Who are you?" demanded Pinelli in a strained voice.

"You know who I am, Pinelli. I am the Phantom. As you have sat in Judgement, so shall I pass sentence on you. You won't spoil, Pinelli. You'll wait. I'll be seeing you again." He turned to the Mad Red's henchmen. "And as for you—rat—lead is too good for you. I'll reserve some special death for you that your crawling soul will be able to appreciate."

He turned from the two men to the girl.

"Ruby, back up around Pinelli's table. Keep out of range of my gun and back to the door."

Like someone in a dream the girl obeyed the order. Standing as she was between Pinelli and Joe, she now had to pass between them to gain the far side of the table at which Pinelli sat.

It was at this precise moment that Joe, the gunman, decided to stake all on a desperate gamble. Instead of trying to get his own gun into action, which would have been futile—instead of charging blindly on the Phantom, he threw himself violently at Ruby's knees.

With a crescendo crash that was seconded instantly by the growl of the Phantom's gun, they toppled to the floor. The Phantom's first shot had missed its mark. Joe came up, firing from behind Ruby's body at the elusive target made by the Phantom as the latter plunged to the right of the doorway.

It was a surprise move and before Joe could shift into position for a second barrage, the gun in the Phantom's hand jerked viciously twice and the gunman's rod was silenced forever.

JUDGE PINELLI sat frozen with fascinated horror in his chair. The Phantom whipped around and pointed his still smoking automatic at him.

"That's another crime you can pass sentence on, your Honor," he said scornfully. "One move out of you and you get the same."

But Judge Pinelli was too wise a man to tempt the fire in the Phantom's eyes.

The masked figure talked to the girl over his shoulder.

"Ruby—are you all right?"

Dazed, bewildered, she climbed to her feet.

"Yes."

THEN let's get out of here. On the run. There'll be a squad of police here any minute."

Ruby stumbled across the room to him, clung frantically to his arm. Together they backed toward the door. The Phantom pushed her out into the hallway and then with his gun still covering Pinelli removed the key from the lock of the door, stepped across the threshold and jerked the portal behind him.

It was but a second's work to turn the key in the lock and snap it off there. Then, half supporting, half dragging Ruby, the Phantom raced down the stairs. He was half way to the front door when the heavy thunder of a night stick resounded against the oaken panel. In mid-stride, the Phantom changed his direction and headed for the back stairs by which he had come.

With a silent prayer on his lips that the house was not already surrounded, he half carried the fainting Ruby to the window he had jimmied earlier in the night. Somehow he lifted her over the sill and dropped down beside her in the courtyard.

Then putting thoughts of all else save escape behind him, he picked up the girl in his arms and sped with her down a narrow alley that ran the length of the building. They emerged onto Seventy-sixth Street and the Phantom got his third break of the evening. A cab was parked at the curb, its driver asleep at the wheel. Opening the door he deposited the limp figure of Ruby on the back seat and jumped in beside her.

He prodded the driver to wakefulness with the point of his gun.

"Get rolling, big boy," he ordered. "Get away from here fast."

The chauffeur stared at the masked face for a moment in startled fear, then jumped to obey. He shifted into gear, stepped on the gas and shot eastward toward Broadway.

Ruby came to for a moment, long enough to get a glimpse of the masked figure beside her. Then, promptly obeying the dictates of over wrought nerves, she broke down in a fit of hysterical weeping. The Phantom tried to comfort her; to still the wracking sobs that parted her lips. But she was beyond words, beyond help.

Joe, the gunman, threw himself violently at Ruby's knees.

Her hysteria increased; she broke down completely. The Phantom realized that she needed care at once.

He rapped on the glass partition separating him from the driver.

"Pull up at the nearest cop," he ordered.

The driver was only too glad to obey. At the next corner he swung over to the curb before a burly blue-coated policeman.

THE Phantom leaned out the window of the car.

"Listen officer, get this straight," he said tersely. "I'm the Phantom. I have a woman here. She's hysteri-

cal. Take her immediately to the City Prison Hospital. Put her under guard. No one is to speak to her. Give her the best of treatment, understand. I want to question her later. It's important."

THE officer nodded his head dumbly, but made no move.

"Take the girl out of the car," ordered the Phantom.

The officer picked up Ruby in burly arms and headed for another taxi. The Phantom snapped out his last order to his driver.

"Get away from here fast. Get to West End."

On a deserted side street he left the cab, saw it disappear around the first corner. Then only did he remove the silken mask from his face and with a lighter step than he had had in days he walked over to Broadway.

He crammed himself into the first telephone booth; dropped a nickel in the slot and swiftly dialed the number of Police Headquarters.

"This is the Phantom speaking," he barked when the connection had gone through. "I want to speak to Inspector Armitage." A pause, then: "Armitage—the Phantom. Two things—important things on the Hesterberg case. There's an hysterical woman in the City Prison Hospital. Ruby Wooley by name. Detail a guard over her, a heavy guard. No one is to be allowed to see her until further orders from me. Secondly, broadcast to your men in the underworld. Have them pick up the trail of every man they see making the following signal."

Briefly he described to Inspector Armitage the signal that Ruby had passed on to him earlier in the evening. Then, sure that the inspector understood his order, he rang off with a curt good-night.

It was with a light heart and a thin whistle on his lips that Van turned his steps at last toward Havens' apartment. For the first time since he had been given the task of tracking to earth the Mad Red, he felt that he had the situation in hand.

HE had passed on the signal of the ring to Armitage; the inspector in turn would get in touch with the Secret Service. Now that everyone of the Russian's men were tagged, they were bound to obtain results.

Not only that, but there was still Ruby to be interviewed. He would see her on the morrow when her hysterics would have subsided. That she had much of importance to tell him he was sure, and he was just as confident that he could induce her to talk.

And then as a final dessert to his evening's adventures—was Muriel.

At precisely eleven-fifty-four that evening, a telephone jangled in the home of the Secretary of State of the United States. Despite the lateness of the hour, he dressed himself, bade farewell to his wife, and stalked into K Street, seeking a cab to take him to the White House.

HE never arrived. Upon anxious inquiry early that morning, the President of the United States denied having telephoned his Secretary of State on the previous evening.

Two minutes after the Secretary of State had left his home Lewis Bond, the international banker, and perhaps the biggest man in the country, received a telephone call from his head groom. Bond was insanely interested in horses, and maintained an elaborate racing stable.

On that particular night he was expecting the birth of a colt from which he expected great things. The groom had instructions to phone him when the delivery was over.

In answer to his head groom's summons, Bond threw on an old ulster overcoat and walked through the spacious grounds of his estate toward the stables.

It is a matter of record that he never got there.

Even while the Secretary of State was searching for the taxicab, even while Lewis Bond was walking ingenuously toward his brood mare and her progeny, Arthur Remis was having trouble with his automobile. Just outside Pittsburgh, as he was returning from a bibulous and riotous evening at his country club, a big Lincoln suddenly cut him off and almost ran him off the road.

Remis stopped dead as did the Lincoln. Then Remis, the munition king, confident in the arrogance of superlative wealth, proceeded to tell the driver of the Lincoln precisely what Arthur Remis thought of him.

The driver took it well, at least a ghost of a smile hovered over his face as Remis came close to him. That faint smile was the last thing that Remis saw for a few hours.

Of a certainty, he never saw his own home that night.

So it was with Naylor, with Carson and others. Most of them knew each other, and if they were not acquainted the Fates provided for that contingency.

They met that night.

CHAPTER XVI

HESTERBERG STAKES ALL

THOUGH it was two o'clock in the morning, the occupants of the Havens' household were very much awake. Richard Van Loan, clad correctly in evening clothes, without an alias, was playing what was presumably a business call upon the publisher.

They sat together in the library. The door was closed as they spoke in low tones. Without, in the room beyond, sat Muriel Havens. She read idly and wished inwardly that her father would choose someone other than the handsome Dick Van Loan to talk business with. She would much prefer to talk to Dick herself.

Even though her father and Van had been closeted together for the better part of four hours she waited patiently until she could play hostess to the most eligible young bachelor in New York, until business should succumb to the social. But had she

known it she was destined not to speak to Van again that night.

In the library a cheery fire flared in the grate, throwing dancing shadows on the wall beyond. Havens sat back in an arm-chair and flicked the ash of his cigar carelessly on the rug.

"YES," Van was saying. "The plans are complete now. Every important member of the underworld is being watched. With the cooperation of the police and Secret Service, my plans are at last working. Unless Hesterberg has already got his coup ready—and I don't think he has—it's only a matter of time now until his machine is completely broken."

Havens nodded. He indicated a late evening paper that lay on his desk.

"It looks as if your scheme is working already. Did you see the paper?"

"No. What's in it?"

"It seems that for the first time in years, in this town, there have been so few arrests in twenty-four hours. Hardly a major crime has been reported since midnight of yesterday. What do you think of that?"

Van breathed deeply. His eyes held the other's.

"I think it's dangerous as hell," he said quietly. "Let me see that paper."

He picked it up and what he read corroborated the statement of Havens.

"This is ominous," he said. "This means that Hesterberg is ready for his big moment. He's going to gamble everything now. He's ready."

Havens stared at him in surprise.

"Why? What do you mean? You read an item in the paper which seems to me to be good news, then you apparently get alarmed."

"I do," said Van grimly. "And I'll tell you why. There have been no arrests here for twenty-four hours. Why? Because there are so few criminals in the entire metropolitan district."

Havens looked at him blankly. Still he did not understand.

"That means," continued Van, "that Hesterberg has at last mobilized his men. He is ready to strike with all his murderous forces. They are mobilized somewhere, God knows where. There is little crime in New York because there are so few to commit a crime. They are all with Hesterberg at his base. We must act quickly, and think more quickly."

HAVENS looked alarmed as the full significance of the apparently cheering piece of news in the paper dawned upon him.

"Then," he said, "you've been too late?"

Van reached for the telephone. "We'll soon see," he said tensely. "But I think you're right."

He put in a call to Police Headquarters and asked for the deputy commissioner in charge. Then he said: "This is the Phantom. Have your men been following everyone who made the sign I told you about?"

Then came the answer which confirmed his worst fears.

"Why no. Our men haven't been able to find anyone making that sign all over town. They've looked everywhere. I think your tip was phoney."

"Perhaps it was," said Van as he replaced the receiver on the hook. He turned to Havens. "So," he said bitterly, "even that plan has gone awry. Hesterberg has made his final move. As I suspected there's not a member of his band left in town. They're getting ready for their coup. And God only knows where they are! I'll try something else."

He picked up the phone again and called a number.

"Hello! City Prison Hospital. Give me the superintendent. Hello! I want to inquire about Ruby Wooley. How is she? Can she be seen at once on a matter of the utmost importance?"

"Wooley?" repeated the voice at the other end of the wire. "Just a minute."

There was silence as the superintendent fingered through his files. At last he said: "Mrs. Wooley's not here."

"Not there?" Apprehension trembled in Van's voice.

"No. She was moved a few hours ago by special order of the commissioner. He sent a car for her. I think it was a transfer to Welfare Island, but I'm not sure."

"Thanks," said Van, and hung up. Then he turned to Havens.

"Well," he said a trifle bitterly. "That seems to be that."

"What's happened?"

"Hesterberg's licked us again. He stole my star witness." He told the publisher the story of his afternoon's adventures. Havens sat openmouthed at the recital.

"Then it must have been Wooley who somehow found out that I was sending the car to take you to the White House."

VAN nodded. "But knowing that doesn't help us now. This is Hesterberg's hour."

Havens rose to his feet. "We *must* do something," he said excitedly. "This apparently is our last chance. I'll go inside and send Muriel off to bed. Then we can plan."

Van didn't answer. He nodded his head abstractedly, and a frown distorted his brow as he grappled for a plan that could stop the Mad Red from the complete consummation of his plans.

Havens went to the study door which led to the living room, and opened it. For a moment he stared wild-eyed across the threshold. Then he gave a shout of alarm.

"Van. She's gone! Look here?"

In an instant Van Loan was at his side. His receptive eyes swept the room hastily. The portieres which hung over the doorway from the hall were torn down. Lying on the floor by the window lay Havens' butler bound and gagged, his eyes turned appealingly toward his employer.

Van raced across the room, and hastily severed the man's bonds. Havens stared ashen-faced, speechless. The butler came to his feet stiffly. Van questioned him abruptly.

"Where's Miss Havens?"

"They took her out, sir. They chloroformed her."

"Why?"

"Two men, sir. Armed with revolvers. They chloroformed her and bound me up."

"How long ago?"

"About fifteen minutes, sir."

"How do you account for the fact that we didn't hear them in the study?"

"They worked very quietly, sir. Efficiently. They had the guns on us and we didn't dare make a move. Desperate characters, sir."

"Yes," said Van grimly.

Havens tore across the room and seized Van by the coat lapels.

"The dogs," he said. "The filthy dogs. Now they've got Muriel in this. We've got to get her out, Van. We've got to."

VAN removed the other's trembling fingers from his coat.

"Take it easy," he said soothingly. "There's no use going off the handle. Look, what's that?"

His eyes noted a white envelope lying on the table in the center of the room. In a scrawling hand, it was addressed to Frank Havens.

Van's index finger ripped open the flap. He extricated a stiff piece of notepaper. He glanced at its message, then folded it again in his hand.

"You may go," he said to the butler. "Mr. Havens and myself will be in the library if you want us. Come on, Frank."

HE took Havens' arm and led him back to the library. He forced his friend into a chair and poured him a stiff shot of brandy. Like a man in a coma, Havens obeyed the other's directions.

"Now," said Van as he seated himself on the other side of the desk, "pull yourself together, man. We can only win this fight, we can only get Muriel back to safety if we avoid panic. Now, come on, snap out of it."

With a tremendous effort, Havens forgot that he was a frantic father. He realized that calmness, coolness were the prime qualities needed in this crisis. He turned a wan face to Van, but when he spoke his voice was steady enough.

"All right," he said. "I'll do my best. What now?"

For answer Van handed him the paper he had found on the table outside. It read:

Havens:
  At exactly 3 A. M., turn your radio dials until you tune in on the message I have for you. Hesterberg.

The publisher crumpled the paper in his hand.

"What does that mean?" he asked hoarsely.

Van was already at the radio. "We'll soon find out," he said grimly as his sensitive fingers fumbled at the dials.

The clock on the mantel indicated that it was slightly after three o'clock. All the regular stations were shut off at this hour. The two men sat tense and silent in the room, as Van twisted the dials. Nothing save the mechanical burr of static came through the speaker.

THEN at last as the condensers whirled beneath Van's fingers, they caught the sound of a human voice—a familiar voice. The dials stopped their timeless whirling. Carefully Van oriented them. The voice became clearer, articulate. The two men exchanged glances as they recognized it as that of Hesterberg.

"Havens," it said. "You should have picked me up by now. I shall repeat this message at five minute intervals for the next hour in any event. I am broadcasting this from my car traveling to my base. You will be unable to trace the broadcast. I sincerely hope that our mutual friend, the Phantom, is listening in with you. What I have to say will also interest him."

The voice stopped for a moment. Havens was frozen to immobility in his chair. His ears ached as he strained them, fearing to miss a word that might deal with the fate of his daughter. Van smoked a cigarette with an air of casualness which he was far from feeling.

"I am ready," said Hesterberg. "I am ready to put into execution the coup that I have planned for so long. Soon my emissaries sail for foreign countries. In their possession are enough international documents to start a dozen wars. They will deliver them to the right people, to the people who have been unwittingly betrayed by other diplomats."

Again he paused, perhaps, to enjoy his complete triumph for a moment.

"There is more than that, Havens. I am now in a certain city not far from New York. I am in complete control. I speak to you via the radio because all lines of communication from here are cut. There is no phone. There is no telegraph. My men have seen to that. But I have other things here. I have the Secretary of State of the United States. I have Lewis Bond, the banker. I have Remis, the munitions man. I have Naylor, the steel man. But I won't bore you. I have other men, influential and wealthy. And their ransom shall be the granting of the credits to Russia that I desire. My men are already in communication with their families. And in a short time the cables will be granting Russia what I demand."

"Good God," said Van. "He's done it!"

But Havens, intent on the disposition of his own daughter, paid scant attention to the fact that the madman who spoke to them was within an ace of wrecking civilization. The publisher sat upright in his chair at the next words.

"Yet, Havens," went on the icy voice of Hesterberg, "there is yet one thing I want. The Phantom still has some fragments of papers that I need. I can do without them, but they will facilitate my purpose. You will get them from him. You will deliver them to my man who will shortly call on you. If you do this, your daughter shall be returned safely. If you refuse, she shall suffer as no woman has ever suffered.

IN a short time my most trusted man shall call on you. It is useless to attempt to get information from him. He is my best man, and for that reason I have given him this assignment. You may capture him, kill him if you will, but he will tell you nothing. If I have not heard from him within a reasonable length of time, I shall assume you have trapped him, and I shall treat your daughter accordingly. Havens! Have you heard me?"

Something clicked in the speaker, then there was silence. The most bitter and awful silence that Van had ever known. Disaster and defeat were imminent. He had failed in the most important mission that had ever been intrusted to him. Hesterberg, the Mad Red, had won!

Havens turned dull glazed eyes to Van. He was in the grip of a terrible emotion. Here he sat, helpless and supine, with his motherless daughter in the grip of a maniac, God only knew where.

"You can't do anything, Van," he said dully, despairingly.

To Van his words were nothing less than an accusation. He flushed, bit his lip and said nothing. Never had he known such a sensation of futility. Despair deluged him. Even his fighting heart, which never before admitted defeat, beat dully in his breast; and as he gazed at the agonized face of his friend he felt as if he had betrayed him, as if the fact that Muriel was in peril was solely his fault.

But after a few minutes the natural driving courage within him asserted itself. His brain cast itself about for a means of yet saving the battle, of outwitting Hesterberg. Then he realized that there was but one answer. He must first find out where Hesterberg had mobilized his army of murder.

THERE existed but a single chance to do that. The Mad Red's man was coming here to get the papers which Hesterberg wanted. That man would have the information that Van wanted. True, Hesterberg had warned them that this man was the pick of his motley crew, a man of courage who would not talk, a man selected for his fortitude and loy-

alty. Yet it was the only chance. *Van must make him talk!*

He rose from his chair with his jaw set. His face was a terrible thing to behold. Dick Van Loan had made up his mind that no matter what torture, what lengths he must resort to, Hesterberg's emissary would talk. That was the only conceivable thing that would save the civilization that the crazy Communist had set out to wreck.

THEN, again, there was Muriel. Van liked the girl more than he would have cared to admit. Perhaps if he had not been the Phantom she might have been more to him than merely the daughter of his best friend. But, as it was, he had no right to declare himself to any woman. Not while he engaged in this dangerous business which was meat and drink to him. His heart was heavy at the thought, but that only stiffened the terrible resolution that he had made.

Havens started at the jangle of the doorbell. He glanced inquiringly, hopelessly at Van. Then, as he saw the other's firm jaw, his purposeful eyes, his set shoulders, an inexplicable new faith was engendered within his heart.

"What are we going to do?" he asked.

Van Loan took a black silk mask from his pocket and fitted it to his eyes.

"Do?" he said, and there was a murderous resolve in his voice. "Do? We're going to make this gentleman talk."

"How?"

"That I don't know. But talk he will if I have to break every bone in his body. If I have to tear him slowly limb from limb. Send your servants to bed and bring him in."

Havens rose slowly. He stared strangely at Van. Never had he

seen him in such a mood; never had
he seen those black snapping eyes
of the Phantom so determined, so
awful, bent on wreaking a terrible
vengeance on his enemies.

Without another word, Havens
turned and left the room. Van
stood on the threshold of the library.
He heard the publisher dismiss his
butler. Then he heard the sound of
the front door being unlocked. He
started as he heard Havens give
vent to a startled expression. Then
he heard footsteps and a steady
thumping noise approaching him
from the hall.

AS Havens reappeared there was
an expression of panicky fear
stamped indelibly upon his countenance. And Van, looking beyond him,
immediately saw the reason for
Havens' newly born fear.

For the messenger of the Mad
Red was Sligo, the cripple, with the
eyes like diamonds, glittering from
a setting of mud!

This, then, was the man whom
Hesterberg trusted most. T h i s
then, was the man that the Mad
Red knew would not betray him.
Van realized now that his hope of
frustrating Hesterberg hung by a
very slender thread. Then a thought
struck him. Perhaps he could—

But he would wait. He would play
that card last. Silently he closed
the library door behind the pair
of them. Havens seated himself in
a chair, his eyes gazing vacantly at
the wall. Sligo grinned sardonically.
He knew the publisher was afraid
to meet his snake-like gaze.

"Well," said the cripple, "what
are we waiting for?"

The Phantom put his hand in his
pocket and walked slowly toward the
cripple. His eyes glittered through
the mask. Sligo shifted uneasily in
his chair.

"Well," he said again, "what about
those papers? For the safety of
everything involved, I'd suggest you
give them to me at once."

Van Loan came a step further.
Havens stared at him, marveling at
the deathly coldness of his manner.
From his pocket he took a knife, a
slim delicate thing with a three-
inch blade, sharpened to nothingness.

As he moved nearer the cripple,
the bridge lamp on the side of the
room caught the blade, and the
light glinted ominously, but the
gleam in the Phantom's eyes was no
less cold and inclement than the
light on the steel.

Van Loan grasped the cripple by
the shoulder with his left hand.
Their eyes met.

"I'm going to ask you some questions," Van said. "You can either
answer them or die slowly and painfully, just as you like. But you'll
do one or the other before you leave
this room."

There was hatred in Van's heart;
a hatred of his own that no one else
could quite understand. But there
was another kind of murder in his
eyes, an expression that no one
could help understanding. Sligo
well comprehended that this man
was not threatening him idly. Yet
he did not flinch.

"If you mean I'm to tell you anything about Hesterberg or his plans,"
he said sullenly, "I'll not do it."

"No," said Van.

HE put his knee on the cripple's
chest. His left hand encircled the
man's neck. His right brought the
knife close to the man's eyes.

"Now, listen," he said in a soft
purring voice which belied the words
he uttered. "When I was in Papua
the natives had a grim form of amuse-
ment which used to entertain them
very much. When they caught a
white man against whom they har-

bored a grudge, they would cut off his eyelids. Now, before I start performing this operation on you, will you consider what that would do to your sleep? And it's a shame to ruin such beautiful eyes as yours. Now, Sligo, will you talk?"

The Phantom brought the knife down close to the man's eyes. The point gleamed like a lonely star and the cripple stared at it, mute and expressionless. Behind Van, Havens stood transfixed, like a man of ice.

"Do you talk?" said Van.

The cripple didn't answer. Instead his jeweled eyes stared straight ahead into Van's. The knife seemed to stick to his hand. His arm seemed suddenly heavy. A faint glaze came over his eyes. He could feel his pulse pounding, and the vein in his throat throbbed. He blinked. Then decided that this whole thing was ridiculous. Why should he worry about Hesterberg? All he wanted to do was sleep—to go to bed. God, he was tired!

But before his body moved itself away from Sligo, his brain fought against the dizziness that was upon him, and gave him a warning.

YOU fool!" something seemed to shout into his consciousness at a great distance. "He's hypnotizing you. Fight! Fight or you're lost."

Van shook his head savagely, as if the mere physical gesture would throw off the daze that insidiously crept over him. His eyes met those of the cripple and held. Havens stood breathless behind Van and watched the strangest battle that was ever fought between two men.

It was literally a battle of intellects. Van Loan was no novice in the arts of hypnosis, and Sligo was a past master. The room was pregnant with silence, broken only by the hissing sounds of men breathing jerkily, tensely, as they struggled for the dominance of their own minds.

CHAPTER XVII

THE PHANTOM TAKES THE TRAIL

NO ONE in that room knew how long the struggle lasted. The gray ghostly fingers of dawn reached up over the eastern horizon and put the night to flight. The clock on the mantel ticked away the minutes, the hours, and still three men remained motionless. Two of them locked in a mental struggle that must end the career of one. And in the background the third man watched, knowing that should the cripple win his own life would hang in the balance.

The battle swayed first one way, then the other. At times Van would feel those glittering eyes of Sligo boring into his. He would feel weak as if he must pay homage to the other's will. Then he would rally. The power of the cripple's mind became less and Van knew that his own will was asserting itself on the other.

Sweat dripped from his face. His eyes glazed with the strain and there was a terrible pounding in his head. Then came the moment that he instinctively knew was the crisis.

Sligo was tiring. He half raised his head. His eyes were bloodshot. He fixed Van's pupils with a malevolent gaze. He staked all on this one moment—and he nearly succeeded.

A terrible lethargy came over Van. Desperately he fought with every ounce of his will power, with every bit of his mentality. Sligo's face was distorted with hate and rage. Now that he had exerted every trick he had, he panted. Then he issued an order, in a final frantic hope that he had subjected Van's will, that he had the Phantom under the influence of his own mind.

"You are in my power," he gasped. "My first order is you release me."

Despite the agony, the weariness that was upon him, Van grinned. When he spoke his own voice seemed to come from a great distance.

"The hell I am," he said. "On the contrary—"

Sligo, his attempt failing, dropped his head back in his chair. Desperately he tried to avoid Van's eyes, but the two black pupils transfixed him through the silk mask. The glittering eyes of the cripple suddenly lost their animation, their brilliance. A glaze came over them. Sligo relaxed in his chair.

Then and only then did Van release him. He stood up and turned to Havens.

"Thank God," he said, "we've got him."

Outside it was broad daylight. The clock on the mantel indicated that it was after nine o'clock. Havens breathed a sigh of relief.

"Now, what do we do?" he asked.

"Now it's easy," said Van. "Listen."

He walked back to the cripple and fixed him once again with his eyes.

"Sligo," he said, "you will answer whatever questions I put to you. I am your master. Do you understand?"

THE cripple nodded his head slightly. "Yes, Master," he said in a dull far-away tone.

"Good. Now where is Hesterberg?"

Havens leaned forward eagerly to catch the answer. Sligo hesitated a moment, then replied:

"At Edgetown."

"Who is with him?"

"Everyone in the gang, and the men he is holding as hostages."

"Is it possible for an enemy to get inside the town?"

"Possible, but dangerous. It is well guarded. However, at night it could be done."

Van turned to Havens and nodded. Sligo slumped forward in his chair. Physical exhaustion had taken hold of the cripple. Van sprang forward and jerked him roughly by the arm. This was Van's chance to get the answer to a question that had completely baffled him.

"Wait, Sligo," he said. "There is one thing more."

The cripple sat up with an effort. "Yes, Master."

"How did Bursage die?"

"The afternoon of his death, I visited him in a wheel chair. I had been wounded the night before. On a pretext I saw him. I hypnotized him into getting himself a dagger and stabbing himself at midnight."

BUT Sligo never spoke again. The tremendous struggle had snapped the thin thread which held his evil life together. He slumped forward in his chair, and Van's finger on his wrist felt no answering pulse beat.

Havens gripped Van's arm excitedly. He opened his mouth to speak but before he could frame his words the telephone jangled imperiously. Instinctively Havens reached for it but Van placed a restraining hand on his arm.

"I'll take it," he said, picking up the receiver.

"Long distance," said the operator, "Millville calling."

Van put a hand over the receiver. "Millville calling," he repeated. "That's about fifteen miles from Edgetown." He removed his hand. "Put the call through."

A moment later a harsh masculine voice came to his ear.

"Hello, Havens? I'm calling for

Hesterberg. Has our man got there yet? If so, why hasn't he left. Why hasn't he reported?"

Van's brain raced faster than light itself.

"Oh, yes," he said. "He's here now. I'll let him talk to you."

"Okay. Put Sligo on."

VAN placed the receiver on the desk. He walked three paces away from the phone, then he turned and walked three paces back again. He picked up the phone and said in a very fair imitation of the cripple's voice:

"Hello! This is Sligo."

"Well?" said the harsh voice inquiringly.

"The trouble is this," said Van. "They're quitting all right. They'll give me the papers, but they're in a vault uptown. I can't possibly get them till about ten o'clock. Then I want a chance to rest. I've had a tough time here. I'll be at Headquarters tonight."

"Okay," said the voice. "As long as we know you're all right. Good luck."

"Good-by," said Van, hanging up the receiver.

"Who was it?" demanded Havens excitedly. "Hesterberg?"

"No. One of his men. I've convinced him Sligo's all right. I've also convinced him that the Phantom's through with the case. That ought to hold him till tonight."

"And now," said Havens anxiously, "what do we do?"

"First," said Van, "we rest. Then I shall go to Edgetown disguised as Sligo. I shall go by night. I must rest first, because tonight will tell the story. Either I die and Hesterberg succeeds in his plans, or Hesterberg dies himself."

"Shall I come? I want to be there. Muriel may need me."

Van threw a fraternal arm about his friend's shoulders and shook his head.

"No," he said, "you stay here. I must play a lone hand. If you have not heard from me by midnight, call the governor. Explain the situation to him. Have him send help, militia if need be. Hesterberg probably has enough men to warrant his calling them out.

"In the meantime, I shall try to foil him. I shall try to prevent his emissaries from slipping through. His men must be stopped from getting to Europe. His money drafts to Russia must be stopped. If I can prevent that by guile so much the better. If not, we must try force. Don't forget, give me until ten o'clock, then send help. Stand by the radio. It's apparently the only way I can communicate with you from Edgetown. Good-by."

He stretched forth his hand. Havens grasped it firmly.

"Good-by, Van," he said. "If anyone can do it, you can. And if"— he hesitated for a moment—"if we don't see each other again, I'll never forget what you've done."

Van was visibly moved by the other's words. He took the mask from his face, wrung Havens' hand heartily, silently, afraid to trust his voice. Then, turning on his heel, he left the room and took a taxi to his own apartments.

KNOWING the secret of complete relaxation, Van lay at full length on his bed. His eyes were shut, but his tired brain was still functioning. He reviewed the information that he had obtained from Sligo and considered the best method of using it.

The story of Bursage's killing cleared up that angle. Van smiled a trifle ruefully as he realized that the explanation was one that he should have hit upon himself. However, it was no use wasting thought on the past, when the future loomed so menacingly ahead.

OF course, it had occurred to him simply to have the authorities despatch a young army to Edgetown to wipe out the murderous throng who rallied to the Mad Red's banner. But that was not as easy as it sounded.

After all, Hesterberg had under his control in his safe-keeping half a dozen of the most influential men in America. Van knew full well that he would have not the slightest hesitation in slaughtering those men in cold blood if it were expedient to do so. Then, too, there was Muriel. For a moment as Van thought of the girl, helpless in the clutches of the maniac, his blood ran cold.

No, first he must go to Edgetown himself. Perhaps he could devise some way of saving the hostages with which Hesterberg planned to foist his will upon the world. If he failed, well, then the troops could take care of the situation. At least they could capture the Russian, even though Van and the others had first been put to death by the former's hand.

Then, too, there was the matter of stopping Hesterberg's messengers. Even though their master should be captured, the documents which they carried could still do their dreaded work. War would ride roughshod over civilization, with the other three horsemen of the Apocalypse galloping grimly in his wake.

Banks would extend the Soviet credit on the cables which were sent by the families of the captured men. And then, again, there was Muriel.

Now, Dick Van Loan had of his own volition eschewed romance for excitement. He had sacrificed his chance at the normal happiness of life for a vivid live-or-die existence. Never would he marry any girl. It would have been too unfair. Yet, now that he realized for the first time the depth of his feeling for Muriel, he felt sick and wretched as he thought of her in alien hands.

Then, at last, after his brain had formulated his plan, he permitted his aching mind to relax. For three hours he slept. Then he rose, dressed, filled a suitcase with a number of things which might be useful to him, and telephoned for his roadster. And in his pocket reposed the torn half of the papers that Hesterberg needed badly.

Half an hour later, as the late autumn sun was streaking down over the horizon to light the other half of the world, he stared out up the Post Road. His face was set and grim, his eyes determined and steady and his heart was a steadfast courage—a courage which he was destined to tax to the utmost iota ere that black night had passed.

For the last time the Phantom had taken the trail of the Mad Red —and this time it would be a battle to the death!

CHAPTER XVIII

EDGETOWN

THE night came down. The twin headlights of Van's car cut two holes through the blackness. Gray lay the road beneath their yellow glare. On either side, trees waved gaunt and ghostly arms to the sky, while far ahead the friendly lights of a town twinkled cheerily for a moment, then were lost to sight as a hill reared itself in Van's line of vision.

From time to time he consulted a map which he had pinned to the dashboard. He fully expected that there would be no lights to indicate Edgetown. Hesterberg had in all probability closed every shutter, cut every wire, to insure that no one could interfere with him now, that no one could take from him his hostages with which he could enforce his will.

Chances were that the residents of the town had been made prisoners also. Hesterberg could not afford to let them walk the streets unmolested. A footnote on Van's map told him that Edgetown was off the railroad line, and that the population was slightly under a thousand.

As he came within ten miles of the town he slowed down and considered some important things. Undoubtedly the Russian had established his guards. A picket line, probably, was thrown out around the village. Van considered his car. Should he drive it through the picket lines or should he leave it without?

Finally he decided to put on the false license plates which he carried in his suitcase and drive right in. It was dark and the pickets would not pay much attention to the car if they were sure that it was Sligo, the evil-eyed cripple who was passing into the town.

WHEN a glance at his map showed him that he was within four miles of the town, he ran the roadster on to the shoulders of the road and came to a full stop.

He opened the suitcase and withdrew a box of make-up. Staring into the mirror over the windshield, he dexterously drew the grease paint over his face. Deft fingers applied black to his eyebrows. Small pieces of flesh-colored wax distorted his features, and slowly before the mirror, the grim face of Richard Van Loan evolved to the ugly countenance of Sligo.

The likeness was so remarkable, so appalling, that it would have certainly passed muster before the cripple's own mother. But Van was not done yet. From his pocket he took an eye-dropper. He lifted it to his eye. His tongue closed on his teeth, for he knew the pain this was going to cause him.

THEN with a firm hand he squeezed the end of the dropper. The drug deluged his eyeball. He grimaced with pain. Then he repeated the process on the other eye. For a full minute he sat there, suffering untold agony. Then, at last, as the smarting died away, he glanced in the mirror, and exultation beat within his heart.

For now the final barrier was past. His eyes of snapping black had become the steely glittering orbs of Sligo, the master hypnotist.

He climbed out of the car, changed the plates, then, as nonchalantly as if he had been in his own bedroom, he changed into the clothes which Havens had taken from the dead body of the man he was impersonating.

Once back behind the wheel he lit a cigarette, stepped on the gas and shot ahead through the night to meet—Death, Triumph, or whatever the gods had in store for him at Edgetown.

He ran the car over the dirt road slowly. Behind him the main ribbon of concrete stretched from New York to Albany, but here on this little muddy highway which led to his destination, the night seemed darker than before, darker and more ominous.

A voice suddenly hailed him.

"Hey, there! Who is that?"

He stepped on the brake and answered: "Sligo. I just got in from town."

A figure approached in the darkness, a revolver held in its hand. It bent over and peered at Van uncertainly.

"What's the password?"

Van swallowed. Here was a contingency he had overlooked. He had figured on his identity as the cripple getting him by. Here was an unlooked-for complication. He assumed an anger he was far from feeling as he threw the car in first, and raced the motor.

I'M SLIGO," he said again. "I just got here. I've important news for the boss. Password, hell!"

The car moved slowly. The figure with the revolver leaped on the running board.

"I don't care who you are. What's the password? What's the—"

Another figure approached and spoke with a voice of authority.

"What's wrong here?"

"This guy won't give the password. He—"

Van cut in. "I'm Sligo. Important message for the chief. I—"

A flashlight tore the darkness away from his face. His heart pounded violently, but he made no perceptible sign of what went on in his emotions at that moment. The authoritative voice said: "Of course, it's Sligo. What the hell's the idea of holding him up? Go ahead, pal."

The false Sligo went ahead, and now his heart beat almost as loudly as his engine raced.

The town was in utter darkness. No light was lit, and with all lines of communication cut, Edgetown was at that moment as isolated as any remote spot of the world.

As Van drove into the single street of the town, he saw a number of men hurrying to and fro through the night. They paid scant attention to him as he parked the car and climbed down from the driver's seat. One or two called his name and he mumbled a reply. Then he left the car and as his eyes became accustomed to the lack of light, took stock of his surroundings.

Lights showed through chinks of the drawn shades of the houses which lined the street. He heard a low hum of voices, and despite the fact that he saw nothing tangible there was an air of bustle about the place. He sensed rather than saw the activity which went on behind those drawn curtains.

A figure passed him. Van touched his arm and said gruffly: "Where's Hesterberg?"

The man peered at him closely.

"Oh, it's you, Sligo. Why, I guess the boss is in his office." He jerked a thumb in the direction of a house across the street. "Did you look there?"

Van did not wait for an answer. He crossed the street, nodded to the man on guard at the door and entered the three-story brick building which was the largest structure the small town boasted.

Despite the inherent courage that was in his heart, Van could not fight off the feeling of apprehension that came over him as he entered the Mad Red's Headquarters. They had been at grips before, but now came the death battle. It was all or nothing for each of them. Only one of them would leave this place alive.

Van had no set plan.

He first must ascertain how far Hesterberg had gone with his plans, and if possible delay his emissaries and guard his prisoners from harm until such time as Havens would send help.

THUS far his disguise had passed muster. It was the most complete thing of its kind he had ever achieved. Yet danger lay ahead. Undoubtedly Sligo was one of Hesterberg's most trusted lieutenants. When they met there would be talk.

He must be wary. A single false move on his part conversationally would arouse the Russian's suspicions.

He mounted a flight of stairs, then stopped dead, pressing himself flat against the wall. A door was open on the landing, and through it the hum of static came to his ears. Then the metallic sound of a voice that issued from a loudspeaker. Van paused a moment and listened. Then a nauseating fear swept over him; a fear that after all his master-minding he was too late.

There were reports that were blaring forth over the loudspeaker. Reports from Hesterberg's lieutenants as each cog in the gigantic whole of his scheme was fitted into place.

"Number 6 reporting to Hesterberg," blared the loudspeaker. "Sailing on *Morganitic* at midnight. All plans consummated."

Van's eyes narrowed and his hands clenched into hard fists as he caught the next message as it throbbed triumphantly out of the speaker.

"Number 3 reporting to Hesterberg. Morton Syndicate cabling credit Soviet. Credit at our terms. Great success."

"Number 8 calling Hesterberg. President guarantees immediate recognition. Sailing *Empire* immediately."

VAN stood there by the threshold of the radio room, stupefied for a moment. In quick succession new reports came in, each one giving the details of some master stroke the Russian had brought to a successful conclusion.

The sudden appalling realization that he had failed paralyzed his limbs. But then a moment later his old, indomitable will asserted itself. He had been tempered too finely in the white heat of conflict to accept defeat until the last shot was fired.

He still had a chance—a wild fantastic chance, but desperate men cannot choose their odds. Pulling himself together, he assumed the shambling gait of Sligo, the cripple, and slouched into the radio room.

HE was quick to note a sheaf of messages before the operator and his trained eyes told him immediately that some of them were in code.

He swaggered up to the operator's desk, confident in his disguise insomuch as it had so far passed muster without question. He reached confidently for a blank form and a pencil.

"How are the reports coming in?" he asked casually.

"Great. In the bag," replied the operator.

Van wasted no more time on idle talk. He applied himself to the blank form and rapidly wrote a message in the code that he and Havens had used on frequent occasions before.

The message was terse, explicit, but emphatic. Havens was to get in touch with the President at once and to stop all boats from sailing from the United States. Further, he was to close down all cable offices and all transatlantic telephone wires. No message, no word, no person should leave the United States that night.

And then, after that had been accomplished — but only after — the President was to rush a company of militia with all speed to Edgetown.

Van signed his name in code and shoved the message across the desk to the operator.

"Here," he ordered tersely. "Hesterberg wants this message sent out at once. Repeat it at five minute intervals for the next half-hour. Important. Clear the air for it."

The operator picked up the blank

and scanned it hurriedly. Van saw the cloud of suspicion pass over his face and prepared for action.

"But this isn't our code," protested the operator.

"No," answered Van with heat. "There's been a traitor some place and the old code leaked out. He's changed it. Get busy and hammer it out."

Assuming that his word was law, he waited no longer to argue the point, turned on his heel and left the room. With a slow tread he mounted the remaining steps that led to Hesterberg's office. A wave of exultation swept over him as he heard the intermittent buzz and whine of the transmitter as his message went on the air.

Please God it would be picked up by Havens; please God it would be in time.

CHAPTER XIX

AN OLD TRICK

HESTERBERG'S eyes lit up as he recognized the man he had sent to retrieve his torn papers.

"Good," he said. "You're back. What luck?"

Van achieved the slow distorted grin that he had seen Sligo use. By way of answer he withdrew the papers from his pocket and handed them to the Russian. Hesterberg took them and gloated audibly.

"Good," he said again. "This is all we need. I'll send a man out with these at once. This, Sligo, is the end. We have won."

Still Van did not speak. He hardly dared presume upon his luck. Apparently, as well as Hesterberg knew the cripple, he had not penetrated the Phantom's disguise. The Russian crossed the room and slapped the cripple heartily on the shoulder.

"Fine work," he said. "By the way, what did Conners say?"

Van's heart sank, and his brain raced. This was the one thing he had been afraid of—that Hesterberg would refer to some subject of which he—Van—knew nothing. He stalled for time.

"Who?" he said.

Hesterberg shot a swift glance at him.

"Conners?" he repeated. "Did you see him?"

"Oh, Conners? Yeah, I saw him."

"What did he say?"

"Nothing. Everything was okay."

Hesterberg's eyes narrowed. A thin cruel smile crossed his lips. "Well," he said with dripping suavity, "isn't that just dandy?"

Quickly he crossed the room and before Van could divine his purpose he drew back his right foot and kicked the detective brutally in the shin.

The sharp pain of the kick caused Van to momentarily forget everything. He sprang to his feet, uttering a sharp exclamation of anguish. Hesterberg stepped back a pace and regarded him with vast satisfaction. Then his voice rang out, clear and commanding.

"Seize that man!"

Strong arms gripped Van's shoulders. A hot shooting pain ran up his leg still. Hesterberg surveyed him with triumphant eyes. He bowed ironically.

I THANK you, Mr. Phantom," he said. "I thank you for bringing me my documents in person. I appreciate the honor you have paid me."

Van said nothing. Hesterberg had penetrated his disguise. Yet he had saved something from the wreckage. At least he had the satisfaction of knowing that by now there was an even chance of the Mad Red's plans being frustrated. If

Havens had picked up his message, the Russian's men could never leave the country. The cables could not be sent.

No, now it narrowed down to his own life, a point which did not trouble him much. But as he thought of Muriel, and the others whom Hesterberg would not hesitate to sacrifice if it suited his purpose, his heart grew heavy within him.

"I would suggest," Hesterberg was saying, "that the next time you assume a disguise, you study the physical peculiarities of your subject. You see, Sligo had an extremely weak chest. I used to slap him on the back merely for the sadistic pleasure I derived from seeing him wince. You did not move."

Van said nothing. He simply stared into the flaming maniacal eyes of the Mad Red, and the message he read there was most assuredly not one of mercy.

"Yes," continued Hesterberg, "then merely to corroborate my suspicions, I invented Conners. There's no such person. Then, to really prove my point beyond all doubt I kicked you in the shin, the self-same shin of Sligo's which has been paralyzed for years."

VAN held his head up. His jaw was firm. Very well, here was Death. He had courted danger. He had eschewed security. Here was the result. The reaper stretched out the scythe to mow him down. And before he went, there was but one request he had to make of the Gods. Let him die as he had lived—game, courageous—like a man.

His eyes met Hesterberg's. A faint smile crossed his lips. "Very well," he said. "It's your trick, Hesterberg. And it's your play. What are you doing?"

Hesterberg smiled too. But the grimace was not engendered by the same motives as Van's. There was hate in that smile—hate and murder. And when he spoke his voice was thick with anticipation of the revenge he would take of this man who had foiled him so often.

"TAKE him away," he said. "Throw him in the cell next to the others. They're in six. Put him in five alone. I'll attend to him personally later on. We must attend to many other things first."

Rough hands dragged Van away. He was escorted down the stairs to a building further down the street. He was pushed up an iron ladder to what he assumed was the second tier of the county jail. On the landing which was unlit he dimly made out the doors of three cells. They were numbered from right to left: four, five, six. That apparently inconsequential fact stuck crazily in his memory; and he lived to thank the fates that it did.

A single guard stood below. Van had seen him but vaguely in the pallid moonlight which poured through the iron bars over the window at the far end of the corridor.

The grated door of the center cell number five was pulled open. Van was flung roughly inside. Then the door clanged to irrevocably. Probably never to open again till the bony fingers of Death himself turned the key.

He heard the low hum of excited voices in the next cell—number six. A voice said ponderously: "Who is that? Another one of us?"

There was no further need for concealment of his identity, Van reflected bitterly. When Hesterberg came to kill him, he would surely rip the disguise from his face to discover the real identity of his enemy.

"It's the Phantom," he whispered. "Who's there?"

He heard a gasp of amazement from behind the wall. The slow ponderous voice said again: "Is there any hope? Or does this madman intend to kill us all?"

Van heard a sharp intake of breath from the other cell. He disguised his voice carefully. "Is the girl there?" he asked.

Then Muriel's voice came to him, firm and clear:

"Yes," she said. "Have you any word from my father?"

HE is well, and you shall soon see him," said Van, relief flooding him as he realized that she was safe.

A babel of voices floated through the wall, as the hostages took new hope now that the Phantom was here. Van silenced them.

"Not so loud," he counseled in a whisper. "We shall be overheard by the guard downstairs. No more talking. I must think. We still have a chance. But I must ask you to remain quiet in your cells if you value your lives. Not a word of conversation even among yourselves. Do nothing until you hear from me."

"He's right," said the heavy voice which Van recognized as belonging to the Secretary of State. "Let us put ourselves in the Phantom's hands. We can have no better protector."

His words of faith once more aroused Van's fighting spirit. After all, the Phantom was not beaten as long as life remained in his body. Hesterberg might yet live to regret that he had not killed his foe out of hand, instead of remanding him to a cell, even though it was for less than an hour.

Van only prayed that Havens had received his code broadcast and acted upon it. Hesterberg would probably assume that inasmuch as the Phantom had discovered the whereabouts of the Mad Red's Headquarters, he had left word in town for help to follow.

The chances were that even now, the Russian was consummating his plans and then after the business of attending to his prisoners, he would flee, secure and triumphant in the knowledge that he had succeeded.

As things stood, the success or failure of the Mad Red's plans lay on the knees of the gods. Havens had delivered the message, if the militia was on its way, Hesterberg, unconscious of these events, was doomed to defeat. On the other hand—

But Van dared not think of that. His present duty was plain. He must endeavor to deliver the prisoners from cell number six. Muriel was there. The Secretary of State was there. Some of the biggest men in the country were there. And even the militia could not save them from Hesterberg's wrath if he decided to wipe them out in mere revenge—a course which was quite probable if he saw all his finely laid plans go slithering from Parnessus to oblivion.

Then suddenly, like a searchlight putting the darkness to flight, an idea came to him. Perhaps, if he could escape from his cell, he could do something. He put his right hand under his left arm pit, and touched something solid and metallic which reassured him.

True, the men that had dragged him here had searched him casually. They had confiscated the .38 in his coat pocket, but they had overlooked the small pearl-handled automatic which nestled reassuringly in his shoulder holster.

Now he withdrew the weapon. He held it carefully in his right hand, then putting his face up against the bars, he called out loudly enough for the guard to hear him: "So, Hesterberg shall never slay the

Phantom. He dies by his own hand."

Before he pressed the trigger he was aware of two things. First, a gasp of alarm, concern and horror from the girl in the next cell; then the rush of feet as the guard from to a low moan and sank to the cold concrete floor of his dungeon.

It was an old trick, but apparently the guard was not an old hand. Unhesitatingly, devoid of all suspicion, he opened the cell door and, rushing in, bent down over

Two hands sprang toward him; one clutched at his throat, the other thudded dully against the point of his jaw.

below dashed up the iron stairway.

A faint mirthless smile wreathed Van's features as he pulled the trigger. The bullet buried itself in the rear wall of the cell, in exactly the opposite direction from where Van stood. Nevertheless, he gave vent Van's prostrate form. That was the last thing he did for the next two hours.

Two hands sprang toward him. One clutched his throat and drew him closer; the other thudded dully against the point of his jaw. Silently he fell on top of his prisoner. Van rose to his feet. He left the cell and clanged the door shut behind him.

Hastily he removed the tricky little pieces of wax from his face. His handkerchief removed some of the grease paint. Then he donned his black silk mask and stood for a moment before cell number six.

"Listen," he said. "Be absolutely silent. Keep alert for a signal from me. I'll see what Hesterberg is up to."

He walked cautiously toward the iron stairs. The door below clanged and he experienced a sinking sensation in the pit of his stomach as two of Hesterberg's men entered. They looked at each other in surprise when they saw that the guard was not downstairs.

THEN they sprang for the stairs together and came up on the run, revolvers in their hands. Three weapons spoke simultaneously as they saw Van. The bobbing heads on the steps presented a difficult target and Van's shot went wide.

He heard the whiz and clang as two rounds hissed over his head and struck against the granite wall of the prison. There was no time for a second shot.

Fearing their master's wrath should anything go amiss, tonight of all nights, they charged upon the Phantom. Van felt himself go down as their bodies collided with his. He heard a chuckle of triumph. One hand gripped his gun arm. Fingers clutched his throat. He was held there helpless.

A hand reached down and touched his mask.

"So," chuckled a voice. "At last the Phantom shall be unmasked."

The hand plucked at the black silk.

For the first time in his life Van knew the full meaning of utter and black despair. His heart turned to lead, and his stomach was suddenly empty. This, then, was the end. The Phantom had lost. Hesterberg had won. And in that last moment he thought of Muriel. The hand on the mask grew tighter. It lifted.

Then a feminine voice said: "Stand back! Drop your guns! Throw up your hands!"

An ecstatic joy surged up in the Phantom's breast. It was Ruby! He brushed away the moment's wonder as to how she had gotten there. It was enough that she had come when he most needed aid.

"Drop those guns!" she snapped again.

The hand fell away from the Phantom's mask. Two guns clattered futilely to the hard floor. With swift steps, the Phantom leaped to the girl's side, snatched the automatic from her fingers.

"Good girl, Ruby," he whispered as he drew a bead on the two men. "Inside there—in that cell. The shade cords."

Ruby understood at once. She was back a moment later and again the gun was switched between them. Swiftly, with deft, expert hands, the Phantom bound and tied the two prisoners together, their arms behind them. Rising to the emergency again, Ruby tore strips from her skirt and fashioned them into effective gags.

THE two men helpless, the Phantom looked hurriedly around for a place to dispose of them. A dark corner beneath the bend in the stairs caught his eye. At the point of his gun he prodded them forward, forced them to lay down, back to back and then tied their feet together.

He straightened up from his work

and looked at Ruby with grateful eyes.

"How did you get here?" he asked breathlessly.

"Hesterberg got me out of the hospital. Had his men bring me here." Her lips curled with utter loathing. "You see—he thinks—he wants me for himself. That's why he tried to keep the drug from me."

THE Phantom looked at her sympathetically, tried to speak, but could find no words. Ruby stooped down and picked up the guns from the floor. She passed one over to the Phantom and concealed the other in her dress. She turned away.

"Where are you going?" asked the Phantom.

"I've got to go back—to Hesterberg. He'll miss me. I discovered you were here in the cell. Came down to see if I could do something for you."

The Phantom gripped her hand fervently.

"You did," he said simply. "Keep your nerve up. We'll get out of this yet."

But the dejected stoop of Ruby's shoulders as she descended the steps gave the lie to his words. The Phantom waited a full two minutes after her departure. Swiftly he inspected the two guns now in his possession. Then satisfied that they were both in perfect working order, slowly made his way down from the iron stairs. Once there he cautiously pushed open the iron door which led to the street and peered out.

Outside there was a loud scurrying of feet. Raucous voices shouted orders. Though it was dark, Van could make out the forms of a hundred men hastening to and fro. Then suddenly he heard the imperious commanding voice of Hesterberg.

"Hold your ranks, men. Let no one take panic. This is something of a surprise, but I can handle it. Every man to his appointed place. And, remember, I still hold the hostages."

At first Van failed to comprehend the madman's words, but then there fell a moment's silence, and steadily he heard the noise of marching feet.

His heart bounded within him. So Havens had not failed him. Aid was at hand. Again Hesterberg's voice split the night harshly.

"Tell the picket to bring the commanding officer to me."

A voice repeated the order, then hurried away to relay it to the outer line of pickets. Van stepped out into the night, confident that his mask would remain unseen in the ado of the moment. He stood in the shadow of the prison. His eyes were riveted to the back of Hesterberg's head as the latter waited to deliver his ultimatum to the leader of the attacking troops.

He heard the clank of rifle butts on the concrete of the sidewalk as the men of Hesterberg prepared to sell their lives dearly should the final test come.

CHAPTER XX

THE GAMBLE OF LIFE

SUDDENLY in the dark distance a staccato command rang out. The marching feet came to a sudden halt. The murderous garrison of the town stood silent, tense, awaiting the next move. Two figures approached through the night. They stopped before Hesterberg. Van, still standing in the doorway, never took his eyes from the Mad Red's back; further, he never took his hand from the butt of the automatic in his pocket.

The picket stood aside and a man

whose uniform buttons glinted faintly in the negative light spoke tersely to Hesterberg.

"Do you surrender?" he asked impersonally.

Hesterberg laughed harshly.

"No."

"Very well," said the officer. "I had hoped to avoid bloodshed. The game's up, you know. When I fire a signal from this Very pistol my men will charge. Now, do you surrender, or do I fire?"

"Neither," said Hesterberg. "You overlook something. I have in my possession a number of people whose lives the country can ill afford to lose. The Secretary of State of the country, half a dozen of its leading financiers, an inconsequential girl, and—the Phantom."

For a moment the officer seemed at a loss. At last he said rather weakly, "Well?"

"They're over there," said Hesterberg, indicating the cells. "In cell number six. If you call your men they die. All of them. Before your men can reach here, one of my men will have mowed every one of them down with a revolver."

AGAIN the officer hesitated. But this time the Phantom did not.

He realized that there was a desperate chance to turn the tables, and he had no alternative except to take it.

He had suddenly remembered that inconsequential fact about the numbers on the cell doors. He raced back into the prison, his knife already in his hand. What he wanted to do was the work of perhaps two minutes. Two minutes which ticked past like two eternities.

When he had completed his task he put his face up to the bars of the cell which held Hesterberg's prisoners.

"Listen," he said. "Not a word.

Your lives depend on your silence. That is all."

Then in less than ninety seconds he was back in the shadow of the friendly doorway below, his keen eyes again boring steadily into the back of Hesterberg's neck. The Mad Red was still speaking to the officer, who seemed wavering.

"So, you see, if you act, my dear Colonel, I shall be reluctantly compelled to commit this murder. Furthermore, in the two churches I have confined the residents of this town. They, too, would be in danger. Surely you would not risk the lives of such eminent hostages as I hold."

The officer seemed greatly troubled.

"I have my orders," he said. "I should obey them. But when so much is at stake, perhaps I should use my discretion. What are your terms?"

HESTERBERG chuckled. He opened his mouth to reply. But the next words that were spoken came from the Phantom's lips.

"He makes no terms, Colonel. Don't move, Hesterberg. I have an automatic trained on his back. He's bluffing you. He has no hostages."

"You lie!" cried the Russian, his face distorted in fury. "You lie!"

The vacillating officer peered through the gloom.

"Who are you?" he said sharply.

"I am the Phantom, and I tell you Hesterberg is in no position to make terms. I have released the prisoners he had in cell six. By now they are safely away."

The officer turned to the Russian.

"Is this true?"

"No! He lies. He—"

"Very well," said Van quietly. Send one of your own men to cell six to investigate. Go on."

"Manning, you heard him. Go to six. See who's there."

A man detached himself from a near-by group and raced away. A second later he returned breathless.

"They've gone!" he yelled. "Six is empty. The guard's unconscious in number five and six is empty."

"You see," said Van to the officer. "Call your men!"

The colonel once more turned to the Mad Red.

"Now," he said, do you surrender?"

His only answer was a scream of rage from Hesterberg. He sprang at the officer. The latter quickly sidestepped, whipped a Very pistol from its holster, raised it and pressed the trigger. A lurid red flare shot across the heavens.

A rifle cracked out from somewhere behind Van, and the officer staggered back, blood dripping from his arm.

Hesterberg turned and shouted to his army. "Fight, or we're lost. To arms, every man—and most of all death to the Phantom!"

SOMETHING black leaped at Van. A rifle butt swung across his face. The muzzle of his automatic moved from Hesterberg toward his assailant. It barked. The man fell, his rifle clattering impotently on the sidewalk.

Hastily Van bent forward and retrieved the weapon. By now half a dozen of Hesterberg's horde were upon him, urged on by the Mad Red himself. Van gave them butt and bayonet. The weapon swung about him wreaking havoc in the ranks of his adversaries.

He heard a ripping of cloth and something cold and biting ran through his shoulder. Then the butt of his own rifle crashed sickenly against the jaw of the man who had bayoneted him.

Then, running at top speed, rifles held at the trail, came the militia. Straight into the ranks of the cream of crookdom that Hesterberg had recruited bore the soldiers. Somewhere a machine-gun rattled its ominous threnody, and the screams of the wounded took up an agonized obligato.

But the battle was brief, though bloody. The henchmen of Hesterberg were no match for the trained soldiers of Uncle Sam. The thugs slowly gave way. Then their lines broke. A few of the less courageous fled. Then—panic.

Van stood with his back up against the wall of the prison which had so recently incarcerated him. Blood streamed crazily down his coat. His face was dripping wet with perspiration. His breath came heavily.

Then, of a sudden, he heard a hoarse scream before him.

A .38 came up in Hesterberg's hand and leveled itself at Van. Summoning his waning strength, the Phantom lifted the muzzle of his rifle. The two shots sounded as one. Then, in an infinitesimal fraction of a second, something white flung itself before Van. Three more staccato reverberations ripped the air.

VAN'S shot found its target. But the bullet of Hesterberg ate its way into Ruby Wooley's body—Ruby who had flung herself before the Phantom and viciously emptied her own automatic into the staggering body of Hesterberg. Even as she fell she fired another round into the bulky body of the Mad Red.

They dropped together. Hesterberg and the woman whom he had desired. Ruby lay there still, with an ugly red wound in her forehead. Yet on her face was an expression of contentment as she entered a world of peace that she had never known on this earth.

Hesterberg, a few paces away, uttered a horrible gurgling sound.

He slumped forward, his hands clutching his heart. But even as he died he turned his maniacal eyes upon the man who had wrenched his ambition from him, who had ripped his dreams of power into shreds.

And as long as Dick Van Loan lived he never forgot that look. It was the epitome of all the evil in the world, the apogee of all the hate, the murder, the lusts that a human heart can know. From Hesterberg's throat came a noise like that of a rattler about to strike. Then he pitched forward on his face, a battered sacrifice to an ambition sired by madness, damned by hate.

THE colonel, arm bandaged, and with harassed eyes, came up to Van with an extended hand.

"Shake," he said. "You've done a great day's work."

Van shook. Then turned toward the cells. "Come on," he said. "It's time we got them out."

The officer stared at him, puzzled.

"But I thought—"

Van grinned.

"No," he replied with a laugh. "They're still here. I'll explain on the way up. I pulled a fast one on Hesterberg, that's all. I knew that it was absolutely impossible to get them out of here under the Russian's guards. I left them locked up and reconnoitered on my own.

"Of course, when I heard Hesterberg's ultimatum to you I realized that I was in a spot. I had to do something and something fast."

"You mean to tell me," gasped the colonel, "that you pulled a magnificent bluff and got away with it?"

"It was a bluff, yes. But not quite as simple as all that," replied Van. "You see, it worked this way. The cell block up above contains four cells—four—five and six. Hesterberg had his prisoners in six. Though the device was an ancient one, and I hardly dared hope it would succeed, I simply switched the numbers on the cell doors. What had been four was now six. What had been six was now four. As far as external appearances were concerned, the prisoners were no longer in the cell in which they had been locked."

"But good Lord, man," expostulated the colonel, "such a simple—"

"Simple, yes, but it worked," grinned Van. "You see, the psychological advantage was on my side. Hesterberg, too, was in somewhat of a spot; his men were excited. It was possible that their entire scheme was about to crash about their heads. I had to gamble that under the strain of the situation the switch would be unnoted."

"My God!" intoned the colonel in a voice of awe, when Hesterberg's prisoners had been released. "You really should be in the cabinet."

VAN smiled and took Muriel's arm. "The colonel will take care of the others," he said. "But I promised to return you to your father, personally."

Down the Post Road they drove. Already dawn had put the night to flight. Already the birds filled the air with melody. The air was soft and cool. Autumn leaves browned the mountain-tops that rose beside the Hudson. Dick Van Loan, very much aware of the slim hand that was tucked through his arm, sighed.

A pair of eyes stared up at his mask anxiously.

"You must be awful tired," said Muriel. "Shall I drive?"

He shook his head. "No," he said. "I'm not tired. I'm just thinking."

For the Phantom who had just won a tremendous triumph, was thinking of the girl beside him. He was thinking that had he been a normal man, a man whose life was clean and simple, he could perhaps kiss this girl, could perhaps ask her to marry him.

But the Phantom could never ask any woman to do that. He had dedicated his life to the wooing of death, and he well realized that it was a suit which would some day succeed. Romance was not for him. And as he came to this conclusion he felt a little twinge in his heart.

The remainder of the journey was made in silence; and less than two hours later, when Muriel had been delivered to her father by the Phantom, Dick Van Loan sat over his breakfast coffee with the publisher. Havens regarded him fondly.

"Dick," he said, "I owe you something I can never repay. You've saved both my life and Muriel's. I'll never forget it."

He proffered his hand. Van took it and smiled. Like all men of action he was slightly ashamed of emotional outbursts. He essayed to pass it off as a joke.

"That's nothing," he said. "It's just a scoop for your papers. You pay reporters fifty a week for things like that."

Havens shook his head. "There's not enough money in the world to pay for some things," he said gravely. "Things like friendship, honor—love."

Van thought suddenly of Muriel, and something stirred within him as he agreed. But he spent little time in vain regrets.

The Phantom was his life. He had chosen, and now he would abide by that choice. Love had been eschewed.

"Yes," he said after a short pause. "You're right, Frank. But I've no time for romance. I must go home and get some rest. Perhaps the Phantom will have a new case soon."

"Perhaps," said Havens.

And neither of them knew then how truly they spoke. Neither knew of the cunning brain, the distorted genius who was already plotting deeds the solution of which would tax the Phantom to his utmost.

FRAMED

Thrills and Excitement in a Fast-Moving Story of a Daring Police Officer's Fight For Vengeance

By WILL LEVINREW

Author of "Murder—For Sale," "The Quadruple Cross," etc.

HIS promotion to the plain-clothes squad had been ratified. But here he was. He was being framed! Framed because he knew too much. Framed because he—*a tough thing for the kid sister, just home from Teacher's College.* Framed because he wouldn't play the dirty game of—his mind snapped to attention.

The bald police commissioner was uttering the sentence:

"Officer Lawrence McGuire, there has been much complaint recently against the personnel of the police department. This must be stopped. Your story that you were in this young woman's room because you were called there in your capacity of patrolman is unsupported by testimony. There is no evidence connecting this young woman with the criminal element of this city; she is a stranger here; she herself denies your story.

"The only mitigating circumstance in your favor is the excellent record you have borne since you joined the department. But discipline must be maintained; the public must have confidence in their servants. You are suspended for one month, without pay, for conduct unbecoming an officer!"

Larry took it standing. He looked at the commissioner, at the other members of the board, at the chief of police, in whose eye he thought he detected a gleam of pity and sympathy. Larry saluted, he turned on his heel and left.

HABIT took him to his motorcycle, but he stopped, a wry grim smile distorting his features. He walked to the corner, got on the bus and went home. He breathed a sigh of relief when he found the little house dark; his sister was not yet home from the movies. He hated the job of facing her just now with the story of his disgrace.

To make certain that he would not meet her coming home, he stole out of the house by the rear entrance, thence across lots to the road that led northward. He had a vague idea that a member of the gang that framed him had followed him on the bus and was watching the house.

When he saw the house in darkness on his return three hours later he once more breathed a sigh of relief. His sister must be in bed by this time. He could postpone telling her the unpleasant news till morning. He let himself in quietly and stiffened to alert attention, all his muscles tense. He scarcely breathed.

There was an aura of gloom that the darkness did not explain, an aura of menace, death. But strain his hearing as he would he could not hear a sound. Knowing the house as he did, he slipped off his shoes, and started a tour of the rooms, carefully avoiding the boards that creaked.

There was nothing, not a sound. Still certain there was something wrong in the house, he drew his gun and switched on the light in the sitting room.

Strong man that Larry McGuire was, master of his nerves, he uttered a hoarse shout—an inarticulate, strangling cry of horror.

His sister! An unspeakable horror! She lay inert, hands clenched, eyes staring sightlessly, one side of her head mashed in.

Larry unbent her fingers. One hand clutched the button from a man's jacket. For a moment the big six-foot policeman went blind, with rage, with grief. His kid sister!

He knew at a glance just what had happened. Not satisfied with having him disgraced, the gang were going to bump him off. He was followed home. The man who followed him did not see him leave by the rear door. His sister had come home and then the intruder or intruders got in some way. And then—his rage and grief mastered him once more.

He straightened his sister's limbs. He took from her clenched fingers the button. He covered her with the table cloth from the dining room. He did not call any one up. He would get the persons responsible for this before the sun rose or he would be dead. He twirled the cylinder in his heavy service revolver; every chamber held its deadly powder and lead-filled copper cylinder. He took a handful of cartridges and put them into the left pocket of his civilian jacket; he put the revolver in his other pocket.

STRAIGHT as a homing pigeon he went toward a night club he knew to be the hide-out of the gang. This was the headquarters of the booze and narcotic racket. He felt in his pocket to assure himself that the button clutched in the fingers of the dead girl was still there. To hell with the law and the police! He would, this night, take the law into his own hands. His brain cleared of the murder madness that had seized him when he looked down at the horror that had been his sister.

He was approaching his destination. Ahead of him, in the dim light from a dimly lit store window, there glided a furtive figure. Something in the slant of the man's head, in his general outline awakened Larry's memory cells. He had it. This was the man who had followed him home. This was his sister's murderer, "Chicago Lew," he was called.

HIS revolver was in his hand; he put it back. A bullet was too merciful for the man who so brutally murdered his sister; blood lust, a mad desire for revenge demanded physical contact. He had to do it with his fists. And a plan vaguely formed. He stepped to the grass-grown strip that bordered the concrete flagging and began running softly.

A pebble, that his racing feet sent bounding across the concrete, carried its message to the furtive figure ahead. The man turned. He had no time to cry out or draw a weapon. With a bound Larry was on him. Larry's iron fingers were about the man's throat, the fingers of his other hand grasped the hand that was tugging at a weapon. Larry's knee came up, the man's forearm was brought hard down on the detective's knee. There was a nasty snap. To the fear in the man's eyes there was now added the pain of a broken forearm.

The man's feature's were purpling. Larry dragged him into an alley where he quickly and deftly handcuffed him and gagged him, using his own and his prisoner's handkerchief for the purpose. Thus trussed up

Larry deposited him in a dark corner of the alley. From the man's coat there was missing a button. The remaining buttons matched the one in Larry's pocket. Into his mind had blossomed and now bloomed a completely formed plan provided this man had not yet reported to his superiors. The plan involved not only revenge for the death of his sister's brutal murder but a clearing of his name.

The arrest and even the killing of the little rat trussed up in the corner of the alley was not enough. He was a tool of someone higher up, the man through whose rapacity and greed it was practically impossible for a policeman to play the game honestly.

He knew what he was going to do; it was a daring plan but—he dodged as a dark shadow leaped at him as he rounded the corner of the alley. He felt the swish of the blackjack.

Behind the dark shadow there came another. As the first plunged forward under the momentum of the missed blow, Larry let drive with his foot. A large number ten shoe propelled by the powerful leg landed flush on the jaw of the stumbling assailant. The figure kept staggering forward a few feet, where he collapsed.

Larry turned to meet the other assailant in time to dodge and throw up his arm protectingly, as he caught the glittering shimmer of steel. The knife ripped through the sleeve of his jacket and he felt a sharp burning pain in the flesh just above the elbow.

FROM the arc light on the street there was just enough light for Larry's purpose. His arm lashed out. Larry winced with the blinding pain that shot through his hand. In the dim light he had misjudged and hit the man on the head. The man's headlong rush was checked for an instant. In that instant Larry stepped close; his left hand came up in a vicious short uppercut that caught the man squarely on the point of the jaw. Larry, without looking at the second assailant, knowing well the result of such a blow, turned to the first who had staggered to his feet and was reeling away, holding his hand to his broken jaw.

Larry leaped after him. His uninjured left hand swung again, a round-arm hook this time. He hit this man in almost the same place he had hit the first.

Then Larry, in spite of two broken bones in his right hand, went feverishly to work. He used his own belt and the belt of his two assailants. Finding that this was not enough for his purpose, he leaped up and caught a clothes line that hung suspended between two windows in the rear of the alley.

AFTER he had both men trussed to his own satisfaction and securely gagged, he deposited them beside the murderer of his sister, making certain that the three men were not close enough to help one another. Larry stole cautiously to the mouth of the alley. Fortunately, all the participants in the fight had reason not to make an outcry. He walked quickly in the direction where he knew he would find the patrolman on post, who was friendly to Larry.

He sighed with relief, when, after walking several blocks, he saw the familiar stocky, uniformed figure twirling his night-stick.

James Halloran and Lawrence McGuire got on the force about the same time. Between the two recruits had sprung up an eight-year friendship.

He started at once into the subject at hand.

"You know, Jim, that I been framed, don't you?"

"We all know that, Larry, and if some of us could only prove it—"

"Never mind that, Jim, I want you to help me now. I want you to help me land the guy that's responsible."

"Gosh, Larry, anything I can do, you know—"

"I know that." He plunged into his story and explained the recent happenings.

"See, Jim. The man behind Lew is Daniel Crowley. There's something I want you to do. Come along with me. "There's a chance he didn't make his report yet. I want you to watch Lew and his two friends; I'm going to Dan's place. The rear of the joint is right across those fences there. If you hear a shot, then you'll know I need your help."

All emotion was wiped from Larry's face by the time he reached his destination. On his way from the gruesome scene in his little home he had stopped at a night bank where he drew on his meager hoard. He was therefore provided with cash, enough for his needs of the night.

Larry was so constituted that he did not react readily to the influence of liquor, provided he did not mix his drinks. He was therefore not afraid that he would spoil his plan by drinking himself into a helpless condition. He also knew that under his present emotional state it was practically impossible for him to get drunk.

He chose a table in a secluded alcove and ordered rye, straight, with water as a chaser. When he was certain that he was not observed he disposed of his drink in a small plant that was on his table to carry out the decorative scheme of the place.

TO the waiter and to others who might have been watching him Larry was obviously getting very drunk. He knew his plan was working when the "hostess" of the establishment sat down at his table. By this time Larry was beligerently drunk, in the state that impels a man to air his grievances.

He became confidential about his load of grief. He began to tell the hostess in more or less guarded language what he had against the public generally and the police department particularly. Larry saw the significant look that was exchanged between the "hostess" and the waiter. The lady excused herself, and in a short time her place was taken by one of the highly decorative entertainers.

Larry gloated with a fierce exultant joy, when, responding to the lady's invitation, they went to an upper private room where there awaited them Dan Crowley and two of his trusted lieutenants, Hy Curtis and Dave Morgan.

The lady cooed softly:

"Tell these men, Mr. McGuire, what you told me, about how you feel."

LARRY stood rocking gently, glowering at the three men.

He lurched toward him, his hand outstretched. Crowley's hand went to his pocket, but he relaxed when he saw that the detective's gesture was not hostile. Larry was saying:

"You framed me, I know damn well you did. Everybody knows it, but the stuffed shirt, the police commissioner. But I don't blame you. To hell with 'em; to hell with 'em all. To hell with you. Suspended for a month. A month—hell! I'm off for life. Hereafter I play my own game, I'm out for myself."

He caught the table for support, and continued.

"I'm a good man, a better man than all the rats you run with put together, a better man with a gun, a better man with my fists. I'm a better man than you are. I know

how the police work. After this I'm out to get mine, and b'lieve me I'll get it. I know police business, and I know how to manage them all right, all right.

"And you!" he leered at the boss of the upper crust of the underworld, the political Tzar, "you can play along with me if you like, if you don't I can get along without you. If you doubt it—"

He drew his gun and backed against the wall.

"I can put the three of you away right now and the jane, too, see, and what are you gonna do about it?"

Dan Crowley smiled; Larry was in an agony of fear for a moment that he had overplayed his hand; he swiftly determined that if he had Dan would die right then, though this was not the end he had planned. He was partly reassured when Crowley spoke:

"I can use a man like you McGuire. I—"

"*You* can use *me?* What the hell do I need you for. I know all about the racket I need to know. I been on the force long enough, too—"

The eyes above the dazzling white teeth grew harder, slightly more frosty, but the voice was still in control.

BUT we have the organization, McGuire. Without the organization you can't do a thing. No man can play a lone hand in this. It's too big."

"Zat so?" His drunken sneer was a fine bit of acting. "Did you have the organization when you started? Think I can't sell dope without your organization? I know every hop head in town. What the hell—"

The voice was still oily, silky. The gun, though it wavered, was nevertheless a dangerous weapon, was perhaps more dangerous because the man holding it was not sober. Crowley was saying:

"Be sensible, McGuire. You're not a child, you ought to know that this is not a one-man game. You can make more playing with me than running alone. Put the gun away and we'll talk. Nobody will hurt you."

The detective nodded grimly. "You're damn right nobody will hurt me." He leered again. "If it makes you nervous to see this gun, I'll put it away. Say what you got to say, but don't start anything; you may not be able to finish it."

He sat down and stared at the three men owlishly. The young woman, at a signal from Crowley, had left the room when Larry pocketed his weapon.

Crowley's cold hard eyes looked appraisingly at the detective for a long time. Larry stood this regard well. He flattered himself that he had played his cards well. Crowley spoke:

"You spoke about selling dope. What made you say that I—"

"Aw, boloney. You know I got the goods on you; that's why you framed me. If you got a proposition to make me, make it, but if you're gonna hand me that kind of applesauce, you can go to hell!"

HE stood up and backed toward the door, his hand in his pocket. Crowley held up a restraining hand. Larry stopped at the door. Crowley spoke, with more decision this time.

"Yes, I've got a proposition to make you, McGuire, but you're drunk. I can't say what I want to say to a drunken man."

"Well, perhaps I am a little plastered. That's all right by me Crowley, I'll be around tomorrow when I've worn off my jag."

"No," for the first time Crowley's voice was raised. We'll talk before you leave, but let me give you something to straighten out. What do you say?"

'Oh, all right."

AT a word from Crowley one of his companions left the room and shortly returned followed by another man. Crowley said to the latter:

"Doc, fix this bird so he can talk and think straight. He's had a lot of liquor."

After the "fixing up" Larry sat up and looked out of streaming eyes at Crowley who spoke softly:

"I've got a job for a man like you, McGuire, a man who knows the inside of the police department as well as you do. If you take it you can write your own ticket so far as pay is concerned. We can go into details later. As an evidence of good faith—" He took from an inner pocket a pocket book from which he took a sheaf of bills. He took some out and spread before the detective, fanwise, ten one-thousand dollar bills. He smiled crookedly as he shoved them toward the detective.

"Lawyers would call this a retainer, what do you say?"

Larry took the bills and put them into his pocket; he looked at Crowley expectantly. Crowley nodded approvingly:

"Now you're being sensible. You might have done that months ago." He picked up the receiver in response to its tinkle; he listened a moment. He turned once more to Larry:

"Detective Sergeant Cross is downstairs now; Cross knows too much, we're afraid. Anyhow he's been snooping around a lot. We tried to reach him but he's pig-headed like you—were," there was a significant pause between the last two words. Crowley continued: "Your first job is to find out what Cross knows. If he knows too much and won't listen to reason—" he made an expressive gesture.

Larry answered promptly:

I CAN tell you right now that he knows too much for our—your good," he noted with secret satisfaction that Crowley had noted the slip. "He knows more than I did. So what?"

"Then we'll have to take care of Cross."

"Does Cross know I came up here?"

"A couple hundred people saw you leave the room with Miss LaRue—"

"I get you, Crowley, so Cross knows. Suppose I bring Cross up here?"

"Cross won't come."

"I'm not going to ask him. I said I'll bring him up here."

Larry returned the long level stare of the other man. Crowley nodded. "Go to it."

The Clover Leaf Night Club boasted a "garden" where drinks were served in the summer time; a small enclosure with iron tables and chairs in the rear of the low rambling structure. This being February this garden was unused at this time. Larry, standing at the door of the garden, caught the eye of Detective Sergeant Cross.

Cross was a man of bulldog courage and tenacity. Even if he suspected Larry he would come in answer to such a summons. Larry counted on that. As Cross followed Larry out to the garden and the door closed behind him, Larry's hard fist was planted squarely on his heavy jaw. Cross slumped to the flag stones, Larry catching him, thus saving him from striking his head on an iron table.

Larry handcuffed his erstwhile superior officer. Then he performed the hardest job in his life. He began belaboring the unconscious man with his fists, each blow designed to disfigure and mar rather than disable. The fourth blow brought the police officer back to consciousness.

He must have thought he was suffering a wild nightmare, when he realized that, as he lay there helpless, Larry, a man who he liked, was doing this brutal thing. Finally came the last blow, mercifully one that once more brought oblivion. Cross was now a very convincing spectacle.

When Detective Sergeant Cross regained consciousness he was in a room with Larry, Crowley, Curtis and Morgan—all of whom Cross knew. In addition to the handcuffs, Cross was now gagged.

AS his eyes fluttered open he caught a swift look from the hard eyes of Larry, who returned his gaze to that of Crowley. The latter was saying:

"A bad job, McGuire. Some of them must have seen him go out with you. I wasn't prepared for—"

"I told you I was going to bring him in. If you didn't mean this kind of thing, why didn't you frame him like you did me?"

"We might have done that, too, but we didn't know how much he had on us. I'm afraid you spilled the beans, McGuire. If he proves pigheaded, we may have to—" he stopped and tapped his dazzling white teeth with a gold pencil. He sighed: "Just when everything was going so nicely, too. We've got a large shipment of stuff in there," nodding his head in the direction of a closed door. "If this flat-floot proves pigheaded," he looked toward Cross whose eyes were now closed, "and we have to put him away we may have to lay low for a while—"

He stopped. Larry had drawn his gun; he was backing toward the window. He said: "Did you hear that, Cross?"

Detective Sergeant Cross opened his eyes and nodded weakly, grunting. Larry flashed a look in the direction of the police officer. As he did so, out of the corner of his eye he noted a movement on the part of Morgan.

Larry's gun roared, the sound reverberating and crashing in the confines of the room. Morgan dropped the weapon he had drawn, his arm hung limp, the bone shattered. Larry's eyes were now blazing. He backed toward the telephone. He picked up the instrument with his left hand without taking his eyes from the three men. In response to his terse growl, there came a voice floating over the wire. After a long wait, he spoke into the mouthpiece:

"Chief, I'm in an upstairs room of the Clover Leaf. There's a shipment of dope here. Sergeant Cross is here, slightly hurt. Bring a squad, Chief, and, Chief, bring the police commissioner, too."

AT this moment there came a pounding of heavy feet on the stairs. Jim Halloran tore open the door and rushed in. He had heard the shot. Before his startled eyes had time to take in the salient features of the strange scene, Larry spoke:

"Those three men there yet?"

"Yes."

"Bring up Chicago Lew, Jim; make it snappy."

Larry walked over to Cross and shoved his gun into his manacled hand. He said grimly: "I'll explain later, Tom; hold the gun on these birds. I'll disarm them."

After disarming the three, he stepped up to Crowley, his eyes blazing hate.

"Chicago Lew's hands killed my sister, but you're responsible. They say you're a good man with your fists. I'll give you one chance. I'm not armed, neither are you. Come at me, if you can get out of this room, you've got a chance to make your getaway."

CROWLEY sprang at him. There was a wild whirl of arms, legs and bodies; then both figures were still. Larry was behind the bigger man. He had the deadly hammerlock; he was slowly pushing the best arm backward; his features were fixed in cold, deadly fury; Crowley's in agony and fear. There was a snap and a howl of anguish. Crowley's arm hung useless.

The door burst open once more. Halloran was dragging in the cringing body of Lew; they were followed by Chief Nelson, the police commissioner and a squad of men.

Larry did not pay any attention to the police. He pointed at the cringing figure of Chicago Lew.

"We've got you where we want you; we've got Crowley. If you talk now it may be easier for—"

"I'll talk, I'll talk!" squealed Lew. There was no interruption while he told the story implicating Crowley. The shipment of narcotics in boxes and packages in the adjoining room came up to specifications. At its conclusion, Detective Sergeant Cross stood in front of Lawrence McGuire, his hands on his hips, his eyes glowering, his face a mass of blood, welts and bruises.

"Young feller, ye made this thing too damned real. You're reinstated now, which makes you my inferior officer. It's ag'inst the rigulations to strike an inferior officer while on duty; we're both on duty. In tin days from now we're both off th' same time. I'll meet ye thin behind the station house and knock hell outa ye." Then he stuck out his huge paw. "Shake!"

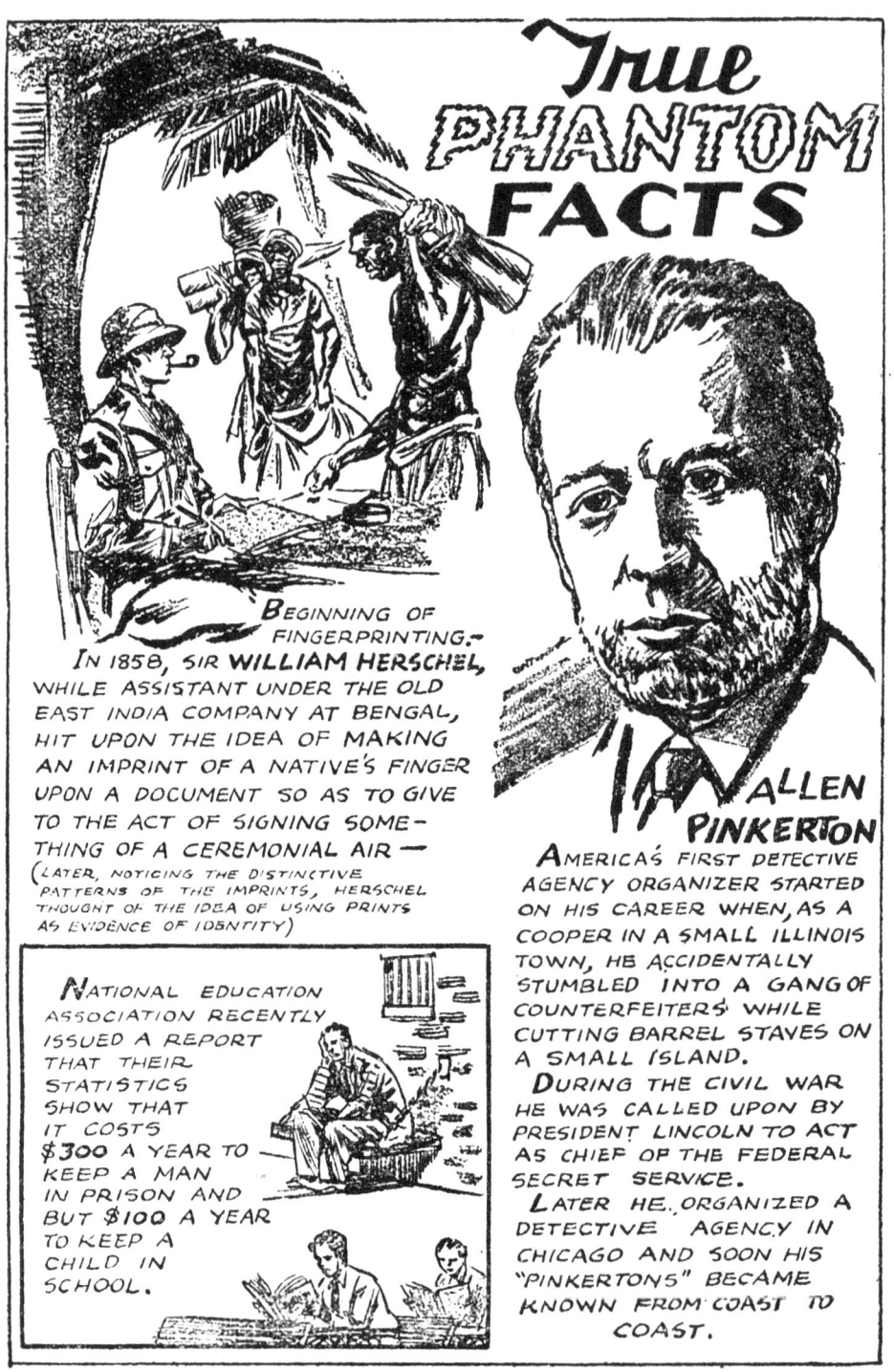

True PHANTOM FACTS

BEGINNING OF FINGERPRINTING.-
IN 1858, SIR **WILLIAM HERSCHEL**, WHILE ASSISTANT UNDER THE OLD EAST INDIA COMPANY AT BENGAL, HIT UPON THE IDEA OF MAKING AN IMPRINT OF A NATIVE'S FINGER UPON A DOCUMENT SO AS TO GIVE TO THE ACT OF SIGNING SOMETHING OF A CEREMONIAL AIR —
(LATER, NOTICING THE DISTINCTIVE PATTERNS OF THE IMPRINTS, HERSCHEL THOUGHT OF THE IDEA OF USING PRINTS AS EVIDENCE OF IDENTITY)

NATIONAL EDUCATION ASSOCIATION RECENTLY ISSUED A REPORT THAT THEIR STATISTICS SHOW THAT IT COSTS $300 A YEAR TO KEEP A MAN IN PRISON AND BUT $100 A YEAR TO KEEP A CHILD IN SCHOOL.

ALLEN PINKERTON

AMERICA'S FIRST DETECTIVE AGENCY ORGANIZER STARTED ON HIS CAREER WHEN, AS A COOPER IN A SMALL ILLINOIS TOWN, HE ACCIDENTALLY STUMBLED INTO A GANG OF COUNTERFEITERS WHILE CUTTING BARREL STAVES ON A SMALL ISLAND.

DURING THE CIVIL WAR HE WAS CALLED UPON BY PRESIDENT LINCOLN TO ACT AS CHIEF OF THE FEDERAL SECRET SERVICE.

LATER HE ORGANIZED A DETECTIVE AGENCY IN CHICAGO AND SOON HIS "PINKERTONS" BECAME KNOWN FROM COAST TO COAST.

"True Phantom Facts" Will Be a Regular

114

JAKE MINTZ, A CLEVELAND, OHIO, DETECTIVE ONCE GAINED SOME NOTORIETY INVESTIGATING A SERIES OF BAKERY ROBBERIES AND THEREAFTER HE BECAME KNOWN AS "THE MINTZ SPY."

NICHOLAS, 1ST, THE "IRON CZAR OF RUSSIA—" KIDNAPPED 100,000 CHILDREN! HE ORDERED ONE HUNDRED THOUSAND CHILDREN BETWEEN THE AGES OF ONE AND EIGHT YEARS TAKEN AND PLACED IN CANTONMENTS AND MILITARY CENTERS TO BE RAISED AS SOLDIERS. (THEIR PARENTS WERE NEVER ALLOWED TO HEAR OF THEM AGAIN.)

LIST OF REWARDS OFFERED THE FIRST LONDON DETECTIVES IN 1830

CAPTURE OF HIGHWAY ROBBER (ALSO THE HORSE, FURNITURE, ARMS AND MONEY OF THE CONVICT.) £20

COUNTERFEITER _____ £10

HORSETHIEF _____ (ALSO A LOTTERY TICKET VALUED AT £20.) £40

OLD JOHN TOWNSEND, THE FIRST LONDON DETECTIVE (1830), OF THE BOW STREET RUNNERS BECAME FAMOUS BECAUSE HE "SOLVED 81 CASES AND PERFORMED VARIOUS FEATS OF DETECTION FOR THE KING." HE LEFT AN ESTATE OF OVER £20,000 WHEN HE DIED, ALL EARNED BY REWARDS.

Monthly Feature of The Phantom Detective

Death *on* Dow Street

*An Escaped Convict Out to "Get" All Who Had
a Hand in Putting Him in the Big House —
and a Detective with Nerve*

By JACK D'ARCY
Author of "Too Many Alibis," "Four Dead Men," etc.

D RAKE wiggled his toes luxuriously in his comfortable slippers, and regarded the cosy fire in the grate luxuriously. He took a deep puff at his pipe and sighed in utter contentment. This was his first night off in a full week, and he was enjoying his idleness to its utmost.

The pleasant clatter of dishes came from the kitchen where his bride of only six months prepared the evening meal. Drake turned the page of his favorite evening newspaper, and silently muttered praise to heaven, that even the arduous job of a detective could offer moments of tranquility like these.

Then the telephone rang.

Even before the sound of its jangle had completely died away, Drake was aware of a vague feeling of apprehension; a fear that perhaps, after all, the night was not destined to be one of peace and contentment. He crossed the room, picked up the receiver and then heard his anxiety corroborated.

A tense voice said: "Drake? This is Summers. For God's sake, man, come over to my house right away."

Drake frowned. Yet his voice was calm and affable as he replied. "What's wrong, Judge? What's happened?"

"Harding's out."

THERE was an imperceptible silence. Drake could hear the other's quick breathing at the other end of the wire.

"Well," said the detective. "What of that, Judge? They all get out sooner or later."

"He just phoned me. He threatened to kill me. For God's sake, Drake, come on over."

"All right."

Drake sighed and hung up. He tossed his dressing gown aside and thrust his head through the kitchen door.

"Got to go out, honey. Don't wait dinner for me. I'll phone later."

A pretty Irish face came close to his. A kissable mouth pouted. A lilting voice said: "Hurry, darling. Get back early."

Drake reached for his coat. "I'll try. Anyway I'll phone."

He kissed her and walked toward the door.

Drake took a taxi uptown. By now he had forgotten his ruined evening. His mind was entirely occupied with the problem of Harding. Summers had been the judge that had sentenced the gangster that all the underworld had thought was too powerful to take a rap. He, Drake, had been the detective who had been responsible for the evidence upon which that conviction had been predicated.

Running back in his memory, Drake recalled that Harding had vowed to get every person connected with his imprisonment. However, with the exception of the yellow press, no one had paid any attention to the gangster's threats.

Now, however, they came back with startling clarity to Drake's mind.

The cab stopped and deposited its passenger at the entrance to the bachelor apartments where Summers lived. Drake rang the bell and waited. There was no reply. He rang again. Another silence followed. He frowned, took a bunch of keys from his pocket and fitted one into the lock. After a moment's struggle, the door opened. Drake walked into the apartment.

On the threshold of the living room, he stood stock still staring at the big armchair over by the French windows. Summers sat with his head slumped forward on his chest. His eyes were dull and glazed. Drake spoke sharply.

"Summers!"

There was no answer. The detective crossed the room rapidly. He bent over the judge's form. A single bullet hole had been bored through the dead man's dressing gown—a hole which continued all the way through to his stilled heart. Drake straightened up. His hand dropped to his coat pocket, and touched the butt of his thirty-eight.

THEN it took all his training, all his nerve control not to jump as he heard a voice say: "Drake, don't move or you're a dead man. Now you may turn your head slowly and look at me. And take that hand out of your pocket."

Drake did as he was ordered. When his eyes fell in line with the French windows, he saw a tall cruel familiar figure standing there holding an automatic which was trained on the detective's heart.

"I'm in luck," said Harding. "You've saved me the trouble of looking for you, Drake."

Despite the pounding of his heart, Drake's voice was steady enough as he answered.

"What do you mean?"

Harding laughed mirthlessly. "Just this," he said, "I'm going to do a complete job now that I'm out. I'm going to kill every one of you. Judge, jury, dicks and all that had a hand in sending me to the Big House. I've just killed Summers. He was the first. You're next. I was going to pay you a visit tonight, but you've saved me the trouble by coming here."

"You're undertaking a pretty large order, Harding," said Drake.

"What if I am? I don't care what they do to me afterwards. But before I go, I'm going to get everyone of you. Summers is gone, and you go now, Drake."

THE racketeer's face contorted with a terrible hate. Slowly he raised the automatic. Drake stood stock still staring at the toy-like weapon which in another moment would spell his death.

Then suddenly, he managed to break through the strange lethargy which held him. Was he to stand here and permit Harding to strike him down in cold blood? No, if he must die, he could at least go out fighting. Already he could see the gangster's finger constricting almost imperceptibly upon the trigger.

Then, like a streak of lightning, he moved. His head went down, and once again his right hand whipped in a flashing gesture to his coat pocket. Harding's automatic spat viciously. Two steel slugs ate into the wall over Drake's head.

A thirty-eight appeared miraculously in the detective's hand. It belched its message of death into the room. The French windows were suddenly shattered. Glass tinkled and rolled crazily all over the floor.

He ran swiftly to the broken windows as Harding suddenly disappeared behind them. As he leaned out he heard the angry snap of the automatic again. Something, humming like a wasp, whizzed past his nose. Hastily he pulled his face inside again.

Then, more cautiously than before, he thrust his head through the shattered frame again. But this time he saw nothing. Harding was not there. He had vanished.

Drake slowly returned to the living room. He dropped his still hot gun into his pocket and lit a cigarette. He sat down in a chair beside the corpse and considered the situation carefully.

Then he came to a decision which almost cost him his life. Harding and he had long had a grudge and Drake wanted to get him personally this time. Instead of telephoning the police, he recalled what the gangster had said about slaughtering every person who had a hand in his imprisonment.

Well, Drake was pretty sure where he would go next. Inasmuch as the prosecuting attorney who had sent the crook to the penitentiary had died two years ago, it seemed to Drake that Harding's next logical victim was the foreman of the jury who had convicted him.

He sat there quietly for a moment racking his memory, then he snapped his fingers and thumbed quickly through the telephone book. Less than two minutes later he was racing cross town.

OF course, this venture which was to cost him so dear was not as completely foolhardy as it appeared superficially. Probably, Harding was not expecting him. He could take the murderer by surprise at Billing's home, put him under arrest for the killing of Summers and it was all over. It was as simple as that.

The cab stopped and Drake got out. Cautiously he approached the two-family brick house where the foreman of the jury who had unanimously decided that Harding was guilty, resided. Slowly Drake approached the building.

Too late he heard the slither of soft steps behind him. Too late, he saw from the corner of his eye a black object held aloft, then descending upon him at terrific speed. For a single flashing moment he was aware of a blinding yellow glare. His skull came into violent contact with something. Blackness enveloped his consciousness.

HOW long Drake remained senseless he never knew. The first sensation that registered in his numb brain was a terrific throbbing in the head.

Slowly he opened his eyes, then finding the light of the room hurt them, promptly closed them again. He heard a harsh mocking laugh. Now, despite the pain, he opened his eyes again and held them open, casting them about the room. His roving gaze abruptly stopped, held by the jeering face of Harding.

The gangster indulged in a low mocking bow.

"You're damned accommodating, Drake," he said. "I lost you before and now you bob up again. I guess it's written in the book of Fate that I'm to kill you tonight."

Drake blinked painfully, orienting himself to the situation. His memory was not yet functioning.

"What—" he began. "Where am I?"

Harding grinned wholeheartedly. "You're at Number 20 Dow Street," he said. "At my headquarters, and your tomb. This is where you've come to die, Drake."

Drake shook his head slowly to clear the cobwebs away. Now he remembered. He had been slugged outside Billing's house. Silently he cursed himself for a fool. He should have called the police.

Harding and his minions were too dangerous to play a lone hand against. Tentatively, he dropped his hand to his coat pocket. Harding laughed again.

Drake smiled weakly and nodded agreement. He was unarmed. He could rely only on his wits now to get him out of this scrape.

"Yes," said Harding. "This is the end, Drake. Over fifty of my men are in this building, so you can see what chances of escape you have. Well, I won't waste any time. If you've any talking to do to your God, now's the time."

FOR the second time that evening, Drake stared blindly into the unwavering muzzle of the gangster's automatic. His pulse and brain raced in unison. He must temporize, stall for time somehow. But how? He began to talk at random, and as he spoke an idea came to him.

"Harding," he said. "You say you're going to bump me off. All right. When I first went on the force, I went on with my eyes open. I'm not squawking. Death is all part of the game. But before I go, I've got a favor to ask."

Harding's eyes narrowed suspiciously.

"What is it?"

"You told me a moment ago that if I wanted to talk to my God, now was the time. I don't want to talk to Him, Harding, but there is someone I like to say good-by to."

"Who?"

"My wife."

Harding smiled cynically. "Nothing doing."

Drake spoke swiftly and desperately. "But, Harding, what harm can it do. Let me phone her. It'll only take a minute. You can listen in. If I attempt to tip her off give me the works at once. Listen, Harding, I've only been married for six months."

"Yeah?" said Harding sardonically. "Ain't that dandy?"

"Listen," said Drake again. "Do you remember Emma?"

HARDING'S eyes softened, then grew hard again. "Well?"

"She died two years after you were sent up. During that time she was ill. Who sent her dough? Who took care of her?"

"The department," said Harding. "I heard about that."

"But who influenced the department to take care of your girl? Did you hear that, too?"

"Well," said Harding grudgingly, "Emma said in a letter that she thought you had something to do with it."

"I did," said Drake. "I did her a favor once. I did your girl a favor once, Harding. Now I'm asking you to return it, to do my girl a favor. Let me say good-by to her. Please!"

Harding hesitated. Then:

"All right," he said. "There's the phone. Make it snappy. And no funny business or you get it at once."

"Thanks," said Drake simply.

He called his home number, and a little thrill ran down his spine as he heard his wife's voice.

"Hello, baby," he said. "I'll be late? What? Sure I'm all right. What can happen to a dumb dick?" He laughed. "Well, if anything does, there's always that twenty-year endowment policy in case of my death. I say," he repeated loudly. "The twenty-year endowment policy in case of my death. Of course, I'm joking. Well, so long, honey."

There was utter silence at the other end of the wire. An aching

question flamed in Drake's heart. Had she understood?

"All right, baby," said Drake. "I'll see you later."

The receiver clicked back on the hook.

"Well," said Harding. "Are you ready?"

Drake calculated rapidly. If his wife had understood his message, it would take her, say two minutes to call Headquarters. The nearest station house was about six blocks away. That meant perhaps five more minutes. If he could stall for ten at the outside, he had a chance. He essayed a grin that he was by no means sure of.

"Let me smoke a butt, Harding. It's not very pleasant to die."

Harding laughed. "Evidently not. You're doing a lot of stalling."

Drake thrust a cigarette between his lips and lit it.

"Just a few puffs," he said. "It's the last thing I'll ever ask you."

"Or anyone else," said Harding. "All right, go ahead. I'll give you five minutes. That's all."

Drake's hand was steady enough as he puffed at what might prove to be the last cigarette he'd smoke.

Drake strained his ears for some sound of his rescuers. But none came. Harding cleared his throat, looked down at the watch again and said: "All right, flat-foot. Ready. Here it comes."

Drake dropped the cigarette and stared into the muzzle of the gangster's weapon. If he could delay only two or three more minutes there still was a chance.

WELL, he would stake all on one turn of the card. After all, he had nothing to lose and everything to gain. He leaned slightly forward, his body ducked, tensed, and sprang.

Harding, taken by surprise, blazed away wildly with his weapon. Something sharp and biting ate its way through Drake's shoulder, but that did not stop his charge. He grappled with the racketeer and the pair of them fell to the floor locked in a grim embrace.

Harding shouted for his henchmen as they rolled over in the dust. Desperately, Drake reached for the other's gun. His hand clamped about Harding's right wrist. The gangster fired the weapon once more and renewed his shouts for aid.

Behind them, Drake heard the door flung open. Excited voices shouted. A dozen pair of hands reached down and attempted to pull him away from Harding. The detective's heart sank. This, then was the end. His last desperate stand had failed. Well, he would go out without a whine. He was ready.

HE released Harding and started to rise. Then of a sudden his heart gave a great bound. A single shot was heard from outside. A single shot accompanied by the thunder of many heavy booted feet. A man cried out. A tremendous thumping came upon the outer door.

Someone yelled: "It's the bulls!"

A score of guns flashed in the light of the room. The outer door crashed in. The room was alive with blue-coated men. Shots flew wildly.

The men in blue were making short work of the men in street clothes. Drake glanced around. Then he raced swiftly across the floor. At the rear was a small door. Now it stood open and disappearing through it was Harding. Drake's hand gripped the gangster's arm.

With a snarl of rage, Harding whirled on Drake. His revolver was still in his hand. Its muzzle pointed directly at the detective's heart.

Without hesitation Drake swung. His right hand moved like lightning, crashed against the point of Harding's jaw. The latter dropped like an ox and went skidding crazily down three flights to the bottom of the stairway.

DRAKE called to a near-by policeman. "Go down there and get Harding, if he's still alive."

Docilely the remainder of Harding's mob were being escorted from the room. Then Drake smiled wholeheartedly for the first time since he had left his fireside that evening. A blue-eyed girl came toward him with outstretched arms.

"Oh, darling," she said. "I'm so glad you're safe. So glad."

They kissed in the centre of the floor, and remained in that position until a gruff chuckle interrupted them. Drake looked up to see his chief grinning.

"Thank God you're still alive, son," he said. "But what beats me is how you got the tip through."

Drake grinned. "I guess it beats Harding, too. It was simple enough though. He let me phone her for a farewell talk. I said that in case of my death my twenty-year endowment policy would take care of her. I accented ever so slightly the syllables twenty, dow, and death. Now it's been a standing joke between us that I've never managed to save enough money to put any in insurance. I figured that angle would arouse suspicion in her mind. The message I gambled on getting over was twenty—dow—death.

"It was a long desperate chance, but the only one I could take. When I married her I gambled on her beauty and tonight I had to gamble on her brains. I think I won both times."

The chief smiled down at them fraternally. "I think you did," he said huskily, then turned away. For the scene that was taking place hardly permitted of an audience.

RUB-OUT

Slugger Morgan Carried Death in His Violin Case—
And Never Hesitated About Playing
a Grim Tune

By JOHN H. COMPTON

Author of "The Death Mummy," "The Clock Struck Two," etc.

I

THE report of the coming rub-out reached Headquarters. Inspector Dineen, sitting in his office high above Center Street, chewed viciously on a big black cigar. His face was almost purple with rage. He glared across the desk at Inspector McGuire of the Homicide Bureau.

"Torrio's gang," he announced angrily, "is preparin' for a rub-out.

Somebody is gonna be put on the spot."

Inspector McGuire nodded, smiled. "Yeah," he said. "I heard about it."

"Well," bawled Dineen, "what are you gonna do about it?"

McGuire looked at his superior in surprise.

"What do you expect me to do? I'm gonna wait till somebody is dead. What else can I do?"

Dineen swore a sizzling oath.

"All right, all right," said Mc-Guire. "Now, listen. These boys of Torrio's have got their slaughter so simplified that they're gettin' care-less—too careless. One o' these days they're gonna make a mistake; and when they do— I've got my eyes on one of them now; and I'm just wait-in'. Bidin' my time."

Slowly McGuire pulled his bulky weight out of the chair across from Dineen. Dineen watched him closely.

"Have you got any idea where they might pull this killin'?" he asked suddenly. "Maybe we could be there an' nab 'em."

"Yeah, sure," said McGuire. "Somewhere we ain't."

II

SHORTLY after midnight that night "Slugger" Morgan stood in a darkened doorway in an obscure, unfrequented section of Brooklyn. The section was desert-ed except for a big, black limou-sine that stood at the corner—its motor purring silently, steadily.

Across the street from Morgan was a dimly lit drug store. Its only occupants were two women and a man who were sitting at the soda fountain.

Morgan stood slumped against the panel of the doorway, humming quietly to himself, and pulling at a cigarette. It was a hot, sultry night.

Morgan hummed.

Suddenly a girl appeared around the corner and Morgan grew alert. When she was directly in front of him she stopped. Without looking at him she said:

"I'll go up to the hotel and get him."

"Put 'im in the phone booth," Morgan said.

"I'll tell him Wally wants him to call him."

"You just put 'im in that phone booth."

The girl nodded, turned around and was gone. Still humming, Slug-ger Morgan stepped out from the doorway and casually crossed the street. He advanced slowly toward the drug store—humming.

Just as he got into the dim, yel-low light thrown off by the store a newsboy came down the street, calling out the morning papers. Slugger, his gray hat pulled down over his eyes, bought a tabloid from the boy and stuck it in his pocket.

Then, as the boy went on, Slug-ger got into a position in front of the drug store in which he could peer over the cardboard advertise-ments and see the entire interior. He took the paper from his pocket and held it up, as if reading.

The soda clerk, a tall thin youth, glanced out casually at him. Slug-ger stuck the paper back in his pocket and stepped on the scales in the entrance way. Then, completely obscured from the soda fountain, he inspected the phone booth at the far end of the store.

He dropped a penny in the scales. A bell rang and a card slipped out of the machine into the bucket. It showed he weighed 165 pounds. He turned the card over and glanced at his fortune on the other side.

Slugger grinned as he read. Then casually, unhurriedly, he stepped off the scales and recrossed the street.

HE had just got back into the doorway when a young man, wearing a cap, came around the cor-ner. A girl came around with him. The girl was in the lead, walking swiftly. They were both headed for the drug store.

Slugger reached down and opened the violin case that rested in the dark doorway behind him. He took out a Tommy gun and slung it under his right arm.

As he turned around the man and the girl were just entering the drug store. The car at the corner was thrown into gear. Slugger quickly ran across the street, the machine-gun poised under his arm. The car at the corner started coming forward slowly.

Slugger leaped across the sidewalk. With a measured tread he marched into the drug store, holding the machine-gun under his right arm.

The soda clerk looked at him blankly. One of the women at the counter screamed and fainted.

"Take it easy, folks," Slugger said. "Nobody's gonna get hurt. Except—"

He ran up to the telephone booth and pointed the gun at the dim figure inside. There was a rasping, metallic scream as the slugs tore viciously through the wood and glass. When the gun was empty, Slugger turned and ran. The man sitting at the counter dropped his soda glass and said, "God!"

A moment later Slugger was jolted to a seat against the soft cushions of the limousine as it shot ahead.

III

INSPECTOR McGUIRE stood in the center of the linoleum floor in the drug store, fanning himself with his hat. Outside uniformed policemen were struggling with a mob of curious, drawn to the scene by the lure of violent death. In the air there was still the whine of sirens.

McGuire stood still for a long time, fanning himself. Occasionally he would glance at the body of the young man that lay, slumped at a grotesque, crazy angle, in the tele-phone booth. Then he glanced out through the windows at the crowd. Then at two or three persons huddled in horror against the soda fountain.

"This act," he said, "should be copyrighted. It's always the same, always the same."

McGUIRE stared curiously at the slim, young woman who was sitting on one of the high stools at the soda fountain. She was weeping bitterly.

"What burlesque show you goin' into?" he asked.

The young woman looked up—startled.

"Why do you ask that?"

"Because," said McGuire, "you put your lover on the spot!"

"I didn't!" she screamed. "I didn't! I don't even know the man. I—I just happened to come in here after him. I—"

McGuire turned away, cutting short her protestations. As an afterthought, he said, almost to himself:

"I'll be damned, though, if I'm gonna give you a million bucks' worth of publicity by throwin' you in jail."

He glanced at the clock.

"Did you get a good look at the guy what did this?" he asked.

"No. It happened so quick I—"

"Of course you didn't," McGuire grumbled. "An' if you did, you'd probably forget about it before anybody was brought to trial."

At that moment Inspector Dineen came charging into the drug store. He was glowering; his face streamed with perspiration.

"Well, well!" he blustered.

McGuire smiled feebly.

"Well, I was a hundred percent right," he said.

"In what way?"

"They did it where we wasn't."

The inspector swore fiercely. Mc-Guire turned to the man sitting at the counter.

"What did you see?" he demanded.

"Sir," replied the man, "I was here buying a soda with two ladies when I saw a healthy, living human being butchered with lead!"

"Cut that," said McGuire.

He walked over and stood beside Dineen who was staring down at the lifeless body in the telephone booth.

"Know 'im?" asked Dineen.

"Yeah," said McGuire. "Not that it matters. He was Joe Mullins, a gunman that got too ambitious." McGuire wheeled around and faced the customer and the soda clerk.

"What I wanta know is what happened before this act," he said. "Did either of you notice anything suspicious before it happened?"

"There was a man outside lookin' in," said the soda clerk.

"I saw him," the customer added.

"What did he do?"

"Well," said the soda clerk, "he bought a newspaper from the boy, that has his stand on the corner; then he looked in over the cardboard signs; then he weighed himself, and—and walked away."

"That," said Inspector Dineen, "was undoubtedly the killer gettin' the lay o' the land."

Inspector McGuire chuckled.

"And that guy," he said, "I think made a mistake."

He turned to the weeping girl.

"I want you, sister," he said, "to come with me while we visit one of our more prominent young gunmen."

THE girl looked at McGuire, a sudden fear flashing in her eyes.

"I—I don't know any gunmen," she protested.

McGuire grinned.

"That don't matter," he said.

IV

INSPECTOR McGUIRE stood over Slugger Morgan with a gun. The gangster, back in bed, stared at him malevolently.

"It took you long enough to let us in," said McGuire.

"I was sound asleep."

"Havin' sweet dreams, huh?"

McGuire slumped down on the bottom of Slugger Morgan's bed. He held the leveled revolver in his right hand. With his left he fanned himself with his hat. Slugger Morgan still glared at him. The girl stood in the center of the room, twisting her fingers nervously.

"This girl here—" said McGuire.

"Never saw her before," interrupted Slugger.

"No?" said McGuire. He looked from the girl to Slugger Morgan in surprise. "Then," he said, "you must have had your eyes closed when she put Joe Mullins on the spot for you over in Waller Street tonight."

Slugger Morgan reached over to the night table and got a cigarette.

"Listen, McGuire," he said, "if you've come to ride me you might as well cut it! I've been here in bed since ten o'clock."

"Yeah?" said McGuire. His eyes traveled quickly around the room. They lit on the tabloid newspaper.

"Morgan," he said, "you've made two mistakes tonight—maybe three. A woman is always a mistake."

The searching eyes of Morgan turned quickly to the young woman.

"Don't know her," he announced.

"I've never seen the man before," said the girl.

McGuire was still smiling. He put down his hat and picked up the paper. He began to fan himself with it.

"No?" he said. Then he sighed. "Then I must be gettin' cock-eyed,"

he added. "You went to bed at ten o'clock—right?" He sighed again. "But I can't understand," he continued, "why all you bums who go to bed at ten o'clock always bring home a *white paper edition* of a morning tabloid which don't come off the press until *eleven o'clock* at night."

He tossed the paper back on the table. The color drained from Slugger Morgan's face. Into the girl's eyes there came a queer, bitter light.

"My pal bought it," said Slugger Morgan.

"Or else," McGuire said genially, "you bought this paper in front of Schuler's drug store at just after midnight."

He got up leisurely from the bottom of the bed.

"You wouldn't mind," he asked, "if I look around a bit?"

"I would!" Slugger Morgan announced.

"Then," said McGuire, "I will."

He walked around the edge of the bed and started across the room. The girl watched his every move. Suddenly McGuire turned around.

"You wouldn't shoot me in the back, would you, Morgan?"

"Of course not!"

"The hell you wouldn't!"

Keeping his gun trained on Morgan, he went to the bed, and, with an unerring aim, plunged his hand beneath the pillows. He pulled out a revolver and slipped it in his pocket.

THEN he walked across to the chair where Morgan had draped his clothes. He ran his left hand through Morgan's pockets. The gangster set his lips firmly. The girl stared at Morgan with increasing distaste.

"You know, Morgan," McGuire said quietly, "I've had my eyes trained on you for some time. I knew that sooner or later you was

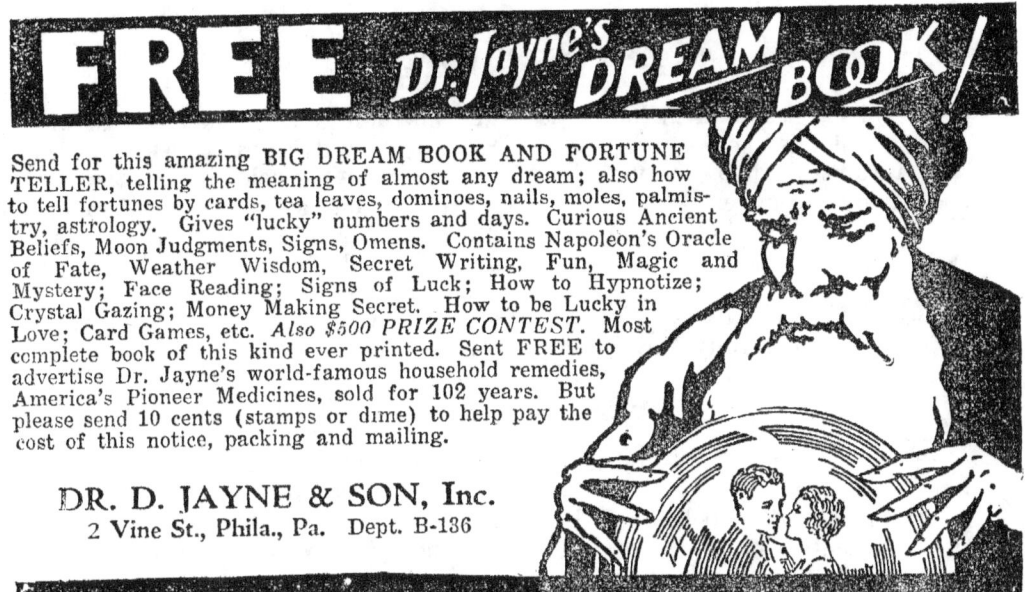

gonna get careless and make a mistake—a bad mistake."

"You can't pin it on me with that newspaper," Slugger Morgan replied defiantly. "You can't do that."

McGUIRE went through Morgan's pockets carefully, examining each object. Suddenly he spun around and pointed his revolver at Morgan.

"Put your hands up—high!" he said.

Slugger Morgan looked at him with a frozen stare.

"What—"

"You're under arrest for murder in the first degree!" said McGuire. "Get those hands up—quick!"

Morgan's hands shot into the air.

"Now, sister," McGuire said to the girl, "you'd better be nice. Very nice. You're in one hell of a hole. I've got Morgan dead right."

"You ain't got nothin' on me!" Morgan yelled.

"No?" said McGuire.

He held out a small piece of cardboard and laughed.

"You, you sap!" he said. "You put yourself right on the spot. You put the finger on yourself!"

McGuire laughed heartily. The girl and Morgan, his hands high in the air, stared at the slip of cardboard McGuire held in his hand.

"You made a bad, bad mistake, Morgan," McGuire laughed. "It's a weight card from Schuler's drug store, at 1470 Waller Street. It's stamped with the address of the store—and the date!"

McGuire shook his head slowly.

"I found it," said Morgan quickly.

"No, no," said McGuire. "It's stamped with *today's date,* and *your weight.*" McGuire laughed again. "The address, today's date—and your *weight!* What a boner!"

THE girl swore softly and walked over to McGuire.

"I know nothing about this. I've never seen the man before."

McGuire turned to her and smiled.

"No?" he said. "Are you sure of that?"

"Please," the girl begged, "please believe me."

"You said you never saw this man before?" McGuire asked. "Well, how was it you didn't recognize him as the man you followed into the drug store and who beat it while you were there?"

"I—" the girl started.

McGuire cut her short as he spun

An Exciting Complete Book-Length Novel of the African
Devil Bush in Which a Famous Hero of the Jungle
Faces New Foes

KWA AND THE APE PEOPLE

By PAUL REGARD

*—in the January THRILLING ADVENTURES. No fiction fan
can afford to miss it! 10 Cents at all newsstands*

around and grabbed Morgan's upraised hand. He twisted Morgan's hand until the table lamp Morgan held had crashed to the floor. Just as quickly did McGuire step back in time to avoid the bullet that went thudding into the wall from the girl's quickly drawn, pearl-handled .22. With his gun he knocked the revolver from the girl's grasp.

Then suddenly releasing Morgan, he stepped back and leveled his revolver at both the girl and the gangster.

"All right, sweetie," he said, "keep your hands in the air!" Then to Morgan: "Get dressed, you, and hurry!"

When Morgan had slipped his clothes on, McGuire tossed a pair of handcuffs to the girl.

"Try these bracelets on Morgan," he commanded, "and you. You ought to look nice together—a nice pair."

When the girl had complied McGuire motioned them to the door with his gun. He glanced once again at the card. He turned it over and read the fortune on the other side. It said: *You will be lucky in your endeavors.* McGuire chuckled.

"What a boner," he said. "*Address, date—and weight.*"

He followed them both down the stairs.

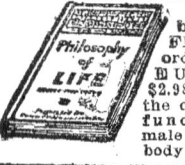

WILDSIDE PULP CLASSICS:
PULP FACSIMILE SERIES

Series editor: John Gregory Betancourt

#1: *Spicy Mystery Stories* (August 1935)

> *Includes Robert Leslie Bellem, Atwater Culpepper, Ellery Watson Calder, Carl Moore, E. Hoffman Price, Jerome Severs Perry, Charles R. Allen, Arthur Wallace, and more.*

#2: **Ghost Stories** (June 1931)

> *Stories by Conrad Richter (best known as the author of* The Light in the Forest*) and E. and H. Heron featuring their psychic detective, Flaxman Low.*

#3: *Spicy Mystery Stories* (February 1937)

> *The February 1937 issue features Robert Leslie Bellem, Lew Merrisll (Victor Rousseau) Hugh Speer, Justin Case (Hugh B. Cave), and many others — plus all the classic "spicy" artwork!*

#4: *Strange Tales #7* (January 1933)

> *This issue features Hugh B. Cave's classic "Murgunstrumm," as well as stories by Robert E. Howard, Henry S. Whitehead, and many more.*

#5: **The Black Mask #2** (May 1920)

> *The second issue of the classic mystery magazine, where hardboiled noir fiction was born!*

#6: *Tales of Magic and Mystery* (February 1928)

> *The second issue of the classic mystery magazine, where hardboiled noir fiction was born!*

#7: **The Phantom Detective #1** (February 1933)

> *The premiere issue of the detective-hero pulp!*

#8: *Submarine Stories* (March 1930)

> *A reprint of a rare pulp magazine, featuring stories and articles about (what else?) submarines!*

#9: *Sinister Stories #1* (Feb 1940)

> *A reprint of a rare pulp magazine, featuring stories and articles about (what else?) submarines!*

- -

Yes! Please send me the following books, for which I enclose payment. (Or order online with a credit card at www.wildsidepress.com, or through your favorite online bookseller.)

- ☐ *Spicy Mystery Stories* (Aug.1935) - $19.95
- ☐ *Ghost Stories* (June 1931) - $19.95
- ☐ *Spicy Mystery Stories* (Feb. 1937) - $19.95
- ☐ *Strange Tales #7* (January 1933) - $15.00
- ☐ *The Black Mask #2* (January 1920) - $19.95
- ☐ *Tales of Magic and Mystery* (Feb. 1928) - $19.95
- ☐ *The Phantom Detective #1* (Feb. 1933) - $19.95
- ☐ *Submarine Stories* (March. 1930) - $19.95
- ☐ *Sinister Stories* (Feb. 1940) - $19.95

Mail to: Wildside Press, P.O. Box 301, Holicong, PA 18928-0301.

U.S. shipping: $3.95 for 1-2 books, $1 per additional book. *Shipping to other countries: please see web site:* www.wildsidepress.com

Name: _____

Address: _____

Address: _____

Email: _____

www.ingramcontent.com/pod-product-compliance
Lightning Source LLC
Chambersburg PA
CBHW080825020726
47501CB00009B/2422